VAIN HOPE

A Selection of Recent Titles by Christine Green

VAIN HOPE

Christine Green

This first world edition published in Great Britain 2002 by
SEVERN HOUSE PUBLISHERS LTD of
9–15 High Street, Sutton, Surrey SM1 1DF.
This first world edition published in the USA 2002 by
SEVERN HOUSE PUBLISHERS INC of
595 Madison Avenue, New York, N.Y. 10022.

British Library Cataloguing in Publication Data

Green, Christine, 1944-
    Vain hope
    1. Detective and mystery stories
    I. Title
    823.9'14 [F]

    ISBN 0-7278-5848-3

Typeset by Palimpsest Book Production Ltd.,
Polmont, Stirlingshire, Scotland.
Printed and bound in Great Britain by
MPG Books Ltd., Bodmin, Cornwall.

For Tony, with love, as always

One

The evening event had been a success. The participants made their way down the wide stone steps and then along the tree-lined path. Some meandered across the lawns, their feet making the dry autumn leaves crackle. The sky's red streaks had been replaced now by a purplish dark and the night had become suddenly cool.

Carla Robins stood at the main door watching them go. Behind her a glass chandelier shone brightly and, just for a moment, she felt like the gracious hostess shepherding her guests safely homewards. But there were no guests, just clients, and the Harmony Clinic had long since stopped being a stately home. Carla began to feel shivery and she had the urge to cross her arms and hug herself warm. But she wore an expensive linen suit that creased easily, so she stood tapping one foot impatiently as a group of three stragglers stopped to talk by the stone gates. Finally they left, turning to wave at her as they did so. That was a good sign. Her job was about creating the right impression, acquiring new clients. She was satisfied that her organization of the open evening had done just that.

'It was a good turnout,' commented Kirsty White, the receptionist. She sat in the reception hall beneath the chandelier at a mahogany table surrounded by vases of white lilies. Carla thought the flowers were way over the top, made the place look funeral. On Monday she'd have words with the housekeeper. 'How many exactly?' she asked.

'Thirty-one signed in,' answered Kirsty, patting a stack of questionnaires. It had been her job to hand them out and help

1

those who needed it. A few of those had been foreign, some dyslexic, some were just nervous of forms. Carla picked up the questionnaires. 'I'll take these to my office and check through them. I want to get the follow-up letters off in the morning.'

As she left reception Carla's high heels made no noise on the carpeted stairs. Most people used the lift but Carla had keeping thin to worry about. Kirsty thought Carla was the most glamorous person she'd ever met. She wore smart suits, had a hairstyle that bounced back into shape even after she'd been out in the wind, clear skin and features that their clients had to acquire artificially. Not that Kirsty actually liked her, no one did. But she did admire her looks. Since the baby, Kirsty had put on weight and her hair had begun to fall out. Maybe I should get mine cut properly, she thought, maybe having fine hair in a ponytail wasn't a good idea.

Stanley Goodman, the security officer, wandered into reception about five minutes later.

Kirsty tried not to be irritated at the sight of him, for sometimes he took over reception a little early, allowing her to catch the last bus. Otherwise she had to pay for a taxi.

Kirsty knew what he wanted. 'Nibbles and sarnies are in the boardroom, Stan.'

'Has madam gone home?' he asked, as he sat down in one of the armchairs. He was stockily built, pug-faced, nearing sixty and hairs sprouted from his ears. His black uniform jacket sat so tightly on his big belly that when he sat down he had to undo the silver buttons to let the bulk spread out.

'She's in her office,' said Kirsty, with a well-practised reception smile. 'She'll probably still be here when I go.'

'You finishing at ten?'

She nodded. 'I'm on six to ten all this week.'

'Have you seen Lyn?' he asked. His tiny blue eyes were almost lost in his moon face and, although he was smiling, his eyes were not.

Lyn Kilpatrick was the new night sister. She'd been in the post for six months and everyone in the clinic knew Stan lusted after her. It wasn't surprising. She was tall, with long legs, red hair, a smattering of freckles and had green eyes. The fact that Stan seemed to think he stood a chance was a joke, for Lyn was a stunner and Stan had as much chance of making it with Lyn as a refuse collector had of making it with a duchess. He was harmless enough, except that Lyn had confessed to Kirsty that she found him 'creepy' and so she did her best to avoid him. Kirsty shook her head at Stan. 'No, I haven't seen her. The first floor's been very busy in the day. Someone had an allergic reaction.'

'Dead?'

'No. But the op had to be abandoned and the woman got transferred.'

Stan shrugged. 'More money than bloody sense.'

'Keeps us in work though, doesn't it?'

'It's worth it for the Carlas of this world,' muttered Stan dourly, as he pushed his cap back and tried unsuccessfully to cross his legs, 'and for the surgeons, but on our wages we wouldn't be hard pressed to find work elsewhere.'

'You don't exactly work your socks off,' said Kirsty. 'There's lots worse places to work.'

Stan seemed to take the hint or the tone and sat for only a few minutes more. 'Who else is still here then?'

Kirsty shook her head. 'I'm not sure. I think the theatre staff have left.'

'What about the boss?'

'He hasn't come through reception.'

At the mention of the boss, part owner and senior surgeon, Saul Ravenscroft – and with it the thought he might still be in the building – Stan stood up stiffly, put his cap back in place, buttoned up his jacket carefully, patted his now supported belly and walked purposefully away. Kirsty glanced at her watch. It was nearly eight thirty. If the boss hadn't left yet she couldn't risk leaving early. It would have to be a taxi again. That would annoy her partner, Mark. When she worked late, she always rang him at eight thirty to check the baby was asleep.

This time he took ages to answer the phone and when he did she could hear Amy screaming in the background. 'I've had enough of this,' were his first words. 'I've tried every bloody thing – a bottle, walking up and down, pushing her in the pushchair . . .' He broke off as the sound of screaming intensified.

'She's probably got colic,' said Kirsty uncertainly. 'Try her with a spoonful of Calpol.'

'Yeah, yeah. I'll try. I think she's doing it on purpose.'

'She's a baby – you have to be patient.'

'Tell me about it.'

'I'll try to get off a bit early,' she said, knowing it was unlikely but wanting to placate him. 'Maybe Stan will stand in for me.'

Kirsty, still hearing the frantic cries of her child, felt her stomach knotting with anxiety.

'I can't promise to be home early. I don't want to lose this job but—'

'Just get here as soon as you can.'

'Yes I'll . . .' she began, but he couldn't hear. The line was dead. She stood for a moment holding the receiver, wishing she could have soothed them both, wishing also that she didn't need to leave both of them – ever. That thought didn't last as she remembered the evenings when she'd been glad to leave the house. When she'd felt young again. Her real age – twenty-one.

Upstairs on the third floor Carla sat at her desk, eased her shoes off and began sifting through the details of those who'd attended. Then she began addressing envelopes and writing short letters of encouragement. To these she added their easy payment plan and a brochure of the clinic's facilities. It was time consuming and she could easily have had everything typed but she thought the personal touch was vital. And her results were impressive. She'd been in the job for nearly two years and the bed occupancy and theatre usage had been at an all-time high. Just three more months and she would be on a profit-sharing scheme. Even now she earned a three hundred pound bonus for every client she introduced and who afterwards went under the knife. But first, of course, she had to gather them in; reassure them; counsel them; convince and finally sell them the surgical package of their dreams.

As she worked she heard cars pulling away. Visitors were encouraged to leave by nine p.m. and the day cases also had to have left the premises by then, even if they had to be carried out. The average stay was two nights. Longer stays blocked beds.

Once she'd produced a neat pile of letters, she checked her diary for the following day. Anyone interested in surgery was offered a home visit and most accepted. Already she had five visits booked – each one would take about an hour but they were worthwhile. She rarely lost clients she'd counselled in their own homes.

She had two expected phone calls that she answered briskly but a few minutes later the knock at the door came as a surprise. She glanced at her watch. It was just after eleven. She slipped on her shoes, picked up her pile of envelopes, slipped her diary into her briefcase and, grabbing her jacket, walked the few steps to the door. She wasn't prepared to hang about for idle chit-chat and anyway it was two-to-one odds on it being Stan. She opened the door a fraction. 'It's you,' she said, as she opened the door wider.

'It's me.'

'I was just leaving.'

'So I see.'

'Your place or mine?'

He smiled. 'Mine's the one with the bed.'

On the second floor, night sister Lyn Kilpatrick sat at the office desk enjoying a cup of coffee while she completed the nightly bed statement. It only took a few moments but from six a.m. it could be bedlam so she crossed her fingers and filled it in early.

BED STATEMENT

Number of beds, first floor = 11
Number of beds second floor = 12
Number of beds occupied, first floor = 8 + accompanying mother
Number of beds occupied, second floor = 6
Total occupancy = 14 + accompanying mother
Empty beds = 9
Discharges = 10
Admissions = 8 + mother
Deaths = 0
Transfers (state where and why) – 1 admitted to Harrowford General Hospital at 7 p.m. following an allergic reaction to the anaesthetic. Condition on transfer: BP 90/60, pulse 110, respirations 32. Now in ICU – condition satisfactory following an emergency tracheotomy. Relatives informed.

All remaining clients appear to be satisfactory at time of report.

Lyn Kilpatrick RGN

She'd signed her name with a relieved flourish. Filling out the bed statement signalled the night was progressing. On night duty most nurses wished their lives away. Daylight was never so appreciated.

Even though she was the only qualified nurse on duty at the weekend it was the easiest job she'd ever had. With a mere fourteen patients tonight she had three care assistants to help her. Hopefully the night would be uneventful.

It was just after midnight and all was fairly quiet. Each patient or client, as Carla and Una Fairchild, the director of nursing, insisted they be called, had his or her single room and rarely stayed long. The only things that really irked her about the job were the account forms. If she gave a client as much as a paracetamol or even a sanitary towel it had to be costed and listed. Often she forgot. She rummaged in her uniform pocket to find her notes from the handover at eight thirty. Tonight was particularly quiet because of the open evening but even so there had been eight ops and they needed careful observation.

She checked her jottings on the scrap of paper – all were run-of-the-mill surgery – rhinoplasties, one breast reduction, two breast augmentations and one major liposuction. On the first floor there were two facelifts, one nose and chin job, a child who'd had bat ears corrected and whose mother was staying by the bedside and a woman who'd had skin folds nipped and tucked. That left nine empty rooms, a real luxury. Lyn wasn't sure which surgeon was sleeping in. There was always supposed to be one, but often there wasn't. In an emergency one of the anaesthetists who lived nearby could be at the clinic within five minutes. In the months since she'd been working at the Harmony there had only been two doctor call-outs but she was always alert for trouble, always on edge, especially when she had an inexperienced care assistant on one of the floors.

Lyn based herself on the second floor, for no particular reason other than that in the mornings the light was better and at the first stirrings of dawn her spirits lifted. An uneventful night was always her main hope and it helped if the care assistants were reliable and didn't fall asleep.

Tonight she had Pamela Miles working with her. Pam was overweight, with flat feet but with a pretty round face and grey curly hair. She was menopausal and suffered hot flushes and the odd dizzy turn so Lyn made sure she sat down frequently. Not that she needed much encouraging, because Lyn was only two thirds of the way through Pam's life history and once she sat down it was, *Did I ever tell you about . . .* Occasionally Lyn wondered if she wasn't being told a load of bullshit, but if she was she didn't care – it passed the time.

Pam worked noisily in the kitchen and sluice. Soon she would appear and give Lyn chapter and verse on conditions, the failings of the day staff and which room – Pam couldn't remember names – would give them trouble. Lyn heard Pam's clogs dragging slightly along the carpeted corridor. All the care staff wore white clogs but Pam hadn't mastered the art of walking in them yet. She appeared at the office door looking pink-faced and flustered. 'I can't tell you what a bloody mess the day staff left. Bits of washing everywhere, visitor's cups and saucers still in the rooms, flowers to still be put in frigging vases.'

'I'll give you a hand,' said Lyn. 'Don't worry about it'.

'I'm not worried, just pissed off clearing up other people's mess.' She paused and sank into the chair opposite Lyn. 'Anyway it's all done. Only rooms three and four to do obs on at one.'

Lyn glanced at her watch. 'I'll do a round downstairs at twelve and make sure that little boy and his mother are asleep.' There was no reply from Pam and when Lyn looked up she could see rivulets of sweat running down her forehead. She was breathing fast and her eyes looked panic-stricken. 'Undo your uniform, Pam. I'll open a window.' Lyn fumbled in the drawer to find the window key, finally did and, once the window was opened, a great gust of cold air blew in. Pam gave a large sigh as the cold air hit her face. Her unzipped dress had allowed her to sag and breathe more easily. 'I'm too fat for this uniform,' she said breathily, as she slipped off her clogs and pulled her dress up past her knees.

'Never mind,' smiled Lyn. 'It'll soon be Monday again.'

Pam managed a half smile as she took a tissue from her pocket and mopped her face. 'No need to take the piss. One Monday I'll start dieting and it won't be over by lunchtime. I wasn't always this fat you know.'

'You're just a well-covered woman,' said Lyn, trying to soothe the effects of her previous remark. It wasn't like Pam to be quite so touchy. 'And at this place the uniforms only go up to an eighteen, so you can't be that big.'

Pam shrugged her shoulders and thrust her hand through the front of her sweat-sodden hair. 'I'm going to wash my face and have a shower. Is that OK?'

'Fine,' nodded Lyn. 'Do you fancy a cold drink?'

'Yeah. Lot's of ice.'

At that moment a bell rang. 'I'll go,' said Lyn. The board in the main corridor showed room six was ringing. As Pam turned in the direction of the stairs to the staffroom she muttered, 'She's a frigging nutcase.' Lyn smiled as she walked to room six. Pam thought most of the clients were nuts anyway.

In room six, the client, Charmaine Reid, was in the bathroom vomiting into the sink. She'd had a breast augmentation and this was her second night. She was tall, slim, with a plaited coil of prune-coloured hair and eyes to match. Cold eyes that no longer crinkled at the corners, a jawline that didn't sag and tightened buttocks that looked great in jeans but close up showed thick keloid scars. Enlarging her breasts had somehow made her look a little more matronly. She was, after all, well over forty. Those who needed surgery to make them feel either younger or more attractive or even less noticeable no longer surprised Lyn. Ms Reid was a veteran of cosmetic surgery and Lyn had nursed her once before. Then, she had seemed to have the constitution of an all-in wrestler, now she appeared to be having a designer temper tantrum. She stamped her bare feet and wiped her mouth swiftly with the back of her hand. As Lyn moved towards the sink, Charmaine switched on the taps and snapped, 'Don't just stand there – do something!' She'd failed to run the taps quickly enough because Lyn had already noticed the smell. Charmaine was vomiting pure gin. Lyn handed her a tooth mug with some mouthwash and said gently, 'Rinse your mouth, Charmaine, and then get into bed and I'll fix you a jab.' Charmaine didn't answer, just rinsed her mouth, wiped her face with a flannel and flounced to the bed.

In the office Lyn read Charmaine's medical notes and her prescription sheet and waited for Pam to return from her shower. She'd been gone fifteen minutes already and Lyn

9

couldn't leave the ward unmanned to go looking for her. Ms Reid would have to wait, because any drug given, even a humble aspirin, had to be checked by a trained nurse and a care assistant. Lyn unlocked the drug cupboard and removed an ampoule of anti-emetic, placed a syringe and needle alongside the ampoule on a plastic tray, then sat down drumming her fingers on the desk. She didn't like to keep anyone waiting for medication and she felt uneasy. The sound of heavy male footsteps coming along the corridor made her immediately alert. It would have been easy to say, as Pam would have done, *It's only Stan*, but Stan bothered her. He was a creepy predatory bastard. Not that he'd ever touched her but there was always the suggestion that he might. Occasionally she hoped he would make a definite approach, then she would have the immense pleasure of . . . she didn't have time to either formulate or anticipate her revenge before he appeared grinning in the office doorway. 'Hello, lovely Sister Kilpatrick', he said, in a low tone that he seemed to use especially for her. His eyes slithered to her legs. 'Uncle Stan has some gossip for you.'

Charmaine, once back in bed, felt a little better. You are one sick bitch, she told herself. Her new breasts were throbbing like crazy but when she touched them they had as much feeling as two grapefruit. She thought that was an oddity in itself but at least they were large grapefruit. Her mouth still tasted of gin and vomit, which made a change from her usual gin and tonic, but she'd had to have a drink. She couldn't have slept without one. Once she'd had the injection and goody wooden clogs had gone on her break, she'd invite Pam in for a drink. She was always good value and honest. 'You're bloody nuts,' she'd told her on her last stay. And of course she was right. At least Pam didn't bother about why she was addicted to cosmetic surgery and she didn't pity her. Charmaine hated to be pitied.

She stared at her bedside clock. Where the hell was her injection? For God's sake, they weren't busy. The night staff had it easy. All they had to do was stay awake. Five more minutes, she thought, and I'm ringing that bell.

She lay back and closed her eyes and was almost drifting off when she heard a male voice along the corridor. Her door was slightly ajar and it was easy to hear the low tones. She guessed it was the security man. He was always roaming the place. What the hell did he expect to find? She knew there was a CCTV screen covering the front and back gates and that he was meant to man it from midnight until the gates opened at six a.m. She glanced again at her clock – it was five past midnight.

Downstairs on the first floor, Alvera Lewis and Wendy Swan had just finished the observations on the two late afternoon cases. Both were stable, so they could be left in peace for a few hours. Only one had been any trouble – the mother of Harry Lloyd-Peters, a boy of six, who'd had his bat ears corrected and just wanted to sleep. His mother didn't seem able to let him. She was concerned about his dull eyes and the tiniest speck of blood on his bandage and the fact that he didn't want to drink. So she buzzed every few minutes for reassurance.

'Shall we ring for Lyn?' asked Wendy, the less confident of the two. Alvera settled her plump body in an armchair in the small dayroom. Then she slipped off her clogs and replaced them with old black moccasins, took out her knitting and began counting her stitches. She wasn't fat but she was solid-looking and barely reached five foot two. She had wide hips and chunky arms, the result, she said, of lifting patients and heavy shopping. Alvera paused in her counting and shook her head. 'She'll be down any minute. She always keeps nice time.' 'Nice' was a favourite word of Alvera. No one knew her real age but her clear black skin and bright eyes made her look far too young for her 'big' children. Born in the West Indies, she'd lived in England, she said, 'for years and years' and her accent was more Birmingham than Barbados. Mostly she'd worked in the NHS and, although she found the work easy at the clinic, she found it hard to pander to 'vain' people.

Wendy watched Alvera's brisk knitting in fascination. 'For a baby?' she queried. Alvera laughed, 'Not for me. I'm making it for the church bazaar.'

They fell silent then. Wendy wanted to talk but Alvera rarely instigated a conversation. She always seemed placid and happy and in a world of her own. Perhaps, thought Wendy, that's the result of being religious and going to Church. Wendy had lived alone since her divorce and she loved working at night, weekends and Bank Holidays in particular. She felt less lonely, slept most of the day away and didn't have to make any decisions about where to go or what to do. She was twenty-six years old and had been divorced for two long years.

'She's late,' said Alvera, as she finished her row of knitting. 'I'll phone.' Just as she picked up the phone Lyn appeared in the doorway. Alvera glanced down at Lyn's feet, now shod in black flat courts. 'You wearing your nice quiet shoes, Lyn?'

Lyn smiled. 'I'm like you. I can only stand the clogs for a few hours. I've just slipped them off.'

Alvera shrugged. 'The black looks better with the dark-blue uniform.'

'How's tricks down here?'

Alvera shrugged again. It was a habit she had and Lyn wondered sometimes if her shoulders were painful. 'All asleep . . . but not that mother in room three. She's fussin' worse than her baby.'

'I'll go and see her. Is young Harry sleeping?'

Alvera laughed. 'He would be if she let him.'

Lyn found Mrs Lloyd-Peters leaning over her child wearing a voluminous black dressing gown. She looked from the back view like a vampire bat diving in for a reviving bite. When she turned round, Lyn could see she looked pale and her forehead was creased with lines of anxiety. She looked far worse than her child, who lay, pink-faced, breathing normally and fast asleep.

'I know I'm being silly,' she said. 'Older mum, only-child syndrome, I suppose, but . . . he's so quiet.'

Lyn gently felt the boy's pulse at his wrist and checked his bandages. 'He's fine,' she said, smiling at the mother's still anxious expression. 'I've got children of my own. I *do* know how you feel and I promise you in the morning, when the anaesthetic's worn off, he won't be quiet any more.' The woman's mouth relaxed into a smile. 'And Harry will feel much better,' continued Lyn, feeling she was winning on the reassurance front, 'than you will if you fret all night. Get some sleep and we'll pop in regularly to make sure he's OK.'

Lyn doubted that anyone could sleep well in a camp bed, but Mrs Lloyd-Peters seemed to be taking her advice, removing the bat cape and slipping under the duvet.

'Thank you so much, Sister,' she said. 'I feel exhausted.'

'Just call me Lyn.'

'I'm Nina. Thanks again.'

Later, upstairs in room seven, Graham, aged thirty, a solo-living single, was sitting upright in bed and in the process of pulling out his nasal packing. Not that he was admitting that it was on purpose. 'It just fell out,' he said to Lyn when she appeared in his doorway. Blood spattered the top sheet and he held most of the bloody packing and his nasal dressing in his right hand. His eyes were mere slits and with the plaster of Paris nosepiece he looked in a sorry state.

'Have you had any sleep, Graham?' she asked as she pressed his call bell to summon Pam.

He shook his head, sending out tiny sprays of blood and mucus. 'I've got a bit of a problem . . . you see . . .' He paused, embarrassed.

'Out with it, Graham. I'm a nurse and totally unshockable.'

Graham smiled, his mouth skewing slightly to one side. 'I've been . . . well . . . sleepwalking. I've always done it since I was a kid.'

Lyn nodded. 'It's quite common.' She was about to say,

13

You'll grow out of it, but at the age of thirty it seemed unlikely.
'How often does it happen?' she asked.

He shrugged. 'Once or twice a week.'

'And do you usually find your way back to bed in one piece?'

'Yes. But that's at home. Tonight I woke up on my travels . . . I'm not sure where . . .' He broke off as Pam entered the room and then left immediately for sheets and rubber gloves and a nasal dressing. Meanwhile Lyn offered Graham a hand to get out of bed. 'I can manage, Sister,' he said. 'I'm quite steady on my feet.' Once out of bed Lyn was surprised to find he was well over six feet tall. He had fair bushy hair and she noticed there were spatters of blood on his forehead. He walked the few steps to the bathroom quite steadily and didn't seem either fazed or made faint by the sight of his striped pyjamas spotted with blood.

Once the packing was removed and a new dressing was in place, Graham washed his face and combed his hair and then sat in the armchair by his bed, while Lyn and Pam made it up with fresh sheets. Even between puffy, beginning-to-blacken eyes, Lyn noticed Graham watching their every move intently. 'Thanks,' he said. 'I hope I won't trouble you again.'

Lyn smiled. 'Get some sleep and I'll keep an eye on your door.'

'Thanks again,' he murmured as he closed his eyes and sank back against the mound of pillows.

Once the door had closed, Graham opened his eyes as far as he could. They hadn't told him his mother had rung, so he had to presume she had not. No visit, no phone call. He really was in her bad books. He put his mother firmly out of his mind – after all, he did his best for her, but some people you couldn't help enough. His hand slid inside his pyjama trousers and he let it rest there like a thoughtful pause, knowing that eventually there would come an exciting prelude, then a little fortissimo and then, all being well, a fast-building crescendo to the finale.

Vain Hope

During his thoughtful phase he thought of Sister Lyn in her navy-blue uniform. She had trim ankles and legs that went on and on. He liked her breasts too, high and pert. And her hands, so soft and gentle. She was a great looker even with the freckles and he could tell by the way that she smiled at him that she liked him too. In his mind his hands played her like a violin, she had the curves of a violin and he was the musician, teasing the sounds of pleasure from her. His full concerto was interrupted only once by the sound of a thud from upstairs. He didn't let that him distract him for long. Sister Lyn was fully in tune with him. His instrument. He was the maestro. Presto! Presto! Presto! He ended with a final flourish and to his great joy remembered the Italian words – *in finire bellezza.* His Italian tapes had definitely paid off.

Later, post-concerto, he felt his pleasure dissipate. He'd had hopes before of finding someone like Lyn and they had all proved fruitless. His ugly nose and skinny body had put girls off. He'd been told the swelling on his nose could take weeks to go down and it would be three months before his new nose would be in its final state. He could wait. He'd been waiting all his life. He would watch over Lyn and when the new Graham emerged he knew she would be bowled over. It was a pity he was going home in the morning; one more night in her company might make all the difference.

Two

C arla drank her breakfast standing up in her tiny galley kitchen. It was Sunday morning and she had a little more time than usual, so she stared out on to her patch of garden that she'd filled with potted trees and potted plants. In the slight drizzle and the half-light, with a drift of steam coming from her central-heating boiler outlet, she thought the garden had a tropical rainforest look.

She'd rented the small cottage on the outskirts of Harrowford because the idea of a mortgage appalled her. As with everything in her life, she preferred transitory to permanent. She thought she had made a good choice. She didn't need either a large house or a large kitchen, because she rarely cooked, preferring to eat out or go without. Her fridge contained skimmed milk, a small piece of brie and two bottles of champagne. Her concession to good nutrition was a full fruit bowl and a medicine cupboard full of vitamins. Vitamin tablets, she reasoned, kept you healthy with virtually zero calories. She'd deliberately sought a one-bedroom place because she didn't want anyone to share her living space.

Her smoothie finished, she washed and dried the glass and placed it in her glassware cupboard. Carla gave a wry smile at her two champagne flutes, her two wine glasses, two brandy goblets and her two tumblers. They were all of the best cut glass but she was a minimalist. If she gave a party, which she rarely did, she hired everything.

In the bathroom, only big enough for one person to stand sideways, she showered quickly, washing her hair at the same time. Then she towelled herself briskly and rubbed on her favourite body lotion. She towel-dried her hair vigorously and then ran her fingers through it. By the time she arrived at the squash club it would be dry and once more she felt grateful for a good hairdresser and the money to pay for such a good cut.

Once she was dressed in her black tracksuit and red bandeau she checked her reflection in the bedroom mirror. She applied a good coat of mascara and a flick of blusher to her cheeks and felt well satisfied with her scrubbed and healthy look. Then, picking up her squash bag, which she'd placed ready by the front door, she left Holly Lodge Cottage.

The roads were fairly empty; the drizzle had now stopped, leaving the roads with a faint black sheen. Conditions were good for driving fast and Carla loved speed. Especially now that she had a brand new car, an Audi, because she admired efficiency and the Germans were renowned for their efficiency.

Outside the Riverside Squash Club she noticed Edward, parked in his BMW, waiting for her. Edward Gray was forty-two, with a wife who probably understood him very well, two children and a career as a stockbroker. He was tall, broad shouldered, had unremarkable features and was both grey by name and nature. Carla had once enjoyed the thrill of the chase – his chase – but once she'd slept with him she'd lost interest. Now she saw him occasionally, but he wanted more of her time and was getting to be a problem. She continued to be seen with him at the squash club because he was her passport to other men. Married men without mistresses, she'd noticed, envied him. She could see it in their predatory eyes. The fact that they saw *her* as an object didn't faze her, she understood it. Men were objects to her in the same way. She'd never loved one and had only once felt any regret at the end of a liaison. Carla didn't know what love was and she didn't want to. She sensed love could be painful and why expose yourself to pain if you had no masochistic tendencies. Far better, she thought, to have variety and be pampered and free. The idea of being a wife horrified Carla, far worse even than being poor.

She sat in her car and waited for Edward to come to her. He waved and beckoned her over. Carla stayed put. Give him a minute or two and he'll give in. He'd parked in a corner near some bushes, probably thinking it would give them a little privacy and a chance to grope her.

Sure enough he lasted a full ninety seconds. He strode across, opened the passenger door and slid in beside her. 'You seem to be in winning mood,' he said, kissing her hand.

She smiled, her expensive capped teeth, courtesy of a besotted dentist, gleamed at him. 'I always am.'

He kissed her briefly on the lips. 'I've missed you,' he murmured. His kisses weren't unpleasant; he was freshly shaved and smelt of expensive aftershave and mouthwash. Carla bore physical contact stoically. And she was always honest with her lovers that she didn't enjoy sex and never climaxed. The challenge seemed merely to spur them on. And she thought it sad that their wives would probably have enjoyed her share.

'Good. You should miss me,' she said, patting his cheek. 'Are you in betting mood?' He nodded.

'OK, if you win you can bed me. If not, you can take me out for a very expensive meal.'

'You're a hard woman, Carla.'

She smiled knowingly. 'And don't you just love it.'

Once on the court, Edward tossed a coin to decide who served first. Carla won. She smashed the ball well above the service line. He returned it easily again and again. They were evenly matched and, although he had more stamina, he tended to lose his concentration. As the point progressed Carla's confidence increased, especially when she saw him beginning to sweat. She'd gained some supremacy at the T and her shots were keeping him well to the back. She had a strong feeling she was going to win and then . . . she stumbled. She'd turned awkwardly on her weak left ankle and had been sent sprawling. 'Sod it! Sod it! Sod it!' she yelled, as she threw her racquet across the court. Edward was by her side in second, full of concern, but she sensed his 'You poor darling' was tinged with glee. She shrugged off his arm and stood unaided and the fact that she could put her foot down and bear weight was enough to convince her that there were no broken bones.

'Your service, I believe, Edward,' she said, coolly.

'I think you should rest that ankle.'

'I'll be fine,' she said. 'If you could just retrieve my racquet.' She smiled to herself as he did her bidding. She knew she was likely to lose now, but reasoned that if he had any balls at all he should *let her* win.

She played on badly and he won by two points. Carla knew he didn't feel any sense of achievement, but he'd won and therefore was on a promise. She couldn't now say, because she'd carried on playing, that it was too painful to lie on her back. Not that it was his favoured position for her, but today he'd have to play missionary.

Standing under a hot shower, her ankle throbbed, but she tried hard to ignore it and reasoned that a few glasses of champagne would ease both the pain and the shagging.

When she met Edward by the bar she didn't limp. Her ankle hurt like hell but she wasn't going to give him the satisfaction of seeing her less than fit. 'Shall we go?' she asked. He nodded and smiled, knowing it wasn't a question but an order. Carla had to be in charge.

Edward had just opened the back door of the squash club for Carla and was offering to carry her sports bag, when a woman rushed from a silver sports car towards them, hair flowing, face flushed. It took Carla a few moments to recognize the obviously disturbed woman – Amanda, wife of Saul Ravenscroft, the clinic's director, co-owner and chief surgeon. Usually Amanda looked immaculate, but now her fine blonde hair hung loose and wild-looking. She wore no make-up and the main colour in her oval face was a red flush matched with red eyes. Definitely an off day for Amanda. Carla had never seen her dressed other than in smart suits or evening dress. Now she wore scruffy jeans and a drab grey tee shirt.

'Where is he, you bitch?' she demanded, jabbing a finger towards Carla's chest. She had blue eyes lurking somewhere beneath puffy lids, her pupils were dilated and her breathing was as fast and frantic as her voice. In the same circumstances Carla would have been much more dignified.

'I don't know what you're talking about,' said Carla calmly. She was used to irate wives and she rarely let it worry her.

'You know very well,' Amanda snapped. 'He's not at home and he's not playing golf, so he must be with you.'

Edward, standing slightly behind Carla, said nothing.

'Hang on a minute,' said Carla with a slow smile. 'I'll just check my squash bag.' She opened her squash bag and rooted through it with slow deliberation. 'No . . . no he's not in here – sorry.'

Amanda's young face flushed an even darker pink, then, as if in realization, paled again just as swiftly. The next 'Bitch,' that emerged had a strangulated tone. Her blue eyes sparkled now in a mute fury. Carla knew the attack was about to commence. Countdown to lunge or slap. Carla, feeling primed, expected the flailing arms and feet. She stepped back swiftly. No contact. Next would come the raking nails and hair pulling. She side-stepped neatly, allowing Edward to step forward and grasp Amanda's wrists tightly. Although she kicked out and caught his shin a couple of times, her trainers made little impression. Amanda was no street fighter and, although she struggled, she was soon reduced to breathless impotent fury. Eventually Edward lowered her arms but didn't let go of her wrists. 'Now calm down and tell *me* what this is all about.' There was a short pause and she took a few deep breaths before answering. 'That whoring slut,' she said, finger jabbing in Carla's direction, 'must know where my husband is. He was meant to be home last night. He's not at the clinic and I've rung our friends and he's not there.' Her voice reached a shrill crescendo and her nose was beginning to run. Carla watched her dispassionately and from her pocket produced a paper hankie that she proffered with a smile. Amanda snatched it angrily but took the hint and dabbed at her eyes and wiped her nose.

'Have you informed the police?' asked Edward.

That question surprised her. 'Of course not. *She* knows where he is. He's probably tucked up in her bed.'

'I don't think so,' said Edward evenly. 'We're going to Carla's now. Perhaps you'd like to come with us to put your mind at rest.'

Amanda's body sagged in misery and not for the first time did Carla wonder how a married woman could get so upset and passionate about her mate. Didn't they have any self-respect?

Amanda Ravenscroft shrugged Edward aside now and began walking away but then she turned for a final onslaught. 'You needn't think your job is safe – bitch!' she screamed. 'When Saul comes back to me – and I know he will – your job will be fucking dust.'

Carla laughed. 'If I see him first I'll ask him for a rise. He usually gives me one.'

Amanda's mouth dropped open but no words came, she just stood there for several seconds. Then she ran to her sports car, fumbled with her keys in the ignition, finally managing to start the car and then rev the engine. Just for a second Carla thought she planned to ram the both of them. Tears were streaming down her face but she wound down the window and yelled, 'I expect you're a married man – can't you see what a tart she is? Can't you see what you're making your wife suffer?'

Then she drove away at speed, her brakes squealing as if to emphasize her point.

'What a drama queen,' said Carla, taking hold of Edward's arm. Edward didn't reply until he reached Carla's car. 'I'll come in your car and come back for mine later.'

Once in the car she placed a hand between his legs. 'My, my, you are a big boy. What's caused that?'

He covered his hand with hers. 'You did – my queen of tarts. You were magnificent.'

She smiled and patted his hand. 'And you, Edward, are a very, very naughty, kinky boy.'

Edward smiled with satisfaction as she drove off, using her right hand to change gear and her left hand in its rightful place.

Graham was in love. There was no doubt about it. Sister Lyn had been slightly concerned about his temperature, but even more concerned about his right-sided bellyache. She'd also placed her cool hands on his bare skin, an act that made him shiver with excitement. Just before she left the floor at eight a.m. the surgeon, Mr Khan, called to examine him, murmuring that he didn't know what was wrong with him, but perhaps he should 'Stay the night, old son, so we can keep an eye on events'. The words were music to his ears. Another night of seeing Sister Lyn and a chance to ask her out.

The day dragged. He tried to watch television but he couldn't concentrate. He fancied looking at some soft porn, but he hadn't dared to bring any in. So he spent most of the day, eyes closed, fantasizing about his first date with Lyn. He didn't eat his meals, partly because he was supposed to be ill and partly because his stomach churned in nervous excitement. By the time she was due on duty he had genuinely begun to feel a little unwell.

He'd combed his hair, shaved, splashed on aftershave, brushed his teeth and used mouthwash. He wore his second pair of new pyjamas and sat by his bed waiting for her. He'd had his operation early Saturday morning, now it was Sunday evening but he felt as if he'd been at the clinic for much longer. He'd had neither telephone call nor visitor and yet he would have been quite happy to stay on and on.

At nine fifteen he was beginning to worry. He'd opened his bedroom door just so that he could see her pass backwards and forwards during the night. Now as time wore on he was convinced something had happened to her. He knew she'd been concerned about him . . . maybe she was sick. When he heard footsteps approaching his door he felt his stomach take a high dive, his heart beat faster . . . it was Pam. 'Good evening, Graham,' she said, flashing him a big smile. 'And how are you feeling?' He could hardly breathe, let alone speak, he felt so disappointed. Eventually he managed to blurt out, 'Is Lyn on duty?'

'She's on the other floor. Did you want to see her?'

Stupid question, he thought, but he smiled. 'When she's not too busy.'

'I'll tell her,' said Pam. 'Is there anything you want?'

Not from you, he was tempted to say. 'No thanks. I'll . . . wait.'

'Please yourself. I'll be round with the hot drinks soon.'

It was ten thirty when Lyn finally arrived, wheeling in the equipment, which reminded him of a trouser press. He still felt agitated but relieved at the same time. She looked rested and fresh and she was smiling. He couldn't imagine her smiling like that for just anyone. She placed the machine close to the bed, then took his temperature with a little piece of high-tech paper under his tongue. Then she attached a small peg-like object on to his finger to register his pulse. Finally she bent over him to attach the blood pressure cuff to his arm. 'That's fine,' she said, 'but your pulse rate is a little high. How's your stomach feeling now?'

'I get the odd twinge,' he replied. Which wasn't a lie, even now his lower body was in a desperate state of twinge. 'Ask her now!' a voice inside his head urged him. '*Now!*'

'Have you had your bowels opened?' she asked, cheerfully. The question threw him. He nodded mutely.

'Here's something to help you sleep.' She handed him a beaker of water and a teaspoon with a capsule in it. He paused. 'Take it, Graham,' she said with a smile. Obediently he swallowed.

As she walked to the door the words of the question he wanted to ask filled his mouth – and there they stayed. With a wave she was gone.

*   *   *

Lyn left Graham's room and walked straight back to Charmaine Reid's room. Not only had she vomited all day, but she seemed to be hallucinating. Mr Khan had just seen her and suggested sending in a physician, but she'd refused. He said privately to Lyn that he thought that she was suffering from delirium tremens and depression. 'Search her room, Lyn,' he said. 'Get rid of her alcohol. I'll prescribe a mega dose of vitamins and start her on some Prozac. One more day and she'll have to go – she's blocking a bed and I'll have the director of nursing breathing fire.'

He'd written up the prescription, adding a strong sleeping pill and an anti-emetic. 'Keep an eye on her,' he said, as he was leaving. Then added cheerfully. 'You don't want to find her hanging from the picture rail.'

'Thank you so much, Jamil,' said Lyn, sarcastically. 'What if . . .', she began, but he'd already turned into the corridor and disappeared from view.

Lyn found Charmaine hunched over in bed, eyes downcast, arms across her breast, face ashen, the smell of vomit lingering in the room.

'You look awful,' she said, gently.

Charmaine looked up slowly. 'I feel like death.' She gave a tight smile, adding, 'In fact, death would come as a welcome relief.'

Lyn sat down beside the bed. She stayed silent, waiting for Charmaine to talk.

'What are you sitting there for?'

'Mr Khan told me you were depressed.'

'That's nothing new. I've been depressed for years.'

'What about?'

Charmaine shrugged. 'My physical flaws, I suppose.'

'Is that why you drink?'

'Who the fuck knows? I've got money. Or at least I spend my husband's money. A fine house, car – a new one every year. What more could anyone want?'

'What more do *you* want?'

'Peace. I want of peace of mind.'

24

'What would you do if you had peace of mind?'

Charmaine looked at her sharply. 'What do you mean what would I *do*?'

'Would you stop having surgery, for instance?'

'Oh yes.' The answer was so swift and certain that Lyn was surprised and the surprise must have shown in her face. 'There's no need to give me that expression, Nursie. Having surgery is no bloody joke, whatever the reason.' She broke off, her eyes filling with tears. 'Oh, for Christ's sake, why am I talking to you? You wouldn't understand. You've got a safe little job and a safe little husband. Just leave me alone.'

Lyn didn't move. 'I don't have a husband, just two hungry kids.'

There was a long pause while Charmaine wiped her eyes with a tissue. 'I see,' she murmured. 'I took you for a contented wife.'

Lyn now thought it best to change tack before Charmaine began to question *her*.

'Mr Khan wants you to have some medication tonight and he wants me to remove your alcohol. How do you feel about that?'

'Will I sleep and stop feeling so sick?'

Lyn nodded.

'You're an optimist,' she said, sourly. 'I'll take the gunk if you let me have a stiff one now.'

'Is it true you've been having hallucinations?'

'I didn't see pink elephants, if that's what you mean.'

'What did you see?'

'Does it bloody matter? Go and get the knockout drops and I'll have a final drink.'

'You won't need a drink, I'm sure,' said Lyn.

Charmaine laughed dryly. 'I *always* need a drink.'

Lyn walked back to her office feeling worried. She couldn't spare anyone to sit with Charmaine all night. They could do a check on her every fifteen minutes, but should she call in a psychiatrist or at least suggest it to Mr Khan? *If* it was a quiet night, Alvera could sit with her for a while. She decided, after a few minutes deliberation, to wait and see if Charmaine settled. The night was young and if they left her door open they could station themselves in the corridor.

Alvera was nowhere to be seen, but she was found eventually in the sluice, tidying up.

'Lordie, Lordie, help me,' she said, looking upwards. 'The day staff are a lazy crowd.'

Lyn didn't want to get into the usual diatribes about the shortcomings of the day staff. They were not, after all, a species apart. 'We need to keep a strict eye on Mrs Reid tonight, Alvera,' said Lyn. 'Check her every fifteen minutes. Jamil thinks she's suicidal. He wants her to start on Prozac and vitamins and stuff.'

'She's a spoilt, selfish woman,' said Alvera sharply, as she began washing her hands.

When Lyn went back with the medication Charmaine was sitting up in bed, triumphantly clutching an empty bottle of vodka. 'I don't feel sick anymore,' she said. 'I feel surprisingly . . . better.' Her words were slightly slurred and Lyn resolved *not* to give her the night sedation. She wanted her to actually wake up in the morning and there was little point in asking how much of the bottle she'd drunk, she'd only lie. Charmaine didn't flinch at the two injections. She merely asked, 'What the hell is that stuff?'

'A massive dose of vitamins to help stop the hallucinations and something to help the nausea.'

'Vitamins? To stop me seeing things?'

'Alcohol causes depletion of essential vitamins and it's thought that's what causes the DTs.'

'Are you saying I'm an alcoholic?'

'Aren't you?'

Charmaine laughed. 'I'm all sorts of *'olics* – a shopaholic, a chocaholic and an op-aholic. There's nothing I couldn't be addicted to. Know what I mean?'

Lyn's pocket bleep came to her rescue. 'I'll see you later,' she said, removing the empty bottle. 'You haven't got any more of this stuff, I hope?'

'Search the room if you want.'

'I might. Sleep it off, Charmaine. You'll feel better in the morning.'

'No I won't,' she said, bitterly. 'I'll just feel sorry to have woken up at all.'

It was Graham ringing his call bell. He seemed half asleep. 'Sorry to be a nuisance, Sister, but I wanted to ask you a question . . .'

Lyn smiled. 'Go ahead then.'

'Will you . . . will you . . .' he stuttered.

'Will I what?'

'Will you go out with me . . . dinner . . . anything, anywhere?'

Lyn took a deep breath. She didn't want to upset him, but if he was the last man on earth, she'd be hard pressed to share a coffee with him. 'I'm really sorry, Graham, but I do have a boyfriend and two kids, so I'm spoken for.' Graham's mouth fell. 'I thought . . .' he began. Then he murmured, almost to himself, 'Two kids are no problem.' He closed his eyes and Lyn said, 'Sleep well,' and left the room.

It was still dark when Graham woke and, at first, he wasn't sure what woke him. He thought for a moment that he'd been sleepwalking again, but he was in bed. The sound was coming from above; not just any old sound but a scream, loud and frightened, followed by a dull thud and a door slamming, lights going on, footsteps. What the hell was going on?

He had to find out. He slipped on his dressing gown, put on his slippers, drank some water to ease his parched throat and then, with a quick glance at the empty corridor, he made his way to the back stairs and the floor above.

Halfway along the corridor a cleaner was sobbing and being comforted by Pam. Lyn was talking to the security man, who began using a mobile phone. He heard one word of the conversation – *police*. Lyn spotted him then and walked towards him. 'What are you doing up here, Graham? This is a staff area.' She sounded cross.

'What's happened?' he asked.

'You'll find out soon enough. Do me a favour, will you?' He nodded eagerly.

'Just go back downstairs and keep an eye on the floor for me. Go to the first floor and ask Alvera to come up to the second floor and ask Wendy, the other care assistant, to look in on Mrs Reid in room . . .' She struggled for the room number.

Above the cleaner's dramatic sobs, Pam supplied, 'Room six.'

'Right, I'll do that,' said Graham. For Lyn he would have danced on red-hot coals – naked.

As he turned to go he heard Lyn tell Pam to take the cleaner to the staffroom and make her a cup of tea.

Once downstairs Graham patrolled the floor. Buzzers began to ring, but he kept his cool and went to each room in turn, explaining that there was an emergency and that the staff would appear as soon as possible. Then he rushed down to the first floor and found Alvera, who left immediately and hurried for the stairs. There was no sign of the other care assistant, so he made his way to room six, so that he could check on Mrs Reid. He didn't know what he would do if anything was amiss, but he was sure Lyn would be pleased he'd used his initiative. He found her sitting up in bed. She'd unwound her chest bandages and was staring at her naked bare breasts. They were bruised and a bit bloody, but Graham had seen very few breasts in real life and he stood, mesmerized, in the doorway. The woman, not a bit embarrassed, said, 'Well don't just stand there with your mouth open. Are they magnificent or what?'

He was about to answer when the sound of police sirens seemed to come from all directions. He walked quickly to the window to see two squad cars screech to a halt and uniformed police rush to reception. In the early morning greyness the lights and sirens and flashing uniform buttons seemed as rousing as a marching band.

'What the fuck is going on, sweetie?' Mrs Reid asked. He turned to look at her. She was good-looking for an older woman and he liked older women. She sounded posh. Even better. She was quite stirring and at that moment, combined with the morning's events, Graham realized he'd never felt quite so excited in his whole life.

Three

O n Monday morning in Harrowford woods Acting Detective Chief Inspector Thomas Rydell was on his third mile and beginning to sweat. It was barely dawn, dry and fairly mild. The leaves crunched as loud as cornflakes underfoot. The birds were singing and the sky, although grey, was lightening in patches. At that moment he was a man at ease; he was fit and healthy, a *mere* thirty-six, he reminded himself; he'd regained his interest in women and was eating and sleeping normally again. An added bonus was that DS Ram Patel had returned to work. Ram had been in a coma for six weeks after being attacked by a deranged killer. His recovery had taken months but, apart from a scar on his bald head and a loss of any memory of the attack, he seemed fine.

Rydell, having counted his blessings, told himself, 'Carry on at this rate, you'll become a human being again.'

The plight of his handicapped son and his divorce three years before had made him depressed and left in their wake a numbness he was only just beginning to shake off. His obsessive–compulsive behaviour had worsened since then, but it was a long-standing problem. Like most psychological problems, his had started in childhood. His father had been an army regimental sergeant major who was often away, and moving house and schools had become a way of life. His father's imminent return from manoeuvres had caused his mother major panics. The house had to be spotlessly clean and tidy. They had to be the perfect family for the soldier's return. And with his return came misery. The RSM's son's shoes had to be the best-polished, his trousers the most sharply creased, his exam results the best. Nothing was ever good enough.

His most vivid childhood memories, though, were of house moving. And the dreaded inspection. As soon as it was known a posting was due, the packing-up began. This was followed by a major house clean. Every kitchen appliance had to be moved from its position so that the backs could be cleaned. His father would supervise and criticize but, apart from a bit of heavy lifting, would do nothing. Then came the dreaded day of the inspection. A hair on the carpet or a sign of grease on the cooker caused his father to scream abuse, his mother to cry and him and Ruth, his sister, to shake with fear. Their houses had never failed an inspection but each one took its toll.

His father had various sayings that they would mouth behind his back. *Attention to detail can be the difference between life and death*, as if perfect shiny shoes was a war strategy. Another one was, *Always check and double-check – especially when leaving*. And when his father checked his bedroom – *A tidy room is a tidy mind*. This was usually followed by a cuff round the ear because his books weren't straight or his shoes not neatly to attention. Even on the food front his father had fixed ideas. *When you're abroad, son – if you don't know what it is, don't eat it*.

Needless to say, he hated his father. The reason he'd learnt to box was that, one day, when he was strong enough and big enough, he'd lay him out. And he had. And that moment had been the best. His father had lost control. Tom Rydell became his own man. Except that his father's legacy went on. One good punch couldn't obliterate the relentless indoctrination.

The cross-country running helped. For a few miles, at least, he could get his head straight, then, when his whole body grew tired and each muscle ached, he stopping thinking and just *felt*. The only problem with running was that it was addictive. If he didn't run for a couple of days he noticed that he developed withdrawal symptoms. He lost some concentration, didn't sleep so well, dwelt too much on the past.

He was on his way back through the woods to his car when his mobile rang. It was twenty-five past seven. He stopped against a tree and caught his breath. 'Rydell,' he answered, his voice sounding husky.

'Suspicious death, sir,' said a voice he didn't recognize.

'How suspicious?'

'A bloodbath by all accounts. The victim's the chief surgeon at the Harmony Clinic. Saul Ravenscroft.'

'I'm on my way.'

Sod it, he thought, there was no time now for a leisurely shower. He'd be lucky to have a brisk rub down with a towel in the car.

Minutes later he was caught, doing just that, by a Neighbourhood Watch type who was walking his yapping terrier. The old boy with white hair and a white moustache banged on his car window and yelled, 'Are you living in that car?'

Rydell wanted to say, *Fuck off and mind your own business.* But he didn't. He flashed his ID, wound down the window and muttered, 'Cop on the run,' producing his running shoes for inspection.

'Oh I see,' the old boy muttered, seeming disappointed. 'Funny things go on in these woods.' By *funny* Rydell understood him to mean criminal. He believed him, but as yet he hadn't seen any human activity, criminal or otherwise, on his runs.

The drive to the Harmony Clinic was short, only about two miles from the woods and traffic was light, so Rydell arrived within minutes. Although the grounds were vast the clinic wasn't isolated. Surrounding the clinic were several new small housing estates. When he'd arrived in Harrowford he'd viewed one or two properties, but they were expensive and they had gardens. Mowing lawns could become obsessional and he could barely contend with those he already had.

The sun's rays now filtered through the greyish clouds and as he waited to turn right into the entrance he noticed the black stone eagles perched on their gothic columns. They shone like ebony and he'd obviously paused too long because a driver behind him sounded the horn. He looked in his overhead rear view mirror to find his DS, Denise Caldecote, waving to him.

The driveway was lined with alternating oak and pine trees. The oak leaves were a variety of colours from gold and russet to pure orange. The rolling lawns on either side completed the stately home impression. Rydell thought that if he was coming here for a facelift, which he'd never contemplated and never would, at least the surroundings were impressive. He neither liked nor trusted medical environments. The unexpected happened and he always felt at a disadvantage. Ram would have accused him of *Lack of balls, guv*, but it wasn't that. It was the lack of being in control, knowing too little about the routine and the jargon.

This would be Rydell's first murder investigation in an institution and he was acting DCI. His immediate so-called *superior*, Superintendent Alec Fenton, had recently had a mild heart attack due to an overdose of pasty, chips, strong ale, belligerence and a fat gut. The surprise shown by his colleagues was not tempered by sympathy. They just wondered how he'd got away with it for so long.

He parked by the squad cars and Denise met him at the stone steps of the erstwhile stately home. 'I've always wanted to see this place,' she said, gazing upwards to the turrets and strange gargoyles interspersed in various high nooks and crannies.

There was nothing tough-looking about Denise. She mostly wore skirts on and off duty and it was reported that in one hot summer she had worn dresses. The barracking and teasing she took didn't faze her. She was blonde and known as *Knockers* for two obvious reasons. There were rumours that she'd had trouble joining the force because of her being under five feet four and not being particularly good at running or punch-ups. She'd once found a gargantuan bra draped around her computer and a straw hat with roses on her desk. 'Thanks lads,' she'd said, slipping the bra on over her dress and wearing it for most of the day. She also wore the straw hat until the superintendent told her she might confuse criminals into thinking they had arrived *at a bloody garden party*. The lads soon lost interest when she failed to rise to their bait and her limitations in battle were accepted.

Rydell valued Denise not only for her feminine perspective, but also for her ability. She was an ex-psychiatric nurse who could cajole and wheedle the most difficult of their customers. She was far better at spotting a liar than the average male officer and, more importantly, she was shrewd and could get a suspect to open up without resorting to raised voices and threats.

'You shouldn't park there,' said an authoritative voice behind him. He turned to find a tall angular woman in her late forties. She wore a grey suit and carried a heavy-looking black briefcase.

'Police,' he said. 'And you are?'

He could see now that she looked slightly flustered. The collar of her white blouse was caught up in her neck, her mascara was slightly smudged and her dark hair only looked part brushed. 'I'm the director of nursing, Una Fairchild.' Rydell noticed her husky voice, caused, he guessed, by drink or fags, or both. She seemed to him the nervous type. 'Could you please tell me what's going on?' she said. 'I had a garbled message left on my answering machine – something about a terrible accident'.

'Not exactly an accident – Miss?'

'Mrs,' she supplied.

'We believe there has been a murder.'

She paled. 'Oh my God – who?'

'It appears to be your chief surgeon.'

She swayed slightly and was lost for words. She glanced at Denise, as if for confirmation, then murmured, 'I can't believe it. I just can't believe it . . .' Rydell hadn't got time to spare for belief to set in, so he led her by the elbow up the steps to the reception area. Uniformed police stood around looking aimless and Una Fairchild shrugged off his arm and moved towards the lift. 'Where are you off to, Mrs Fairchild?' Rydell asked.

'To see my night sister, of course.'

Rydell shook his head. 'Oh no you're not. Just sit down . . . here!' He pointed to one of the armchairs in an alcove and she resisted for only a few seconds.

'Body's on the top floor, sir,' said a young round-faced constable. 'The lift only goes to the second floor,' added the PC.

'Police surgeon and scenes of crime officers?' queried Rydell.

'On their way but it could be a while.'

Rydell nodded. 'Start doing the personal descriptive forms, Constable, and make sure you keep anyone down here who comes in or tries to get out.'

The constable nodded, not at Rydell, but at the main door, as if to say, *look at this lot*, as the day staff arrived in droves. If Rydell hadn't guessed how difficult coping with a murder in an institution might be, he could see now and, as yet, he hadn't even *seen* the body. The staff looked around apprehensively. They were quiet at first, but soon a hubbub of questions began. 'What's going on? What's happened?' they asked each other.

Rydell stood in the middle of reception feeling like a ringmaster. 'Quiet, everyone.' He paused, waiting for silence. 'There has been a serious incident here and I would appreciate everyone staying put until I've had a chance to assess the situation.' He waited a second or two for any signs of dissent then signalled Denise to the lift with a slight nod of his head.

On the second floor buzzers were ringing, with no staff in sight and one lone male patient wandering around. They made their way up to the third floor and into a long dim corridor. A uniformed constable stood halfway down, guarding a door with a *do not disturb* sign hanging from the doorknob. Rydell knew him vaguely – his name was Andrews, known as Liver Salts, usually shortened to Liver. He wasn't very bright, but he was good-natured. 'The sarge has just gone downstairs,' explained Liver. 'He says to have a look around but I think he's gone to throw up. He's not keen on blood.'

'Who is?' muttered Rydell. Already he felt uneasy. Maybe this place wasn't a conventional hospital, but the smell and the atmosphere were the same. He felt Denise's hand on his back as they walked into the room. She wasn't exactly *pushing* him and he found it vaguely reassuring.

The room itself showed no sign that anything was amiss: there was a bed, a wardrobe, bedside table with an alarm clock, two wine glasses and an empty bottle of Barolo. He'd steeled himself for a bloody body on the bed. But the bed was stripped and the curtains were pulled back. There was only one door and, when he turned to look, it was slightly ajar and blood had seeped from underneath to spatter the cream carpet.

Denni had already slipped her surgical gloves on. Now he did the same, fumbling a bit as he did so. He kicked the door open slightly to see the bathroom floor awash with blood. A naked man lay face down on the floor. Rydell stood trying to concentrate on the scene but for several seconds he was only aware of the warmth of the bathroom and the smell of blood mixed with aftershave or perfume. Denni stooped down to get a closer look from the doorway. 'His throat's been cut,' she said. She didn't need to add that his wrists had also been slashed.

Rydell noticed the toilet-paper holder had been wrenched from the wall. The roll of toilet paper was still attached but soaked in blood. And then it struck him. 'Poor sod was pissing at the time.'

'There's something else, guv . . .'

'What?'

'The blood's not that fresh. He looks as if he's been dead for some time.'

From where she stood Denni could see grey in the man's hair and, although he was lean, she guessed he was middle-aged.

Heavy footsteps along the corridor signalled the arrival

of the SOCOs and they vacated the room immediately. The police surgeon, Dr Jem Parkways, tagged along at the end of the team and, as he passed, he winked at Denni. 'I'll be as quick as I can,' he said.

Rydell was tempted to talk to whoever found the body, but Jem was always in a hurry and so they waited outside, sending Liver off to help with the PD forms. The sound of clicking cameras and voices filled the room and Jem reappeared in five minutes.

'What a bloody mess,' he said, cheerfully. Jem was still in his thirties, with the sort of physique and dark good looks that could have made him a film star heart-throb. He knew by the way that Denise looked at him that she rated his looks. 'Well folks – cause of death – his throat and wrists were cut with a scalpel.'

Denise was impressed. 'How do you know it was a scalpel that was used?'

Jem laughed. 'It wasn't genius on my part. The scalpel was lying underneath his chest. There's considerable frontal lividity and I reckon his throat and wrists were cut almost simultaneously. There's no sign he tried to protect himself. Taken unawares undoubtedly – mid piss – he does have a bruise on his forehead.'

'Cause?' asked Denise.

Jem smiled down at her. 'I think he came a cropper either on the cistern or against the lavatory bowl. He could well have been kneeling down at the time.'

'Time of death?' asked Rydell.

'You're an optimist, Tom,' said Jem. 'The post-mortem will help but all I can tell you is – he's been dead at least a couple of days.'

Rydell found it hard to believe that a surgeon could lie dead undisturbed for two days, but he thanked Jem and he and Denni walked along the corridor to the staffroom, where the cleaner who found the body sat tearfully drinking tea. She was a thin woman in her forties with a straggly haircut and pale face that gave her a harassed appearance, which

Rydell thought was due to life itself, rather than having made
a shocking discovery. She looked up with watery eyes as they
walked in. 'He was ever such a nice man,' she said. 'Who
would want to kill him? He only did good and he always had
a friendly word. I just can't believe it . . . I just . . .'

'You're Jacky Watson?' asked Rydell, halting the flow.
She sniffed and nodded. 'How long have you worked here,
Jacky?'

'Ever since it opened two years ago,' she said, sipping her
tea. 'I work Monday to Friday. I do the top floor on a Monday
first, because they only have one cleaner at the weekend.'

'I see,' said Rydell. 'So tell me what happened this
morning.'

She took a deep breath. 'I always do the on-call room first
– just my little routine. The *do not disturb* sign was up, but
it's usually empty anyway – know what I mean? – I knocked
and there was no answer, so I walked in. I always strip the
bed first, so I did that and I put the sheets in the dirty linen
skip. Then I collect the towels from the bathroom. As soon
as I got to the bathroom door I noticed the stain. I opened the
door – I was that shocked. I tried to scream, but my throat had
dried up. I rushed out into the corridor and saw Pam Miles
coming out of the staff toilet, so I screamed out then for her
to get the night sister.'

'You only touched the bed?'

'Yeah. Like I said. I put the sheets and stuff in the
linen skip.'

'Thank you, Jacky. We may need to speak to you again.'

'Yeah, well I hope you catch the bastard. He was a
good bloke.'

Carla's first home visit on Monday morning was in the middle
of Harrowford. She planned her visits carefully, using a map,
so that she never went back on herself and her afternoon visits
were nearest to the clinic.

She found the end-of-terrace house easily enough. The
front door was painted in a garish pink and the window

frames in dark blue. She quickly made up her mind that here lived someone of little taste. She checked her notes – Karen Oaks – in brackets she'd written (*Tummy tuck – needs it!*). A snotty-nosed boy of about four answered the door. Karen appeared behind him wearing a pink towelling robe decorated with tea stains and grubby finger marks. She was twenty-nine but looked thirty-nine. Her bleached hair was not brushed and her eyes were baggy. Carla made a mental note to suggest a facelift at some time in the near future.

'Make yourself comfortable in the front room,' said Karen, 'and I'll get Shane's breakfast – that'll keep him quiet.'

Shane sat cross-legged in front of the television and, as Karen disappeared into the kitchen, Carla prayed the kid would stay put. He did and moments later Karen returned to hand him a bowl of cereal. 'I wanted Frosties,' he whined and wiped his nose on the sleeve of his pyjamas. Carla was beginning to feel quite nauseated. She disliked children, loathed this sort of house, and the warmth from the gas fire and the lack of ventilation gave the room a smell she recognized from her own childhood – damp sheets and urine.

'It's really good of you to come,' Karen was saying. 'I used to be ever so fat and I've lost the weight but my stomach is a mess.' Then, to Carla's horror, she lifted up her robe to show a tumbling mass of loose skin above skimpy briefs. Carla swallowed and said calmly, 'It certainly needs doing, doesn't it?'

'Yeah. But there's quite a few questions I'd like to ask.'

Thankfully she ceased to expose herself. 'Fire away,' said Carla.

'Is it painful?'

Carla suspected that it was but she merely smiled. 'It will be uncomfortable for a while.'

'How long will I be in?' asked Karen, as she began picking globs of Weetabix from Shane's hair. 'I've got two other kids at school and I'll have to arrange for my mum to look after them.'

'Two full days and for a couple of weeks afterwards you may feel rather weak.'

Karen gave a sharp intake of breath. 'I thought it was a simple op like liposuction.'

Carla smiled her most reassuring smile. 'Every operation has its risks, Karen. An abdominoplasty – that's a tummy tuck – takes three hours or so.' She paused as Shane crept on to his mother's lap. 'And for a few days you won't be able to sit up straight, as that would put too much tension on the stitches.'

'There's more to it than I thought,' said Karen, gazing fondly at little snot nose.

'I like to be totally honest with my clients,' said Carla. 'Is there anything you'd like to ask?'

'Will I have a scar?' she asked.

You silly bitch, thought Carla. 'Yes, Karen,' she said slowly. 'You will have a scar around the navel and along the bikini line. It will look red and angry at first but over the months will fade to a silvery line.'

'Mum,' yelled Shane. 'I want a drink.'

'In a minute,' said Karen. 'This lady hasn't got all day.' Shane poked his tongue out at Carla, wiggled off his mother's lap and began banging his toys about. Karen seemed inured to the noise, but Carla would have cheerfully banged *him*.

'What about the surgeon?' asked Karen. 'I saw Mr Ravenscroft and he seemed very nice. He did explain what he was going to do but I didn't really take it in.'

'Mr Ravenscroft will be doing the op himself and he *is* an excellent surgeon – one of the best.'

'That's reassuring,' said Karen. 'It's such a lot of money.'

'Have you got enough?' asked Carla, finding it hard to believe that she had.

Karen passed a worried hand over her face. 'My mum's lending me the money. I don't know when I'll get round to paying it back.'

'Perhaps I can help you there,' said Carla, honing in for the clincher. 'I'm allowed to offer certain selected clients a very good discount if you'd be prepared to sign up today . . .'

she paused. 'It has to be today to guarantee the surgeon and book a bed.'

Karen frowned anxiously. 'I'm not a hundred per cent sure . . .'

'Do you have a partner?' asked Carla.

Karen shook her head. 'Not any more. He liked me fat. Once I'd lost weight he left.'

'Well, good riddance to him then,' laughed Carla. 'You'll feel a lot more confident in yourself when you've got a lovely flat stomach.' Karen smiled broadly.

And Carla knew that vain hope and her discount offer were on the home straight. 'It's something just for you and you alone, isn't it?' she said, in her best soothing voice.

Karen nodded. 'Yeah. You're right. Just for me.' Then she added, 'Would I be able to get that discount?'

'I've got the paperwork here,' Carla smiled, as she opened her briefcase. She scanned a few printed sheets and then said. 'With a five hundred pound discount the surgery and a two-day stay would be three thousand five hundred pounds and, to be honest, that's a real bargain. The same op at a London clinic would cost twice as much.'

Shane began to whine now and bang at the same time. Carla wanted to say she would have thought that amount was a small price to pay for being away from the brat for a few days.

'So I have to sign today? When would I have the op?'

'If you sign up now you'll have the surgery next week.'

'Next week,' echoed Karen, uncertainly.

'Confidence and peace of mind is beyond price or time.' Carla thought that was a pretty good line, and it worked. There was only a short pause. 'OK,' said Karen. 'I'll do it. I'll sign today.'

By twelve thirty Carla had seen three more prospective clients. Two signed up straight away and she felt really pleased with herself. This was one of the best jobs she'd ever had, second only to being a croupier. Her worst job had been as a travel rep. Without the holidaymakers it would have been fine, but mostly they couldn't follow instructions, were often out of control and, worse – they expected her to *care*.

She drove back to the clinic feeling well pleased with herself. It was only when she saw the police cars her mood changed. What the hell was going on? Whatever it was, she had a feeling it would ruin her day. As she left her car a uniformed officer stopped her. 'Are you Carla Robins?' he asked. She nodded. For some reason her mouth had gone dry.

Four

The director of nursing managed to waylay Rydell as he came down to reception. 'My night staff are exhausted, Inspector, and they have to return to work tonight. Could you please allow them to go home and get some rest?'

'That's fine,' he said, 'as long as they have left their details with the uniformed staff.'

Rydell delegated the setting up of an incident room on the top floor to DS Ram Patel. It was a political choice in the knowledge that everyone would rally round to ease the burden on Ram, who in theory was still on part-time hours.

By eleven thirty Rydell was driving to Saul Ravenscroft's home to break the news to his wife, now his widow, he reminded himself.

Denni sat beside him not saying much, just staring out of the passenger window on to the countryside. 'You're quiet,' he said. 'Problems?'

She shook her head, 'Nothing a mother transplant wouldn't cure.'

Rydell knew of her mother, had even seen her once. She had a face like granite, a mind like a sieve and, from all accounts, Denni was under considerable pressure to move in with her. He sometimes wondered if the reason for Denni being unattached was due solely to the hours of care her mother demanded. 'You should get the professionals in,' he suggested once more.

'She won't have strangers in the house.'

'You're too soft with her.'

'Can we change the subject, guv?'

Silence fell for a few miles then, straight-faced, Rydell said, 'Male cellulite. You don't hear much about cellulite in men, do you? Is it like dimples?'

She watched his face. He, unblinking, watched the road. 'You're taking the piss, guv.'

'Me? Never!'

'I was actually wondering,' said Denni, 'why our victim's wife didn't report him missing. He seems to have been lying there unnoticed for the whole weekend.'

'I've been wondering that too,' said Rydell, as he scanned the side roads for a signpost to the village of Turncliff. 'There's several possibilities, I suppose. One – she didn't know he was missing, thinking he was somewhere else. Two – she's been away for the weekend. Three – he's gone AWOL before and she's stopped caring and, of course, four – she's the perpetrator.'

Denni resumed scenery watching and wished the drive would go on and on. Telling the next of kin was always traumatic. It was the very worst part of the job. Tears she could handle better than the male officers, but the shock and stunned silence – the disbelief – that was difficult. There were no words that helped and at that moment the idea of Mrs Ravenscroft being the killer seemed the most stress-free option.

The village of Turncliff was small enough to be called a hamlet; there was no village shop, one pub and a handful of cottages around a village green.

'This land used to be owned by Lord Turncliff,' explained Denni. When there was no response from Rydell, she added, 'The former owner of the Harmony Clinic.'

'Know-all,' said Rydell, good-naturedly.

The Ravenscroft home lay in several acres of ground on the west side of Turncliff. The surrounding trees, swaying together in the gusts of late October winds, may have been long established, but the building was new – a bungalow so long it resembled a stretch limo. There was a paddock at the back and Denni could just see the top of a stable. A Range

Rover was parked on the front drive and the double garage doors were open to reveal a silver sports car. Rydell rang the doorbell and they waited and waited.

Denni peered through one of the front windows into the long living room; she expected modern, but the style seemed to be a mixture. Two maroon Chesterfields sat divided by a circular glass coffee table, in the middle of which a vase of red roses was reflected in mirrors at either end of the room. The pictures on the walls were mere bright splashes of colour in large frames. The corners of the room were dominated by tall, tropical-looking plants that at least provided some evidence of life. Otherwise there was none.

'Come on,' said Rydell. 'We'll go round the back.'

The kitchen door was slightly ajar to reveal an expanse of white cupboards. Denni repeatedly called out, 'Mrs Ravenscroft,' but there was no response, only the hoot of a lone wood pigeon and a rustling in the trees. Rydell nodded at her to go in then footsteps sounded from behind. Denni swung round to see a young woman in jodhpurs, Barbour jacket, hard hat and carrying a riding crop. 'Who the hell are you?' she demanded. Her accent was that of a southerner, someone who said *barth* for *bath* and *parth* for *path*.

'Mrs Amanda Ravenscroft?' queried Rydell. She nodded, the seeds of anxiety already showing in her pale face. 'Police,' he said, showing her his warrant card. 'May we come inside?'

Denni noticed that she was clutching the riding crop so tightly her knuckles were turning white. She sat down heavily and stared at Rydell. Her make-up was perfect, except that her eyes were red and slightly puffy. 'He's dead, isn't he?' she asked, solemnly. It wasn't a question. It was more a statement, tinged with the hope of a denial.

Rydell sat down beside her. 'Yes. I'm sorry,' he said, slowly. 'Your husband was found dead this morning at the clinic.'

There was a long pause before she said, 'Murdered, of course.'

'You sound as if you were expecting it,' said Rydell, trying not to show his surprise.

Amanda stared at him; she still held the crop in a vice-like grip. Her other hand she'd clenched into a fist. She had long nails and Denni knew that she was deliberately digging her nails into the palm of her hand. Trying to hang on and stay in control. 'I knew she wouldn't let him go,' she said, between clenched teeth. 'That bitch isn't the type to give up. If she couldn't have him . . .' She broke off, trembling and, as her hand shook, the riding crop tapped on the kitchen table.

'Who is *she*?' asked Rydell.

Amanda stared at him as if he was slow on the uptake. 'Carla Robins, of course.'

His raised eyebrows obviously confirmed to her that he was both slow and incompetent. She sighed in exasperation. 'She's the PR person,' she said. 'Known as *the ugly chaser*. My husband had been having an affair with her for a few months – it was inevitable that, once I found out, he'd give her up.'

'He's had more than one affair?' asked Rydell.

She nodded. 'Women around surgeons are like wasps around a toffee apple. He's susceptible. I prefer him to have his flings with married women.'

'Why is that?' asked Denni.

'Because,' answered Amanda slowly, as if speaking to a child, 'they are likely to be discreet and are less likely to take it seriously.'

'And you think Carla Robins took their relationship seriously?'

There was a long pause before she answered. Her eyes glittered with tears, but whether tears of anger or sorrow Denni couldn't tell. 'Seriously enough to kill him. It's quite obvious.'

'She may have an alibi,' suggested Rydell.

'Well, does she?' snapped Amanda. 'You've spoken to her. You're detectives. Surely you can recognize a cold calculating bitch gold-digger when you see one.'

'We haven't spoken to her yet, but I'm sure we'll make the right judgements,' said Rydell, 'based on the evidence.'

'What evidence is that?'

Rydell smiled. 'Forensic evidence, interviews, looking at the circumstantial stuff.'

'You need look no further, Inspector, than Carla Robins.'

'I'll try to bear that in mind.'

At his trace of sarcasm she changed tack. 'Please go before I say something I'll regret.'

'When did you expect him home?' asked Denni. Amanda had by now begun to shiver and she had to struggle to keep her voice sounding normal. 'I expected him home late on Friday.'

'And you didn't ring the clinic?' asked Rydell.

Amanda looked at him sharply. 'Of course I did. I rang after midnight. The security man told me he wasn't signed in. It's a fire regulation to sign the sleeping-in book. And his car wasn't there. So then I presumed he was with her somewhere and I just had to accept that he wasn't home on Friday night.'

'And Saturday night?'

She nodded wearily. 'What was I supposed to do? Ring the police to let them know my husband was shagging away from home two nights running?'

'So what *did* you do, Mrs Ravenscroft?'

'If I answer this, will you go? It may have escaped your notice but I loved my husband – he may not have been the faithful type but it was me he was married to.'

'It's a deal,' said Rydell, with his best reassuring smile.

'On Sunday,' she began, without looking at either of them, 'I went searching for them both. I found *her* at the squash club with a married man, but she denied having seen my husband.'

'The man's name?' asked Rydell. Amanda passed her hand wearily over her face. 'Edward Gray.'

Denni waited a moment, then stood up to leave. Rydell followed her reluctantly. 'Is there anyone you'd like us to call?' asked Denni.

'No. No one.' Now that the realisation was beginning to set in, Amanda's colour had become ashen.

'Perhaps we should call your doctor,' suggested Denni.

'And what will he do – give me some Valium and pat me on the head and tell me time heals all?'

Denni shrugged. She hated to leave someone recently bereaved on their own. 'You must have a neighbour who would come and stay with you.'

Amanda stared at Denni. 'Do I look the type who doesn't have friends? I don't need nosy neighbours. I want to be on my own – for God's sake – I should be allowed that . . .' she broke off. 'And – I want to see his body.' When there was no immediate response, she glanced beseechingly at Rydell.

'As soon as that's possible, we'll take you to him.'

A long sigh of relief escaped her. Rydell signalled at Denni to sit down again. Denni sat and Amanda turned away from her irritably, although when she spoke, her voice was even and controlled. 'I've asked you once to go – I'm not suicidal – in fact I'd been half-expecting it. Carla Robins is a mad bitch and my husband wanted rid of her. She wasn't going to allow that to happen – she's the one who ditches men. She had to kill him.'

'Other than Carla Robins, can you think of anyone else who may have had a motive?' asked Rydell, as he stood at the kitchen door, one hand on the handle, wanting to leave, wanting to get on with organizing his team.

Amanda's answering laugh was totally humourless. 'He was a brilliant surgeon, everyone liked him – men as well as women. He was one of the good guys.'

'Jealousy maybe? Some people can be jealous of the successful good guys.'

'Not that I know,' she replied, dully. 'There's only one person who could have had a motive.'

Rydell judged that, although naturally upset, Amanda was in control of herself and seemed able to cope. It was time to go. They were both at the door when the question was asked.

'How did he die?'

'Very quickly,' answered Rydell. 'He wouldn't have known what was happening.'

'I asked – *how*.'

'His throat was cut with a scalpel.'

She stared bleakly ahead and muttered, as if to herself, 'How ironic.'

Carla had been studying the WPC for half an hour. Not that she made it obvious. She'd been told to wait for the chief inspector and so she waited, silently, observing the young police officer sitting opposite her in the staffroom. Carla let her eyes flick occasionally at the impassive face. It wasn't a face that needed any surgical help, with its neat nose, good chin and unlined eyes. Maybe her skin needed a little more care but she didn't need any abrasive therapy. The only fault Carla could find with this slim brunette was that she had thick ankles and even cosmetic surgery couldn't cure that. So far she hadn't seen her teeth.

'Do you think he'll be long?' she asked, smiling, hoping for a glimpse of enamel in return.

'No idea,' said WPC Nearly Perfect. There was no smile and, to Carla's disappointment, no sight of her dentistry.

Eventually Carla *had* to ask the question, although she knew Miss Nearly Perfect wasn't going to give her a straight answer. 'What's happened?'

'The chief inspector will tell you when he gets here.'

'It must be murder at the very least. If it was a bomb scare we wouldn't be sitting here, would we?'

No answer. Carla shrugged, picked up a fashion magazine and flicked through the pages. She wanted to get to work. This was such a waste of time. A streak of sunlight from the high window shone on the overflowing ashtray on the coffee table. She looked at it in disgust. Later on today she'd make a formal complaint.

Five

Rumours spread around the Harmony Clinic within hours, like fast-flowing lava. In the telling, Saul Ravenscroft had died in several different ways – shooting, stabbing and battering. Suspects ranged between his first wife, his second wife, his present wife, the co-director and, ultimately, the gossip settled on the idea of a deranged psychopathic killer stalking the grounds. The fact that Ravenscroft had been single until three years previously didn't matter. What the staff didn't know they made up.

Stanley Goodman, the security man, wearing his semi-police type uniform, spread the rumour just as easily as volcanic dust. The rumour clung to him and then was passed on in every quiet whisper, every knowing glance. As he stopped on his rounds he shook off his theory and managed to make it stick. Soon everyone shared what they thought the police suspected. A mad killer was stalking the clinic.

The day the police had found the body Stanley had arrived home late, but his eyes were bright and shining. 'You wouldn't believe it,' he told his wife, Freda, who lay in bed banked by pillows and smiling at him, waiting for him to get her up. Stanley had phoned her on his mobile to tell her the news. Not that she really cared, but she loved to hear news and gossip from outside her own four walls. 'Police everywhere,' he said, pulling off his tie. 'Of course, I was a key witness. The inspector spent ages talking to me. He said my memory was second to none.'

'You've got a good memory, dear.'

'I always knew I had, but it's nice to get it confirmed,

50

especially by a cop.' He began taking off his uniform. 'I'll see to you in a minute, Freda. I'm all of a doodah. I wish you could have been there. Of course, the police think the same as I do – there's a deranged killer on the loose. One of them psychopaths who hears voices – that's who's done it.'

'How did he get in?' Her high-pitched voice halfway to a whine irritated him.

'Trust you to ask a silly question.' He paused to slip on a tracksuit bottom and allow himself time to think about her question. 'I reckon he was hiding somewhere. Probably came in the crowd for the do.'

'Seems likely,' she murmured, not knowing if it was or not.

'Ravenscroft was the best surgeon in that place. Bloody shame some nutter cut him up and I bet the police don't catch him and, if they do, all he'll get is a few years in jail or a mental hospital. Hang 'em – that's the answer.'

'But if he's mentally ill . . .'

'Mad dog! That's what he is. And what do they do with mad dogs? Shoot 'em!'

Stanley hung up his uniform ready for the evening and walked through to the kitchen to put the kettle on. He'd begun to feel tired now as the excitement left him, but first he had to get Freda up. I ought to get help with her, he thought, but it cost money and he could care for her better than anyone. He put a tea bag in each mug then added sugar and milk to both, finally he topped the mugs up with boiling water. He let the tea brew to a darkish tan then removed the tea bags with sugar tongs.

'Stan, I'm getting desperate,' she called out.

'Tell me about it,' he muttered, as he walked the short distance to the bedroom.

The tea had to wait. She wanted the bathroom. He took a quick sip of his, then put the two mugs on the dressing table. 'Come on then, you old bag of bones,' he said, as he pulled back the duvet. It was his little joke. Freda was fat, arthritic and asthmatic. In fact, she had more medical problems than he could remember. He pulled her upright and then, hands under her arms, he lifted her on to the commode chair. It strained his back and made him sweat but he'd been doing it for five years and he was used to it now. Then he wheeled her to the lavatory, left her there and walked back to his mug of tea. His next job would be to shower her. He didn't mind the showering bit, it was getting her dry afterwards that irritated him. She had more crevices than the Grand Canyon and she would whine, *I'm not quite dry yet* at least three times. Dressing her was not such a problem. Just knickers, a tracksuit top and bottoms and her slippers. Two years ago he'd abandoned tights and bras and slips. Once he'd hauled her into the wheelchair she could wheel herself around the bungalow and make him some breakfast. Then he'd have a smoke, read the paper and get into the single bed next to hers.

It was nearly half past eleven by the time he did get into bed. He'd be up again at five. 'Have a nice rest, Stanley,' she said, as she always did. He lay in bed listening to the sounds of the television, which stayed on all day. He'd been married to Freda for nearly forty years and she'd ailed from day one, but he often had the feeling now she would outlive him. It didn't matter whichever way it went. He would be more lonely if she went first, but he just tried to get through each day without dwelling on their future, which could only be worse than the past.

As he was falling asleep he relived his police interview. He'd liked the young detective sergeant. She looked soft and had gentle eyes. She didn't stir his imagination like his queen of the night, but if he was hard-pressed for a face and a body to fantasize about, she would do. You're a sad old bugger, Stanley thought. It was a big disappointment to him that he hadn't had sex for ten years but a much bigger disappointment to realize that he might never have sex again – ever.

At five the click of the door and the thud of the wheelchair hitting his divan woke him. He felt lousy. He had to force his eyes open. Freda was smiling down at him. She'd brushed her wispy hair and put some lipstick on, but nothing could help her pasty flabby face now. He roused himself to smile at her and take the mug of tea she offered him.

'I've done you a nice bit of haddock,' she said. 'It's been on the news about your murder. A real loss, they say he is, in the world of cosmetic surgery. They've interviewed a couple of actresses and they looked ever so upset.'

'Don't expect they know where their next facelift is coming from,' said Stan.

'That's no way to talk, dear.'

'It's true enough though. He was a good surgeon. Pity he didn't do more with his talents.'

'You know best, dear,' she said, knowing he wanted her to disagree. Stanley drank his tea. In his groggy state he wasn't up to an argument and Freda was an old hand at placating him.

She wheeled herself off into the kitchen and the smell of the smoked haddock cheered him up. He just hoped she'd cooked a poached egg as well. Together with some bread and butter it would set him up for a night's work. He sat down to eat and she set the plate awkwardly in front of him. Everything she did was awkward but it couldn't be helped. She did the best she could.

'I expect the police will want to interview me again,' he said.

'You be careful,' she said, her mouth half-full. 'If a maniac is on the loose, you could be first in line.' A trickle of egg ran down from her mouth.

'Wipe your mouth,' he said. She wiped her mouth with the back of her hand. He finished his meal before he spoke again. 'I'll try to get back to put you to bed about midnight but if the police are there, I won't be able to manage it. So you'll have to sleep on the sofa.'

'I'll be all right. You don't want to get caught, do you?'

They washed up together in silence. Stanley didn't like to leave her at night, but it was against the rules to leave the clinic at all while he was on duty. Even so, every night he returned, just after midnight, to put her to bed. He'd made a gap in the fencing at the far side of the grounds. From there it was five minutes brisk walk to his housing association bungalow. Sometimes it took him half an hour to get Freda organized and ready for bed. He was gone for an hour – maximum. Lucky for him the CCTV camera didn't pick up every square inch of the grounds.

As he was transferring Freda from her wheelchair to the sofa, the thought crossed his mind that it was possible the killer had used the same entry and exit point. Even worse, the killer could have followed him and maybe even knew where he lived.

'Not so rough, Stanley dear.'

'Sorry, love. This murder business is on my mind.'

'Well, don't you worry about me. I'll be fine – don't forget my catheter bag, will you?'

'Do I ever?'

'No. You're the best, Stan.' He smiled and patted her face. It wasn't her fault she was barely sixty and an invalid. Neither of them had much of a life, but it was all they had and he didn't want some deranged killer spoiling even that. Stanley was Freda's life. Without him she'd be reliant on strangers. She couldn't bear the thought of that. She'd be better off dead.

The walk via the front of the clinic took ten to fifteen minutes. He did have a bicycle but it needed new tyres, new gears, plus a new saddle and, so far this year, he hadn't been able to afford to get it repaired. There was slight drizzle starting but he didn't mind – it was refreshing – made him feel wide awake.

As he walked into the clinic grounds and saw, in the half-light, a van parked near reception and uniformed police clambering into it, he realized what they'd been doing. A fingertip search of the area. He slowed down. Had he left anything behind near that bit of fence? A thread from clothes or a cigarette end? They might think he was the killer. It was a chilly evening but he could feel himself growing damp under the arms. He had a feeling that tonight was going to be a long hard night.

Lyn Kilpatrick had finally left the clinic that Monday morning at ten thirty. She hadn't been interviewed as such because Una Fairchild had intervened, telling the chief inspector that the night staff had been on duty for twelve hours and that they couldn't think straight, let alone answer questions. A PC had filled out a personal descriptive form and asked her for a date at the same time. She refused as always, saying she was spoken for. Saying that didn't constitute a lie, it was just nicely ambiguous. Her two children more than spoke for her. She lived next door to another single parent and between them they shared babysitting.

Seeing the body had been a tremendous shock. The cleaner's scream followed by *Sister! Sister!* had made her dash up the stairs thinking a patient had wandered up there and collapsed. Instead she'd found the cleaner crying outside the on-call room and in the bathroom a sea of blood with Saul's naked body in the middle of it. At first she'd stood there taking in the scene, hearing her heart drum in her chest. The arrival of Stanley made her pull herself together. She didn't want him, of all people, gawping at the body. She told him to call the police, then she closed the door and stood guard until the police arrived.

Eventually the police had allowed her to do the handover to the day staff and Una had insisted on hot sweet tea and they'd sat in Una's office, saying little, but trying to accept that their chief and best surgeon had been murdered. Una sat at her large desk looking fresh and businesslike, in contrast to Lyn, who felt as if she had been in a war zone. Her eyes were gritty, her chest felt tight and her feet and head throbbed as one.

It was Una who asked the question that Lyn wanted to ask. 'You don't think his wife . . .' Then she muttered to herself, 'No. I'm sure she didn't.'

Lyn wasn't that sure. But she thought it more likely to have been a jealous cuckolded husband or boyfriend. Saul, the good surgeon, was a known womanizer. But his wife knew that and she wouldn't risk being seen at the clinic if she'd planned some sort of violent showdown. But then, who would? Only one name came readily to mind.

'We'll have to advertise as quickly as possible for another surgeon,' said Una, as she sifted through a pile of letters. 'Martin won't be able to cope on his own even with a registrar.' Martin Samuels was a major shareholder and surgeon number two – now elevated to number one.

'He hasn't got the same pulling power as poor Saul,' Lyn said. Una looked up sharply, and Lyn, being tired, didn't realize what she'd said. Una, recognizing a Freudian slip and noticing the exhaustion in Lyn's eyes, picked up the phone and summoned a cab. 'Best not to drive,' she said. 'I'll send a taxi round for you tonight.'

Lyn felt grateful even though it was only a short distance to drive. As she stood up she felt a little faint. 'Get plenty of rest,' said Una briskly.

Once home Lyn stripped off her uniform and underwear in the hall. She gathered them up and put them straight in the washing machine, adding to that the washing that her two children had stuffed in the space between the machine and the work surface. She decided against having a bath, being so tired she might fall asleep in it. She checked her phone messages. Sean and Zoe had slept well, except that Sean, who was six, had wet the bed. Zoe, aged eight, had decided she hated her new teacher. Holly's phone message ended, 'Is it true? Has Saul been murdered? Are you OK? See you later. I'll fetch the kids from school – get some sleep.'

Lyn viewed her bed with its cream duvet and soft plump pillows with as much, if not more, desire than a woman in the first throes of love. She suspected, though, that the bed, like sex, might be disappointing and that she might lie awake reliving events. For a while she did, even wanted to, but within minutes of lying prone, she was fast asleep.

'Mum! Mum! I've had a horrible day – can we have some biscuits?' Lyn struggled to sit up, her eyelids felt swollen and her mouth was dry. Zoe had little patience. 'Come on, Mum. Get up!'

'Where's Sean?'

'Holly's downstairs with him. I'm hungry.'

'I'll be down in a minute.'

Zoe shrugged. 'Well, don't be long. Holly's made you some tea.'

Lyn splashed her face with cold water, slipped on her dressing gown and walked downstairs to the kitchen. Holly was busy mopping rusk from baby Sophie's mouth. She was twenty-two but looked about eighteen. She looked up. Her blue eyes were full of concern. 'I'm really sorry,' she said. 'I bet it was a shock.'

'Mum, what's Holly talking about?' asked Zoe.

Sean, who was playing with his cars, looked up. 'I got a star today, Mum.'

'Jolly good,' said Lyn, easing herself on to a kitchen stool.

Holly pressed a mug of tea into Lyn's hand. 'You look knackered,' she said.

'I am. I feel as if I've been in an accident.' She glanced at Sophie, aged five months, who sat in her baby seat, seriously regarding everyone. Lyn smiled and cooed and Sophie's face, round and dimpled, broke into a huge smile. Lyn couldn't resist kneeling down to kiss her forehead and inhale her baby smell.

'Come on, Lyn,' urged Holly. 'Drink your tea and tell me all about it.'

By now both children had gone into the living room, but Lyn felt reluctant to talk. She noticed Holly's eager expression. She had the baby but little else. She couldn't afford a TV licence, hardly ever went out and, if it wasn't for Lyn's full fridge and freezer, she would have gone without food. Sophie was the result of a three-month love affair. At least it was love on Holly's part. As soon as her boyfriend found out she was pregnant he disappeared. Neither she nor the DSS could track him down.

'I'll let you feed the baby if you tell me the details,' she said, with a winning smile. Lyn nodded. Holly wasn't insensitive, it was just that she didn't know the whole story and she loved hospital gossip. In some ways she lived her life through Lyn – they shared the children, shared cooking, outings in the summer, even Lyn's bed was a shared item. While she worked, Holly and Sophie slept in her bed.

So, as she cuddled Sophie on her lap, Lyn told her the events of that night. Holly hung on to every word. It was only when she asked for more description of Saul's body that Lyn began to feel choked. 'I didn't really look properly,' she lied. 'There was a lot of blood.' That wasn't a lie.

'So who do you think did it?'

Lyn shrugged, 'Stan the security man thinks it's a psychotic on the loose.'

'Do you think that?'

Lyn shook her head. 'No. It was someone who knew he was staying overnight. He wasn't on call. He must have given the locum the night off, if there was one booked. Maybe he'd had a drink and he didn't want to drive.'

'But why did no one find him till Monday morning?'

'Search me. The *do not disturb* sign was on the door. The cleaners don't do the staff floor at the weekends. And there was no call-out over the weekend.'

'I reckon it was a jealous husband,' said Holly, bright-eyed and animated.

'I think it was more likely to be Carla Robins.'

'You didn't tell me he was shagging *her.*'

'Didn't I? I thought I had.'

Holly looked at her quizzically. 'You're not usually so secretive about what's going on at the clinic.'

'I'm not being secretive. It's common knowledge that they were at it.'

'So it could have been one of *her* exes?' suggested Holly.

'Yeah – I suppose,' said Lyn, reluctantly. 'He could have been in the building with the others for the open evening.'

'Maybe she did do it,' said Holly. 'A crime of passion. He refused to leave his wife and she cut him up.'

Lyn was non-committal. 'The police will find out.'

'Will they? They don't always. Perfect murders do get committed.'

Lyn was about to answer when Sean and Zoe came running in. Sean was trying to batter Zoe with a plastic sword and her high-pitched shrieks seemed to pierce Lyn's eardrums. 'For God's sake – SHUT UP!' she yelled. Zoe paused mid-scream. 'It's his fault. He was hitting me.'

Lyn took a deep breath.

'Just go in the other room and watch TV – quietly. I'm trying to talk to Holly.'

'There's nothing on the telly. You're horrible!'

When they'd left the room Lyn noticed her hands were shaking and the baby responded by waking and screaming loudly. Holly picked up the baby and she immediately quietened. 'You're in a state, aren't you?' she said. 'I've never heard you yell at the kids like that before.'

'I'm just tired. It's been a shock.'

'It's a good thing you didn't really know him, then.'

'Yeah,' mumbled Lyn.

Later, when she left in a taxi for work, Holly and the children stood waving at the door, watching her go. The hall light lit their faces and for a moment she thought she saw suspicion on Holly's face. Once the taxi had driven off, Lyn told herself she was being paranoid – after all, one fleeting expression could easily be wrongly interpreted. As friends they shared care of the children, they ate and drank and laughed together, but in reality, Holly knew only what Lyn wanted her to know.

Six

R ydell's experience of murder investigations was that the first twenty-four hours were not only the most vital time, but were also a real test of stamina. After thirty-six hours, with only three catnaps, he was beginning to realize he couldn't hold out much longer. Always a list maker he now seemed to be making lists of lists. He'd organized the team, the fingertip search had been completed and the post-mortem performed, but not yet reported on. The scenes of crime team had bagged up, dusted, sampled and photographed the murder scene. They had also videoed the murder scene plus the whole of the clinic. The personal descriptive forms had been filled in, and he had the names and addresses of all those attending the open evening. Plus they had briefly interviewed the security man, Kirsty the receptionist and one or two of the patients.

Now it was nine p.m. and he was sitting with Denni in the staffroom on the top floor of the clinic. Not that Denni was actually *with* him, she had fallen asleep on one of the bench-type sofas and it was all he could do not to join her. He had to struggle to keep awake until eleven, when they could then begin interviewing the night care staff. The director of nursing had explained that, regardless of murder, the work of the clinic must go on and that the clients must come first. He couldn't really argue with that, but in his opinion, a tummy tuck was a damn sight less significant than catching a murderer.

There was no computer, as yet, in the staffroom, so he was planning tomorrow's briefings by hand. The press were hungry for news and he knew they had converged on the

60

window like starving seagulls. The uniformed men at the gate had so far managed to keep them out of the clinic, but soon, keeping officers on gate duty would become too expensive and they would swarm in. Rydell had no time for journalists. They were only doing their job, he knew, but the truth got distorted or at least dramatized and he thought they preyed on the vulnerable. No, he didn't think that, he knew it. At least a press briefing meant they had no excuses to become creative and they might even print the truth. Anyway, press coverage was almost academic because he was confident that this investigation would be a short one. An inside job. With any luck it should all be over by the end of the week.

He began making neat piles of the paperwork on the coffee table. The staffroom had been a tip and he'd helped tidy it up. His attitude was that if you couldn't control your environment then it controlled you.

Denni lay sideways facing the wall, her breathing deep and regular. All he could see was the back of her blonde hair. She'd kicked one shoe off and the other was half off. For all her good points she was not a tidy person. She'd been a psychiatric nurse before joining the police and he'd assumed nurses were tidy and methodical. Not so in Denni's case. Ram Patel was more organized and, although he gave the impression of being laid-back and carefree, Rydell sensed his anxiety, especially since his head injury. Ram would have described all three of them as sad bastards and perhaps that was true. The significant other in their lives remained the job.

Denni stirred just before eleven. Her roundish face had red crease marks down one side, reminding him uncomfortably of a child's face after sleep – his child.

'At last,' he said. 'Sleeping Beauty awakes.'

'I feel more like Lady Macbeth.' She brushed her hair and checked her face in the staffroom mirror. 'I don't just feel like her – I look like her.'

'No you don't,' said Rydell. 'I'm sure Lady M was a brunette.'

Denni managed a weary smile, took a notebook and pen from her handbag and checked her interview list.

'Who are we interviewing first, guv?

'Alvera Lewis. Only because she's on first break and that's from twelve thirty to one thirty. I'm mostly interested in what she knows about Carla Robins.'

'Hospitals are just like nicks – all gossip and rumour. Most of it untrue.'

'You do the talking, Denni. I'll play the strong silent male part and listen, while you do the two-women-over-the-garden-fence bit.'

'Thanks, guv. I'll do you a favour one day.'

When Alvera did arrive, Rydell made coffee for them all.

'I don't drink coffee,' said Alvera.

'Tea then?' suggested Rydell.

'No thanks.'

Denni noticed Alvera's strong arms and rather lumbering walk. She had checked the PDF and found that Alvera was fifty-nine. She didn't look it, but the heavy way she walked suggested to Denni that Alvera suffered from backache or worn hips or both. Something in her attitude also suggested she didn't like or trust the police.

'Sorry to interrupt your night,' said Denni, with a friendly smile.

'I got to be here.'

'How long have you worked at the clinic?'

'A year.'

'So you knew Mr Ravenscroft?'

'I didn't know the man. He smiled at me and said hello – that's all.'

'But I expect the others talked about him.'

'Some did, some didn't.'

'Did you hear he was a good surgeon?'

'Yes. I heard that.'

'What did you think when he was found murdered?'

There was a long pause before she answered. 'I think the Good Lord has his ways.'

'How do you mean?'

'The Good Lord knows those who repent their sins.'

'You think he was a sinner?'

'Of course. We're all sinners.'

'How did he sin?'

Alvera sat back in her chair and folded her arms. They reminded Denni of hams.

'His sins were of the flesh. He was *the* fornicator.' Denni noted the defining *the*. Obviously to Alvera he was not merely a devil, but the devil incarnate.

'Would you tell me why you're so sure of that?'

'I'm sure.' Alvera looked towards Rydell. 'You don't say much?' she said, coldly.

'I listen,' said Rydell. 'And I can tell you are a woman of principles.'

'The Good Lord help me. I put my trust in the Lord.'

'So,' said Denni. 'You think Saul Ravenscroft was a fornicator because you heard other people saying he was. Jesus was condemned to death on rumour and suspicion.' Alvera stared at Denni and pursed her lips. 'Our Lord was pure – and praise the Lord for that. You shouldn't speak of Him in the same way you speak of bad people.'

'How do you know Mr Ravenscroft was a bad person? You said yourself he was a good surgeon.'

'He just wanted money from people who only think about themselves. Vain people always looking in the mirror. What do they see in the mirror? Ugly – they don't see their souls. The soul is what matters, not what you look like on the outside. Only the Lord matters. People forget that. The Lord will redeem all sinners who repent.'

Denni looked across at Rydell, who raised one eyebrow as much to say, you're stuck with this one.

'Why do you work here, Alvera?'

'I work here 'cos it's not hard work. My back is painful and my doctor said I should take light work at my age.'

'I see. I did hear,' said Denni, softly and slowly, so that

Alvera would think it significant, 'that Mr Ravenscroft was planning to stop seeing Carla Robins.'

'She not the only one,' snapped Alvera.

'There *were* other women then?'

'Men like him ain't satisfied with one woman,' she said, with more than a touch of venom in her voice. 'They're always searching, like foxes looking for food. Their souls need feeding, not their bodies.'

'OK Alvera – name names!'

Alvera seemed taken aback by Denni's sharp tone. 'I got no names to give you. I've seen him.'

'Where did you see him?'

She pursed her lips again. 'Come on, Alvera,' urged Denni. 'You're a Christian woman. It's your Christian duty to tell us the truth.'

'I seen him. I seen him take women in that room. I heard him talking to women.'

'How many are we talking about here – a baker's dozen or the odd tartlet?'

Alvera didn't think that was funny. 'I saw him with Carla Robins on Friday night. I came up to this floor to . . . I saw her going in the on-call room.'

'Where were you when you saw this?'

'At the end of the corridor.'

'What time was this?'

'I didn't take no notice of the time.'

'Why did you come up to this floor?'

'For the staff toilet.'

'Isn't there one on the second floor?'

'There's a visitor's toilet and at night the girls use that, but I don't. I'm fussy.'

'OK Alvera. We've established you saw Carla – who else have you seen?'

'I don't say I saw them. The Lord knows I couldn't swear on the Bible it was her – I only saw her back as she went in the room.'

'And who was it?'

Alvera unfolded her arms and sighed. 'It was the director of nursing.'

'You mean Una Fairchild?'

Alvera nodded. 'I was shocked. She's a nice woman – a married woman. I know her skinny backside. It *was* her.'

'Did you see him?'

'No.'

'So it could have been someone else in the room?'

'He was in the clinic that night.'

'Can you remember the date?'

'No.'

Denni glanced towards Rydell. 'Is there anything you want to ask, guv?' He smiled and gave a slight shake of his head.

'Nearly finished then, Alvera,' said Denni, smiling but getting a stony stare in return. 'In your opinion, Mr Ravenscroft was seeing Carla Robins, Una Fairchild and who else?'

'Lord help me – it was the girl I work with – Wendy Swan. I thought she was a nice girl, but I see them together.'

'Here in the clinic?'

'No, in town. He was buying her flowers. I saw them together in the shop.'

'It doesn't mean to say they were sleeping together.'

Alvera looked about to concede that point. 'The Good Lord knows about that,' she said, looking upwards. 'He watches us all. On judgement day all the sinners will be lined up before the Lord. Only a few will enter the kingdom of Heaven.'

'It would be a very long queue.'

Alvera wagged a pudgy finger in Denni's face. 'I think you're a nice woman, but you should take Our Lord more seriously. You're never too young to prepare for death. Remember – the Lord is waiting.'

Denni tried to keep a straight face. 'I'll try to remember that – thank you.'

The actual details of Friday night Alvera couldn't remember. She remembered the place was untidy and that Lyn had had her break in the day room from two to three. 'One night here is like the next,' she said. 'I do my job and what other people do is their business.'

When asked if anyone was missing from the floor for any length of time, she shrugged. 'We're in and out of rooms like jack rabbits. The bells ring and we answer them. I don't care what the others do. All that matters is the Good Lord knows I do my job properly.'

Once Alvera had gone, Denni breathed a sigh of relief, mostly because she had laughed. She'd nursed many mentally ill religious fanatics. They made her uneasy.

'Nutter?' asked Rydell. 'Or harmless zealot? Maybe she's our killer. Her arms are powerful enough. She could crush walnuts in her elbow.'

'You still haven't told me about the reports,' said Denni. 'Play fair, guv.'

'That's what I'm trying to do. I don't want to jump to any hasty conclusions and let you jump with me.'

'I do have a mind of my own.'

'And that's precisely why I asked you if Alvera Lewis is a fanatic capable of murder.'

'I'm not a shrink – that's hardly a fair question. I'd have to get to know a bit more about her background. She's on the surface just a respectable church-going woman with very fixed ideas. But those fixed ideas would probably keep her on the straight and narrow – unless . . .'

'Unless what?'

'Unless something traumatic happened and she took a detour.'

'I suppose that could be said about most of us,' murmured Rydell. 'Anyway – check her out. Criminal record, any psychiatric history, pay a home visit. You know the score.'

'You think Carla Robins did it, don't you?'

'I'm keeping an open mind. All the circumstantial points that way. She's the coldest woman I've ever met.'

'Cold is good,' said Denni. 'You need real emotion for unpremeditated murder.'

'I think this murder was planned like an army manoeuvre,'

murmured Rydell, as he tidied the growing pile of personal descriptive forms.

'She'd need a good motive to risk everything. What motive could Carla have? She wouldn't benefit from his death – would she?'

'Not financially. Maybe she was looking to be a shareholder, a major shareholder in the clinic. Ram can do some financial digging on that. He can add in double figures.'

Ten minutes later Wendy Swan arrived. She smiled nervously at both of them. Denni could tell that this one was to be Rydell's interview. She was young and attractive and unlikely to be a religious fanatic. Rydell's face had a more animated expression now. Denni sat back in her chair and felt curiously relaxed, as though she was in the judgement seat, only, thankfully, the queue wouldn't stretch to infinity.

Denni read the personal descriptive form – Wendy Swan was twenty-six, divorced and living alone. Her hair was described as shoulder length and blonde, although Denni could see dark roots. She had eyes the colour of strong tea. In the summer she'd had a tan, but now it had faded, leaving her complexion sallow. Night duty had given her dark rings under the eyes, but it hadn't yet affected her figure. She was listed as being five foot five of slim to average build. Her features, although neat, were spoilt, Denni thought, by her small taut mouth.

Rydell listened to her carefully as she told him that, although she'd been on duty that night, she hadn't heard or seen anything. 'Tell me about Saul Ravenscroft,' said Rydell. Denni noted the surprise on her face.

'I'm quite new here but I've heard he was a very good surgeon.'

'You didn't know him socially?'

'No. I saw him once or twice late at night and early morning. He did his rounds then, but the trained nurse always accompanied him.'

'You didn't meet him outside the clinic?'

'No.'

Rydell took notes. This seemed to worry her. 'Why are you writing everything down?'

He smiled. 'Just so that I have a record of everything you say. These are only preliminary interviews.'

'So you could interview me again?'

'Does that bother you?'

She shook her head. 'No – but I didn't see anything. I can't be much help.'

'Did you leave the floor that night?'

'No.'

'You're sure? You didn't come up to the staffroom during the night.'

'No. I think it's creepy up here at night.'

'Did any of the staff come up here on that Friday night?'

'Is that when he was killed?'

Rydell nodded. 'Yes. Did anyone leave your floor that night?'

'I can't remember. We're moving about all the time.'

'Have you heard the rumours about Carla Robins?'

'Everyone's heard them. I don't believe it.'

'Why not?'

She shrugged. 'All sorts of rumours go round this place.'

'But you don't believe Carla and Ravenscroft were an item.'

'No, I don't believe that,' she said, sharply. 'They may have had a one-night stand but I'm sure that's all.'

'Why are you so sure?'

'She had other men.'

'You saw her with them?'

'Yes.'

Rydell smiled. 'You sound peeved, Wendy, as if you fancied him.'

She paused and watched Rydell, as if trying to read in his expression the answer she was supposed to give.

'A lot of women fancied him rotten.'

'And you? What did you *really* think about him.'

'If I was his wife I would have killed him.'

'Really?'

She shrugged. 'Who knows? No one knows what they'll do until it happens.'

'So no man has ever cheated on you?'

'I didn't say that. Anyway, my personal life is my business.'

'Fair enough. We'll be speaking to you again. In the meantime, I'd like you to think about what you'll write in your statement about Friday night.'

'Statement?' she queried.

'Yes. A record of what happened from when you came on duty to when the body was found.'

'I can go now, can I?' She half stood, eager to get away.

'Is there anything you want to ask?' Rydell asked, looking across at Denni.

'Just one thing,' she said. 'Do you have any hobbies, Wendy?'

Wendy stood up. 'I don't have much time. I go clubbing sometimes in Birmingham.'

'So you're not into flower arranging?'

'No. Why should I be?'

By now Wendy Swan was on her feet.

'And Alvera?'

'What about her?'

'Do you think she's an honest woman?'

Wendy raised her eyebrows in surprise. 'A bit too honest at times. She's very strait-laced.'

'Thanks for your help, Wendy.'

They waited in silence as she closed the door and they heard the dull thud of her clogs on the carpet.

'Well, what do you think to her?' asked Rydell.

'You want me to be blunt?'

'You often are.'

'I think she was either shagging him or wanting to.'

'Is she worth a follow-up?'

'Definitely. A bit of delving into her background might throw up why she's working nights.'

'Does she have a choice?'

'Oh yes. It's not internal rotation. She's a volunteer. She works overtime too. She should work four nights one week, three the next, but she often works five or six nights a week.'

'So you're saying,' said Rydell, 'that she's nuts too. A workaholic?'

'Could just be short of money,' conceded Denni, 'although I think she might have wanted to catch a glimpse of you know who.'

'You think she was that besotted?'

'I do. But maybe it's just a gut feeling rather than what she actually said.'

'She didn't give much away.'

'Enough,' murmured Denni to herself. 'Enough.'

Seven

G raham Coombs was discharged from the clinic, much to his disappointment, at ten thirty a.m. on Tuesday. A taxi drove him home and, after he'd paid the taxi driver, he stood staring up at the attic room paid for by the DSS. He was reluctant to go inside, but he told himself that from now on his life would change for the better. After all, now he had a new nose. Tomorrow he would begin planning for his new life. Once the swelling went down he would look normal. People would notice *him*, not his nose. He would find a job and, in a few weeks, he could start dating Lyn.

As he turned his key in the lock and opened the door he realized there was something different. The dull brown and cream paintwork was just the same, the green floor tiles were just as scuffed, but there was no smell and for that he was grateful. For once, having lost something was an asset. Before the operation, whenever he came into the building the smell had always bothered him. He'd previously rushed up the stairs to escape the cooking smells – garlic and chips and old stews. Today he walked up slowly, delighting in the fact that he could smell nothing.

Once in his room he felt quite tired, so he sat at the table by the window and stared down at the street. The sun shone weakly and grey clouds threatened rain. The litter and a few dead leaves, swept along by a breeze, were the only movement he could see. Once Oakdale Road had been upmarket, with its grand four-storey houses. Now they were all flats and bedsits, window frames rotted, paint peeled and the only cars that were parked outside were old bangers.

Graham couldn't drive. He'd had three lessons once, but he'd been so nervous – his leg trembled violently and clutch control was beyond him. His instructor had recommended tranquilizers. Graham had called him a stupid bastard and resolved to live his life via trains and buses. For years he'd taken a real interest in trains, but he'd met so many cranks who were obsessed by timetables that he resolved not to associate with such people.

After a while the view palled and he walked into his kitchenette and measured a mug of water and poured it into the kettle. He hated waste. He looked at his watch – it was eleven fifteen. He had the whole day to kill.

Wendy Swan and Alvera compared notes on their interviews that night. By midnight the floor was quiet and they stood in the clinical room to talk.

'What did they ask you?' queried Alvera, as she sprayed antibacterial spray on to a trolley. Wendy, checking supplies, opened a drawer noisily. 'Nothing much really – did I see anything? Did I go upstairs to the staffroom? The woman cop, for some reason, asked me if I liked flower arranging.'

Alvera coughed nervously. 'I did say I see you in a florist's with Mr Ravenscroft.'

'You did what?' Wendy couldn't keep the irritation from her voice.

'I just told the truth . . . Our Lord said . . .'

'Don't say any more, Alvera. He might be your Lord but he isn't mine. You grassed me up because you think your religion protects you. Next time I speak to them I'll tell them you *did* leave the floor that night. You'll be a suspect then – religious maniacs are always suspects.'

Alvera, spray in hand, opened her mouth, closed it again, banged down the spray bottle and said, 'You're a wicked woman and may the Good Lord forgive you.'

'Go take a running jump, Alvera.'

Alvera clumped to the door but stopped in the doorway. 'You *could* have left the floor that night.'

Vain Hope

Wendy turned her back and it was only when she heard Alvera stomping along the corridor that she noticed she was trembling.

Pam Miles was off duty. She should have been grateful but she wasn't. At work she had vague worries about patients, but as long as she reported any abnormalities to the nurse in charge, it was then her responsibility. At home abnormalities were normal and she was the one who had to do all the thinking. Somehow she'd managed to bring up her three boys to be lazy, irresponsible and showing no ambition in any direction. Some mornings she dreaded going home so much that, once she was in the car, she thought she would just drive on and on and on and on. It was her dream. She'd have her clothes and some of her belongings crammed in her car and her life savings, which didn't amount to much, and then, when she could drive no more, she'd stop. Nestling in some small sleepy village would be a bed and breakfast or a small guest house with stark white net curtains and hanging baskets and roses and ivy creeping up the walls. She'd stop, have a late breakfast and then take to her bed. After a night or two, she'd drive on until she found a little house to rent. Eventually she'd find a job, buy a bicycle, become slim and go dancing again.

Since the murder she knew that dream was on hold. She'd been interviewed twice, more of a chat really. She told them she was bothered by hot flushes and her concentration wasn't good. And she told them that Friday, Saturday night and Sunday night had all merged into one, so she wasn't reliable about that particular night. It wasn't much use the cops saying, *When did you do that*? or asking how many times the bells rang that night. Wendy Swan had made her laugh. 'Don't the cops realize,' she'd said, 'we're all zombies on night duty?'

One day, she told herself, as she gathered up beer cans, emptied ashtrays and gathered up the dirty clothes dropped on the floor, I'll be away from all this . . .

* * *

73

Wendy Swan, having worked five nights in a row, felt spaced out. She had to work and the clinic didn't use agency staff. The bells had rung all night. Perhaps the new patients sensed the unease in the clinic, or maybe they thought the killer would strike again. Either way there had been no peace.

She hadn't spoken to Alvera since their row. In fact, none of the staff spoke much. Even Stan seemed depressed. He was a funny bloke. She didn't know if he was married or single but she suspected single. He probably watched porn on the internet.

When eight o'clock came, Wendy dashed off quickly and stood behind one of the bushes to smoke a cigarette. She didn't like smoking in her own car. The cigarette helped a little and she didn't have far to drive. She lived in a starter home – a one-bedroom box – on an estate of the young and childless. In her *cul de sac* of six boxes she was the only one living alone. She was planning to move in the future, but she could still afford the mortgage if she worked long hours and anyway, she was never quite sure where she actually wanted to live. Not since that night two years ago.

She'd been working nights at the local hospital but she'd felt ill during her shift and had been sent home. Once she'd got into her car the nausea had disappeared. She'd been feeling tired and a little off colour and her breasts had been uncomfortable for days. Pregnancy hadn't occurred to her until then because her periods had always been so irregular. Tingling breasts, feeling sick – tired all the time. 'I'm pregnant,' she'd said aloud, as she drove. 'I'm pregnant!'

By the time she got home she'd felt fine, elated even. She'd surprise Lee – she'd wake him and they'd make love and only then would she tell him she was pregnant.

She'd crept into the house, slipped off her uniform and underwear in the hall and padded up the stairs. She'd paused at the door to listen to his heavy breathing. Oh yes, he'd been fast asleep. She opened the door. It creaked. The bitch beside him woke first. Her mouth opened but no sound came out.

74

Then Lee woke to see his wife standing naked at the door. 'Fuck!' he shouted.

'You've already done that, you bastard!' she'd screamed back. She'd run down the stairs to the hall cupboard and fetched the axe. By the time she returned the bitch was pulling on her pants. When they saw the axe they ran round the room in a panic, like headless chickens. Lee used his mobile to ring the police while Wendy hacked and hacked at the bed. She was demented. Lee and the bitch dashed out of the house leaving her to destroy the bed. By the time the police came she was panting and exhausted, surrounded by foam, springs and feathers.

The police were surprisingly sympathetic and, although she had to spend a night in the cells, they sent for a doctor, who prescribed sedation which she declined to take. She told no one about the pregnancy. No charges were brought against her and, within a week, she had decided to have the pregnancy terminated.

It had taken all of that two years for her to feel relatively normal again. She did have regrets. She'd wreaked vengeance on an innocent bed – she should have hacked his balls off and killed the bitch.

Alvera arrived home at her terraced house, took a bath and then filled a bowl of cornflakes and ate them to the sound of gospel music from her CD player. She lived alone but she never felt alone. The Lord was with her. In everything she did she was conscious He was watching her. She finished her cornflakes, washed her mug and bowl, cleaned the sink and then listed her jobs for the day.

Once she'd been married with children, but her husband had chosen the heathen path and her daughters, Gloria and Yolande, had followed him. Gloria had been sixteen, Yolande fourteen. She'd never seen them since. She'd heard, via a distant cousin, that they were all in the USA. She'd been lost at first without them, but as the years passed, she realized it was God's will and the cross she had to bear, but He would be a source of comfort and would never leave her.

When she'd completed her list she walked upstairs to her bedroom. Her legs felt like lead and her ankles were swollen. She was nearly sixty, but she told no one her age. Every day she prayed for her church, her daughters, and the clinic. She prayed for the clinic because she hoped God would let her carry on working. Living on the old-age pension she wouldn't be able to give her weekly contribution to the Church.

Once in bed she put her hands together and began her prayers. On the far wall the Light of the World watched her. 'Praise the Lord,' she began, 'I was a sinner. Now I have repented.'

Carla Robins carried on working as if nothing had happened. It was unfortunate that Saul had died and she had been very shocked. In fact she'd felt numb. It wasn't the fact she'd lost a lover. Lovers were easy to find. She'd lost a true friend. And the shock was all the greater because she couldn't think of anyone who would want him dead. Even Amanda. But she supposed no one went through life without making an enemy or two and, one day, it was inevitable they would catch up with you. At least his end was quick.

Martin Samuels had visited her office and they'd revised their business plans. A new surgeon was essential and she would be part of the interview panel. Martin had already put out feelers and Carla hoped the new surgeon would be a little more prepossessing than Martin himself. Now that Saul was dead he was busy angling, trying to get a hook in her knickers, but, so far, he hadn't provided the right bait. Once he did, Carla would be more than happy to reap the benefits. Long ago Carla had recognized that she was a tart. Not a tart with a heart, but a tough bitch who would achieve her ends by using whoever crossed her path. The only emotion Carla ever allowed herself unreservedly was anger. Anger was useful. It fired the adrenaline, fuelled ambition and kept fools at bay. Any other emotion was depressing and unproductive.

She'd already rung the prospective clients who'd attended the open evening to reassure them that the clinic was safe, that the police were on the premises and the killer would soon be caught. Most were still interested but undecided. She offered them as many home visits as they required. That worked like a charm. 'One will be enough,' seemed to be the majority answer. So now Carla had a diary full of visits and only one that she would find hard work – visiting the stupid Karen again to reassure her that the new surgeon was just as competent. It was a lie of course but no doubt Karen would believe her.

If the police were satisfied with her good recall of the evening, she hoped she wouldn't be interviewed again. But she was trying to remain positive. She hadn't admitted to sleeping with Saul that night. It was none of their business whom she pleasured. She wasn't stupid. She knew she might be a front-line suspect, but he could have been killed at any time over the weekend. Pathologists were clever but they couldn't name the exact hour of death.

The trouble was that she'd lied and she should have told it as it was. Why on earth had she told them she walked to and from the clinic? That was very stupid of her. She should have told the truth. Who was she protecting anyway? Some people you couldn't protect and her gut feeling was, that very soon, she'd be charged with murder.

Stan had felt quite important showing the police his two CCTV monitors. One viewed the car park and the front gate, the other the back of the building. The cops didn't seem so impressed. On the left of the building was a side entrance with a coded entrance device. 'Who knows where the cameras are?' asked the inspector.

Stan had to admit that all the staff knew. When they were installed there'd been an open invitation for everyone to admire them. 'I do patrol the grounds every hour,' Stan protested. 'I'm very thorough. The staff know they can rely on me.'

'Do you get much trouble?' asked the woman cop.

'Once a drunk wandered around the grounds about three in the morning, but he couldn't get in, because he didn't know the code to the entry systems.'

'So,' said the DI, 'the cameras roll, you patrol and only people who know the code can get in at night. There was no sign of a break-in. So what does that tell you, Stan?'

Stan shrugged, unable to think. Eventually though, he managed a response. 'I suppose it means it was an inside job.'

'You sound unsure,' the cop had said.

'I thought it was a nutter.'

'No nutters on the staff? Could have been a patient.'

Stan hadn't thought of that. Perhaps that was why he was a mere security man. He'd tried to get into the police once and they'd turned him down.

'I don't see much of the patients,' he said.

'But you would have noticed one wandering around?'

Stan, a bit agitated, responded, ''Course I would. I told you. I'm very conscientious – my job is very important to me.'

'Just one question then, Stan. Did you see Carla Robins on Friday evening?'

'I knew she was in the building but I didn't see her.'

'You're sure?'

'Yeah. I don't like her but she's attractive.' Maybe that was the wrong thing to say. Both cops had given him a funny look.

The cops had left it at that but Stan was worried. He was worried about them finding out he left the building at night. Maybe his loose bit of fencing had been discovered. Perhaps they'd find something . . . he didn't know what. They might suspect him of being the killer. After all, he had access to everywhere. They may even think he had a motive.

Eight

A few days later it was decided from above that the operations room at the clinic should be abandoned. There
were no explanations but at least Rydell and Denni were
delighted. Since the discovery of the body they had hardly
left the clinic. Rydell had begun to feel institutionalized, but
at least his fear of hospital had declined, not that he'd strayed
far from the top floor. A lecture room had been made into
a temporary dormitory and they'd taken it in turns to snatch
a few hours' sleep. Rydell had managed to run around the
grounds on dry days – three in a row. Usually it helped him
to think, but the investigation was still without major forensic
reports and now running only seemed to blank his mind and
crucify his leg muscles.

Communal living disturbed him too. Everywhere he looked
there was disorder – stray coffee cups, takeaway cartons,
overflowing ashtrays. He even found a pair of socks stuck
down the side of a chair in the staffroom. There was only one
lavatory and one shower for ten people and at least four of the
team worked at night. The cramp in his leg muscles could
easily be relieved, but his brain couldn't function properly
in chaos. Sometimes he felt he could hardly breathe, but
he didn't tell anyone and if anyone did notice they didn't
comment.

Now that they were back at Harrowford station Denni
complained of headaches so severe she could see flashing
lights and, when she read, words danced in front of her eyes.
She had a desk near the window, which provided natural
light, but clouds the colour of pewter hid the sun and she

was obviously having difficulty seeing. Rydell had noticed her adjusting and readjusting the written statements she was reading. 'You need your eyes tested,' he said. 'Go home and take the day off tomorrow.'

'It's not my eyes, it's a headache,' she said. 'I can always buy some reading specs at the chemists. If we're one down it will . . .'

'Who's ADCI here?' asked Rydell. 'I'll tell you what. I'll set up a focus group – get it?'

Denni wasn't amused.

'There's nothing wrong with my eyes. The only reason I can't focus properly is because of the headaches.'

'Go home!'

Denni wasn't sure why she didn't want to go home. She felt ill enough. It was pride really. Everyone in the team had been working virtually round the clock, so why should she be the one to crack? Rydell began sifting through photos of the crime scene and Denni sat undecided. She'd taken a couple of painkillers but they hadn't helped. Now she felt slightly sick. After a few minutes she realized there was no point in her sitting in the office doing nothing. She'd just slipped on her jacket when Ram walked in. Since his return from sick leave he'd thinned, so he was a little less cuddly and just lately he also looked a tad shabbier. 'Is the end of the world nigh or are you just practising?' he asked.

'And you, Ram, look like an unmade bed,' said Rydell.

Ram swivelled across to Denni on his office chair and put his arm around her. 'I need a wife,' he said, giving her arm a gentle squeeze, 'and Denni here would be perfect, but she suffers from baldism and she's fussy. She wants a man with a full head of hair, his own teeth, rock-like muscles and an IQ above one hundred and fifty. I just don't qualify. I'm just a slightly sadder sad bastard than I was before. Have a humbug.'

Before Denni could answer he popped a humbug into her mouth. She felt waves of nausea rising up into her throat. She took the humbug from her mouth and threw it in the wastepaper bin at her feet. 'I feel really sick,' she said miserably.

'Take her home,' said Rydell, 'and don't be long! And, Denni, don't come back until you're better.'

'Sorry, Denni,' muttered Ram.

She smiled feebly, still feeling sick.

Outside in the fresh air she felt a little better and took several deep breaths. Ram drove her home and sat her down on the sofa. 'It's just lack of sleep,' he said, as he helped her off with her coat. 'And I'll sort you out.'

'How?'

'Trust me. I'm from the mystic east – well, my genes are. Now, sit with your back towards me and put your feet up.'

She felt his cool fingers on the back of her neck begin to rhythmically massage her neck. The gentle kneading and stroking motion soothed her stomach almost immediately and time meant nothing. She noticed that the muscles at the side of her neck began to feel as if they were deliciously dissolving. Then after a while he began massaging her head in a raking motion, ending finally with feather-like circular movements to her temples. She was vaguely aware that he'd removed her shoes then pushed her back gently on to the sofa and placed a pillow under her head.

When she woke her duvet covered her. The lamp was on and the curtains drawn. There was no sign of Ram. Her headache had gone and she felt great. She walked into the kitchen to make coffee and switched on the radio. There was a serious discussion going on – *Farming Today*! She had slept for fourteen hours! Ram needed a new nickname, she decided. He was called Sabu by the wags at work. Ram, Ram the Magic Man suited him far better. She'd always had a soft spot for him, but now she'd have to be careful – she could become addicted to his head and neck massages.

When the newspaper was delivered just after seven, she noticed that the murder itself had been relegated to page four – 'detectives are still interviewing staff and patients'

– Amanda Ravenscroft had obviously provided her story –
the angle being that, although she knew he'd had affairs, she
would have stood by him no matter what. She didn't name
names, but she knew he was about to end a short affair with a
member of the clinic's staff. When asked if she would now be
involved with the management of the clinic, she'd answered
ominously, 'Yes. And heads will roll.' Denni thought this
an unfortunate phrase in view of her husband's throat being
cut. Had she actually used those words or were they mere
journalistic licence?

In the incident room by eight a.m., Rydell had beaten her
to it and was sifting through neat piles of paperwork. His
summer tan had already begun to fade and now he looked
grey and exhausted. He glanced up and smiled. 'You look
better, Denni.'

'I'm feeling great, boss – thanks to Ram.'

He looked at her quizzically. 'I won't ask any questions,'
he said. 'Let's just crack on. There's a briefing in an hour.'

An hour later the room was packed. Rydell stood in front
of an array of photographs of, not only the scene of crime,
but also the clinic staff. Denni sat at the back of the room
by the door wondering why Ram hadn't turned up on time.
'The rogues' gallery,' Rydell announced, 'is by courtesy of
the Harmony Clinic.' As he began summarizing the findings
of the post-mortem Denni felt hands on her neck and Ram
whispering in her ear, 'Good kip?'

Ram's fingers traced her neck, but she tried to concentrate
on Rydell's main contention that they did now have considerable forensic evidence – all they needed was a match.
If necessary, everyone at the clinic that night, including
patients, would be DNA tested. The time of death had
now been loosely established, thanks to analysis of the
stomach contents, between around midnight on Friday and
the early hours of Saturday morning. 'That doesn't mean that
an outsider wasn't involved,' said Rydell. 'One of the group
of potential clients could have hidden in the clinic. But for

now we'll concentrate on the staff and patients. And we need to know far more about our victim. Any questions?'

Someone at the back called out, 'Could the killer be female?'

Rydell nodded. 'The victim was taken by surprise. Whoever came up behind him, he either trusted or he didn't hear. According to the PM there was no sign of a struggle. It was an efficient killing.'

'A contract killer?'

'Possibly. But let's not jump to any conclusions. It's still early days. It's a case of interview and re-interview. Forensic are doing their work – now it's our turn.'

As they all filed out, Ram murmured in her ear, 'Bet you a fiver his widow had him done in.' Before Denni could answer, Rydell had come alongside her. 'It's time we had a word with Amanda – she's had more than a week to get over the shock.'

Back in the incident room, Rydell reorganized the papers on his desk, checked his in tray and his out tray, repositioned them by a few centimetres, then checked that his computer was switched off. Finally, he turned to Denni, who waited patiently, and asked, 'Are you ready yet?' Denni pretended not to hear.

Within half an hour Denni and Rydell were knocking on Amanda Ravenscroft's front door. She wasn't alone. They heard voices and noticed two cars in the drive. It was Martin Samuels who opened the door. 'She's in a bit of a state,' he said. He too looked worried.

'It's early days,' said Rydell. 'We'll be as brief as we can.'

'No, no, you don't understand. She's had a real shock today . . .' he broke off at the sound of Amanda's high-pitched shout, 'Martin!'

'I'm coming,' he shouted back.

Martin signalled for them to follow him. Amanda sat, head in hands on the sofa, with a bottle of brandy and a half-filled tumbler on the coffee table in front of her. She looked up as they entered the room. Her eyes were red and puffy, she wore no make-up and her old jeans and sweater had seen better days. 'Why the hell haven't you arrested her yet?'

'We'll sit down, shall we?' said Rydell. 'And then you can tell me why I should.'

She stared at them blankly and didn't answer, so Rydell and Denni sat down on the sofa opposite her. Martin stood, looking awkward and even more worried. 'Shall I tell them or will you?' he asked.

'You tell them . . . No. I'll tell them.' She took a deep, sighing breath. 'That bitch – that evil bitch . . .' she broke off. 'You tell them, Martin. I'll choke on the words.'

Martin managed to look both worried and embarrassed at the same time. 'Amanda's heard from their solicitor. It seems, unbeknown to Amanda, that in the last six months Saul made changes to his will . . .'

'Changes!' sneered Amanda. 'Come off it – he altered the whole fucking thing. He's left me with nothing except this house.'

Martin put a consoling hand on Amanda's arm, but she shrugged him off and angrily swigged at her brandy. 'Saul changed his will completely,' continued Martin, nervously passing a hand over his hair. 'He left everything – his share of the clinic, his stocks and shares, his capital, to . . .' He paused and looked anxiously at Amanda, who was now sitting staring straight ahead. 'To Carla Robins.' Then he added, swiftly, 'We're going to fight it, of course.'

'And this came as a complete surprise?' asked Rydell. Amanda's withering look made him feel foolish. Of course she'd been surprised – devastated would have been a better word. Rydell looked towards Denni and gave her a slight nod indicating she should take over. Denni sat forward on the edge of the sofa, her body language signalling interest.

'How long were you married?' she asked.

'Three years!' she answered, as if it were thirty-three. Time, thought Denni, was relative to age. Amanda was still only twenty-eight.

'Was Saul in a relationship when he met you?'

'No. At least, he wasn't living with anyone.'

'So there was no one else at the time?'

Amanda gave a brief laugh. 'I wouldn't know.'

'Did you ask?'

'I wasn't interested in his past life. It was me he married. That was all that mattered.'

There was a slight pause before Rydell said, 'We are trying to establish motive here. You're not being very helpful.'

'You're wasting your time. The bitch Robins is the only person I can think of who would have been capable of murder and obviously had a motive.'

'So as far as you were concerned,' said Rydell. 'You were happily married?'

'Yes,' she said, crisply. 'We were very close . . . or at least I thought . . .' she broke off, obviously remembering he'd left the bulk of his money to another woman. She shrugged. 'I might be younger than him – than he was – but I knew the score. He told me he couldn't be faithful, but that his sexual conquests meant nothing.'

'And yet he made his will in favour of Carla Robins. That indicates he may have been in love with her.'

Amanda's eyes flashed but then dulled, as if suddenly realizing that he *had* been in love with her. 'That scheming evil bitch,' she muttered. 'She's clever, cunning. She'll outwit *you* if you're not careful.'

Denni ignored that. 'How often exactly did your husband stay out all night?'

She shrugged miserably. 'He did the occasional on-call – if he was worried about a patient or I suppose if he wanted to sleep with *her*.'

'When you didn't find him at the squash club, what did you do?'

'What was I supposed to do? I came home.'

'Did you assume he was with Carla?'

'Yes, of course. But he wasn't. The tart was with someone

else – a married man, of course. She was only interested in married men.'

'Edward Gray?'

'Yes. I told you.'

'And now some other poor cow's life is ruined,' she said, before gulping down the last of her brandy.

Denni guessed Amanda's misery was only partly due to being bereaved. Being scrubbed out of her husband's will seemed to have really shaken her and she wondered if they were both playing away from home. Was Martin Samuels' presence an indication of a closer relationship? She glanced at him as he poured another brandy without being asked. His eyes still followed Amanda's every move.

'Tell me about the on-call rota,' said Denni. Amanda's first response was to look at Martin. And it was Martin who answered. He sat down beside Amanda to do so. 'Being senior, neither Saul nor I did more than one or two nights per month on call. We had a list of locums who would sleep in but occasionally we were let down. Sometimes if we worked late it was convenient to sleep over.'

'And that night. The night Saul was murdered. Whose turn was it?'

Martin stared into his glass. 'It was mine.'

Denni glanced at Rydell. 'Your lucky night, then,' said Rydell.

'What's that supposed to mean?'

'Who else knew you were meant to be on call?'

Martin's right hand balled into a fist. 'How the hell do I know. It wasn't a secret. The on-call details were kept quite openly in Saul's office.'

'We didn't find them.'

'That's not my fault.'

'Has it crossed your mind that *you* could have been the intended victim?'

'Of course it has.'

'So you feel it more likely that someone wanted to kill you than Saul?'

'I didn't say that. You're twisting things. Why would anyone want to kill either me or Saul?'

'Why indeed?' muttered Rydell. 'Are you telling me you knew Saul was staying overnight?'

'No, I didn't know – it's not as simple as that.' Martin began to look very uncomfortable.

'What is it, Martin?' asked Amanda, suspiciously. 'What aren't you telling me?'

'Saul didn't plan to stay the night, not the whole night. He told me not to bother about sleeping in.'

Amanda now sat rigid, looking daggers at Martin, who mouthed, 'I'm sorry.'

'Look, Inspector, regardless of whether my husband planned to be with that slut all night, that's not the issue. She killed Saul. And now we know her real motive. The money-grabbing murderous bitch!'

Rydell stared long and hard at Amanda. 'I'm left wondering why a man would cut his wife so completely out of his will without good cause. The way I see it, he would have to be a very angry man indeed. So what had you done to deserve such treatment?'

It was Martin who answered, his face white with anger. 'For God's sake, hasn't Amanda suffered enough? She was a good wife. She's done nothing wrong. It wasn't her fault Saul was swayed by a gold-digger.'

'I don't suppose she twisted his arm,' said Rydell.

'No, but she twisted his thinking,' snapped Amanda. 'If he was thinking at all, which I doubt, he would have listened to his brain rather than his cock.'

'I think there was more to it than that,' said Rydell, 'but my . . . doubts . . . will keep till our next meeting.'

Rydell stood up. 'I shall want to talk to you again very soon, Mrs Ravenscroft.'

He looked towards Martin. 'Is there anything you want to tell me before I talk to your wife?'

Martin slammed down his tumbler of brandy. 'Why the hell do you want to speak to my wife – she doesn't know anything!'

'Did she know Saul socially?'

'Yes . . . yes, of course.'

'Then, knowing the victim, she will, I'm sure, be able to shed new light on –' he paused – 'recent events.'

'You bastard!'

'Part of the job, sir.'

Back in the incident room Rydell found Ram studying computer readouts of the clinic's finances. He looked up, frowning. 'I know now why I gave up accountancy – there's no risk to life and limb. Take me off this, guv, please. I'm fit enough to return to normal run-of-the-mill mayhem.'

'No can do at the moment, Ram,' said Rydell, giving a cursory glance at the sheets of figures, 'but if you want an update which might make a difference – I could manage a drink at lunchtime.'

'You don't mean – male bonding?'

Rydell laughed, 'No, Denni will be there.'

'Does it include solid nourishment?'

'Of course.'

'You're on! Denni and food are two of my most favourite things.'

'Don't let Denni hear you calling her a thing.'

At that moment Denni walked in. 'It's all right boss. Ram is allowed to insult me any time.'

Rydell glanced at them both with a puzzled expression. 'You two aren't . . .'

Denni shook her head. 'No, boss. Ram is a good friend and magic at neck massages.'

'You any good with tortured leg muscles?' asked Rydell. Ram stuck a thumb up in the air. 'The best.'

'I'll let you know if they give out.'

Later in the Three Tuns, a pub with no place to stand at the bar but a good line in standard pub fare, they sat at a round table in the corner and discussed the quality of the beer. 'I'll never be a beer drinker,' said Ram. 'Lager's not so heavy.'

'Just as fattening,' said Denni.

'I could go off you,' replied Ram. 'So what's new on the case that merits lunch, guv?'

Rydell, having lined up the pub's place-mats edge to edge, said, 'Ravenscroft's wife doesn't stand to inherit the clinic or his money.'

'Who the hell does?'

'Carla Robins.'

'Did the wife know?'

'It appears not. She seemed genuinely shocked.'

'Well she would,' said Ram, 'if she'd topped him for his money.'

'Is that your theory?'

'I don't have a theory – just a negative thought.'

'Which is?'

'Not a professional hit man.'

'Why not?'

'He left too much evidence behind. No match on finger-prints, so probably no previous. Could be an amateur hit, I suppose, but it must have been planned. I looked at the photos – didn't look like a crime of passion to me. What do you think, Denni?

Denni, glad to be included at last, paused, thinking about the scene. The carefully made bed, the closed bathroom door, the two wine glasses left on the bedside table. And finally the blood and the scalpel.

'Whoever did it,' she said, 'must have acquired the scalpel from theatre and, I think, wore theatre greens and overshoes, maybe even a mask.'

Rydell smiled at Denni, 'I agree, but why leave the scalpel?'

For some reason, Denni had found his approving smile irritating. Condescending. 'A symbol maybe,' she suggested. 'I think the bloodstained theatre gear would have been placed in the appropriate plastic bag and sent to the laundry.

Tracing yet another bloodstained gown would be well nigh impossible.'

'Only a member of staff would know that,' said Ram.

Rydell agreed. He did have some information, but he'd been reluctant to share it because his attitude at the start of an investigation was to share out the suspicion. The neat pile syndrome. Equal piles he found more satisfying, more easy to cope with than the unequal. But, of course, they would find out anyway and maybe knew already.

'Two members of staff do have criminal records – both for violence,' he announced.

'We know,' said Denni.

'And we do have some good fingerprints from the scene, plus the odd strand of assorted hair. Want to hazard a guess?'

There was a short pause before Ram and Denni answered in unison, 'Carla Robins!'

'Could be an early close on this one, guv,' said Ram, cheerfully.

'We'll pick her up for more questioning as soon as we've finished here.' Rydell too sounded cheerful.

The food arrived then. Denni had just picked up her knife and fork when her mobile rang. Reluctantly she answered it.

'Denise, is that you?' Her mother's slurred voice seemed like a slap in the face. 'I'm on the floor – I slipped. I can't get up.'

'I'll send for an ambulance.'

'No, you come. I haven't broken anything. I just need a hand to get up.'

'I'm on my way.'

'Trouble?' queried Rydell.

'I've got to go,' said Denni. 'My mother's fallen.'

'I'll come with you,' responded Ram immediately.

'No,' said Denni sharply. 'She doesn't weigh much.'

As she drove to her mother's house she thought Jean might not weigh much physically, but emotionally she was as heavy as a drowned corpse with lead weights attached.

She found her trying to scramble aboard her recliner chair. Next to her on the carpet lay a wet patch of whisky with cigarette butts in the middle, the sight of which reminded Denni of a ministry of health shock-tactic poster.

'Don't just stand there,' Jean ordered, her voice thick with fags. 'Give me a hand. I've sprained my ankle.'

Denni stared at the sight of her mother's shabby dressing gown, with its hem hanging a trail of cotton over spindly legs, rip-tided with varicose veins. Without answering, she hauled her back on to the recliner. It was only when she felt the bones of her mother's body, how little resistance was in her slight frame, that the anger subsided.

'My bloody ankle gave way,' Jean said, easing herself into a more comfortable position.

Denni couldn't see any swelling or bruising or any deformity. 'Do you want me to bandage it?' she asked.

'Leave it.'

'I'll make some tea, shall I?'

'If *you* want one, I'll have one

In the kitchen Denni looked at the debris – soup congealing in a saucepan, mouldy bread in the bread bin, plates with half-eaten crackers, dirty plates and full ashtrays. She found a clean mug and made tea.

'I can't cope with this mess,' she said, as she handed the tea to Jean.

'Have I asked you to? I'll get round to it in time.'

'I can't stay,' said Denni. 'We're interviewing our prime suspect.'

'Well you mustn't miss that, must you?'

Denni sighed. 'I have to go. I'll ring you later.'

'Don't put yourself out.'

Denni slipped on her coat and gathered up her shoulder bag. As she got to the living-room door she looked back at her mother. Tears were sliding down her face. Denni carried on walking but a feeling of anguish thudded into her chest, making her gulp for air. Once outside she took a deep breath. Why the hell did she feel so guilty? What had she done to deserve this? And when would it ever end?

Back at the station Carla Robins was already waiting in an interview room and Rydell had chosen Ram to help him conduct the interview. Denni went to the canteen and sat with a plastic cup of coffee, on her own at a table by the window, and stared at the murky white sky. She minded very much that she wasn't to be present at the interview. She minded, not least, because she'd already made up her mind that Carla Robins wasn't the type to commit murder. She didn't feel it was mere intuition. Logic had its place too. It was more her understanding of Carla's personality, based, she reminded herself, on just one meeting and the opinions of others. Carla may have lacked passion but she was intelligent enough *not* to leave fingerprints and Denni was sure hers would be there. And she was intelligent enough to provide herself with some sort of alibi. But why lie about sleeping with Saul? She'd also said she'd walked to and from the clinic. It was at least two miles to her cottage. Would she really have walked home in high heels? She'd said her car was playing up and she didn't want to risk a breakdown. What purpose did that lie serve? Unless she was protecting someone.

Nine

Freda Goodman had managed to answer the phone the moment it rang. It wasn't fair on Stan to let it ring and wake him up. Sleeping in the day was difficult enough, especially during the last humid days of summer. Stan noticed every noise that drifted in through open windows, the sound of lawns being mowed, the steady thump, thump of pop music, running water, cisterns being flushed, even the sound of marching ants, she didn't wonder. Now it was autumn and the windows were closed and it was Freda who got the flak for waking him up. The telephone call had changed things – she *wanted* him to wake. She stared around the kitchen looking for some way to make some accidental noise, either with a saucepan lid or by dropping a spoon or two. After deliberating for a few minutes she put the kettle on to boil. Making decisions wasn't easy for Freda, so making a cup of instant coffee gave her a little longer. Drinking it a little longer still.

Once she'd finished the coffee she caused a bit of clattering at the sink, dropped two spoons on to the vinyl floor and banged a saucepan lid loudly. Then she wheeled herself to their bedroom door, which was always slightly ajar, and listened intently. There was no sound of him stirring. He wasn't snoring or clearing his throat. On other occasions when he was this quiet, it crossed her mind he might be dead. What on earth would she do then? She nudged the right wheel of her wheelchair at the door and watched it slowly open.

He lay, sheet pulled up over his head, a big mound on the

bed. Freda couldn't hear him breathing at all – she could hear the slight wheeze in her own lungs but nothing coming from him. She eased her chair towards him and as she got to the bedside she tugged at the sheet. His response was slow but positive – he yanked the sheet back over his head.

'Stan,' she said, softly. 'Stan – wake up, pet. The police have been on the phone. They're coming round to see you at three o'clock.'

'Bugger,' came the response. Freda knew him well enough to know he'd been awake for some time. Normally if she had to wake him he didn't speak for ages – he just grunted.

'I'll make you a nice cup of tea,' she said.

'What's the time?'

'It's nearly ten to three.'

'Christ Almighty, woman, why didn't you wake me before?' he shouted, as he threw back the bedclothes. Freda backed out of the bedroom and wheeled herself the short distance to the kitchen. It made her nerves bad when he was irritable. Her hands trembled as she put two tea bags in the pot. When she poured the tea, some slopped into the saucer. She couldn't stop trembling.

'Anyone would think the police are coming to talk to you,' said Stan, as he took the cup from her. 'And you know I prefer a mug. Pull yourself together, woman.'

The police didn't turn up until three thirty. Freda watched them arrive and stand talking beside a dark-blue car. There were only the two cops, both men, one tall and slim, the other balding, Asian, stocky and wearing rimless specs. He didn't look like a copper at all. She couldn't help but feel a little excited. Stanley, after all, was an important person at the clinic. He was bound to be a source of information.

'We won't take up much of your husband's time,' said the inspector. She heard his name as Rider but she wasn't sure. The other one was called Patel. She was very disappointed when they closed the living-room door on her. A low muttering began and went on for some time and Freda realized that, as usual, her being in a wheelchair made her invisible. They were not going to ask *her* if she knew anything. And until they did she wasn't going to volunteer any information. It was her legs that didn't work – not her ears or her eyes.

Once the police had gone Stan's mood improved and he whistled as he began peeling potatoes. 'I'll make the tea tonight, love.'

'You're cheerful,' Freda said. 'Why are you keeping it a secret – what did they say?'

He shrugged but didn't turn from the sink. 'I'm not keeping secrets, Freda love. I reckon from what they say that there'll be an arrest made soon.'

'Who are they going to arrest?'

Stan, finishing the last potato, turned and smiled. 'Carla Robins – who else could it be?'

'Why are they so sure it's her?'

'She lied about being with him that night. The evidence is all there, you see.'

'Did the police tell you that?'

'They didn't have to. I know about forensics and such like.'

'Of course you do, dear,' she said, trying to keep him sweet. Freda had long ago realized that she was in no position to start arguments or make a fuss. All she could do was appear grateful. '*Why* did she kill him, then?'

Stan bristled at that. 'I'm not sure about the whys and the wherefores. Could have been a crime of passion.' He stared ahead out of the kitchen window to the small shed at the bottom of the garden and imagined having Lyn Kilpatrick tied up there. He could understand a crime of passion.

'What are you thinking about, Stan?'

'I think I'll have another go at runner beans in the spring. Your favourite veg, love.'

Freda gave a little sigh of contentment. Her Stan was the best.

Denni sat alone in her office, wading through various reports but pausing every few minutes to stare into space. Rydell and Ram were off on some mission from which she'd been excluded. It worried her a little but she tried to make light of it, deciding that she felt like Cinderella. All she needed now was the fairy godmother. The prince wasn't a high priority. For Denni, a man could provide sex, fun and companionship but the idea of settling down, like dust on a flat surface, didn't appeal. For Denni, hitting thirty had been liberating. Now she realized she might not marry, might not have kids, but she could have a good career, money in the bank and holidays abroad. She could treasure both male and female friends, if she ever had the time, she reminded herself. All in all, she thought, her thirties were the best years so far. Only two things marred her life – occasional broodiness and Jean.

It was in the canteen, over a damp egg and cress sandwich and a cup of stewed tea, that Denni heard the news. Rydell and Ram had gone to interview Carla Robins again.

Denni, normally fairly placid, felt a mixture of anxiety and anger well up in her chest, until it seemed suffocating. She took a deep breath, gulped her tea and then hurried back to her office. There she stood by the window, took some deep breaths and rehearsed silently her main concern: *You bastards are trying to sideline me and I'm not having it*!

Rydell turned up a little later in her second, less emotional, run-through. 'There you are,' he said. 'I've been trying your mobile all morning. You'd better get down to the interview room now if you want a crack at Carla. I'll join you in a few minutes.'

Denni thought Carla Robins was probably the most glamorous suspect ever seen in Harrowford nick. She wore a pale grey suit with a vivid green blouse and black court shoes with four-inch heels. She half smiled at Denni as if to say, 'I've no idea what I'm doing here but I'm sure it will get sorted.'

As Denni sat down opposite Carla, the uniformed police-woman sitting in the corner of the room winked at Denni. Was it a come-on or a symbol of solidarity?

Rydell's appearance signalled the beginning of the formal

interview. The tape recorder's whir Denni found quite distracting, but more distracting still was Carla's continued air of confidence. It felt as if she wasn't in the frame – *they* were.

Rydell's questioning was in a quiet, low tone. A deliberate affection that could lull suspects into a false sense of security. Denni found having to strain to hear both tiring and irritating. It was a technique worth a try.

'So Carla,' he was saying, 'tell me why you lied to us about sleeping with the deceased? We know you did lie. There is a witness.'

Denni knew Rydell chose his words carefully. He made *sleeping with the deceased* sound either perverted or as if it was intended to unnerve a woman who may have once loved the man. Carla smiled. '*Acting* Chief Inspector,' she answered, 'I wasn't sleeping with the deceased – I was shagging Saul, who was very much alive at the time – and when asked, "Did you sleep with the victim?", I replied, "No, I did not sleep with him." I always tell the truth when asked the right questions. And in this case I didn't even come close to feeling drowsy.'

'You're obviously going to be pedantic,' said Rydell.

'I'm surprised you even know the word – Acting Chiefie.'

Denni saw Rydell's shoulders stiffen and his top lip tighten. Carla Robins was getting the better of him. She managed to catch her boss's eye. 'Did you have *any* feelings for Saul?' she asked.

Carla looked down at her perfectly manicured hands then looked at Denni with an expression of resignation. 'If you must know, he was a good friend and a good lay. I had a certain amount of respect for him.'

'What about Edward Gray?'

'What about him?'

'Do you have any feelings for him?'

'No. I'm arrogant enough to think that any man who cheats on his wife isn't worthy of my affection. If all mistresses – what a lovely old-fashioned word – could see their love objects merely as weak-willed prats, many affairs would end abruptly.'

'You obviously don't have a high opinion of men?'

Carla paused before answering, her sharp eyes flicking over Denni's hands. 'I notice you're not married, Detective Sergeant.'

'No. I'm not,' she said, but added, because she thought she should, 'but I do like men. Just waiting for the right one, I suppose. Did you think Saul was the right one for you?'

'Maybe as far as any man could be. As I said, I liked him and respected him, but anything more than the odd few hours together was out of the question.'

'Did you ever ask him to leave his wife?'

Carla laughed. It lifted her face and the sound was unexpectedly infectious. 'What would I want him *for*? I have a good job, a home, money in the bank, car, a regular sex life. What could he provide me with?'

'Approximately one point five million pounds.'

For the first time Denni saw Carla genuinely surprised – her mouth opened and then closed. 'What *are* you talking about?'

'Did Saul never discuss his assets with you?'

'Not his financial assets. Do you mind explaining? I am, after all, being questioned about murder.'

Rydell sat forward and murmured, 'Are you trying to say you didn't know that he was worth so much?'

'I would have thought he was worth *more*, but so what?'

'He left it all to you.'

'I beg your pardon, Chief Inspector?'

'He left everything, including his share of the clinic, to you.'

Carla lost that air of calm superiority. Anxiety flickered in her eyes. She began twisting her hands together. 'Why would he do that?'

'Perhaps he was in love with you.'

'He may have been, but even so, I'm very surprised. Has his signature been forged? I take it you're not talking word of mouth. He signed a will?'

'It seems genuine – why would it be forged?'

There was a long pause. 'I'm being set up,' she said. 'Someone is trying to give me a motive for killing him. I didn't kill him. It wasn't a crime of passion – there was no passion involved. I didn't do it and you can't prove I did.'

'All the forensic evidence points to you,' said Rydell. 'You do have a previous conviction for violence. We have fingerprints and samples. We will need to take your fingerprints again, samples of hair et cetera. If they also match, the chances of anyone else entering the room after you left are remote – since they left no trace.'

Carla regained her composure quickly. 'I don't consider a tussle with a drunken holidaymaker would convince anyone I was capable of murder.'

'You were charged with assault. So it was slightly more than a tussle.'

'The silly bitch needed a slap in the mouth. Unfortunately she bruised easily. So I spent a month in a Greek jail but there, if you pay enough compensation, you get released.'

'So who paid up?'

'Saul. I told you he was a good friend.'

'Your affair is a long-standing one then?'

'Yes.'

Denni watched the interview proceed with a growing sense of unease. Rydell disliked Carla intensely, that was obvious. She came across as cold and brittle but that didn't make her a liar. As for the inheritance, Denni recognized her genuine surprise and, if money wasn't the motive, what else could there be?

Ten

It was midnight and blowing a gale. The trees outside the clinic swayed in frenzy and the wind tore at windows, hurtled bins and crates outside, until torrential rain joined in the battering. Lyn Kilpatrick stood at the nursing station, staring at the mayhem outside. She did have the time to spare and there were ten empty beds and, so far, no problems with clients. The bad weather Lyn found oddly comforting. For the past few days she had sensed or imagined she was being followed. Nothing definite, just the odd urge to look over her shoulder. She hadn't seen anyone and she dismissed the idea as being due to anxiety following the murder. Why would anyone follow her anyway?

A bell rang and then another and another. The high winds were proving too noisy for even those recently anaesthetized. Lyn checked the board for the room numbers. Wendy Swan was answering one, Alvera the other. Lyn was left with the fat-suck in room three. In the past she'd assisted in theatre and had seen the fat sucked out via a wide suction pipe. If the pipe could have stayed in position it wouldn't have been so off-putting but the vigorous, even rough, sweeps of the sucker made her teeth go on edge and, of course, the results were not always as the client imagined. The surgeon had to assess how much fat to suck from each area – a little too much on one side meant lopsided patches. Too much overall and the result was like sucking the innards from a sausage – all that was left was wrinkled skin. A few weeks on, the client returned for the excess skin to be removed. Lyn wasn't sure what happened to those who regained their fat cells – did they give up then and accept they would never be perfect and that they might even burst?

It was as Lyn approached room three that she turned abruptly at a sound behind her. There was no one there. The wind whined and howled like some demented soul and, as she put her hand on the door handle, something made her turn and look again. Stanley was at the end of the corridor – grinning. Just as she decided to stay and confront him he waved and walked away. *Perv*! *You horrible perv*! She took a deep breath, put a cheerful professional smile on her face and opened the door to find out what ailed Miss Fat-Suck.

It was later in the night that Lyn realized that this Sunday night the staff were the same as on the night when Saul Ravenscroft was found dead. Since Carla had been arrested, the police presence at the clinic had ceased. Everything should have gone back to normal, but it hadn't, at least not for Lyn. Yesterday she'd been shopping in the town and she wasn't normally nervous in the multi-storey car park, even after dark, but yesterday, she had felt nervous. She'd forgotten on which floor she'd parked the car and had had to walk via the ramp. Unusually she'd stared at the dark insides of the parked cars to make sure they were empty. For the first time she noted where the cameras were. Even with the reassuring thought that there *were* cameras, she used her remote to unlock her car several yards before reaching it and practically threw her shopping in beside her on the passenger seat. Once inside her car she locked herself in. Only then did she feel safe.

During her break Lyn sat in the day room with Wendy Swan and, when Wendy looked up from her *Hello* magazine, said, 'Do you think she did it?'

'She wouldn't have been arrested if she hadn't done it – would she?'

'The police can get things wrong.'

Wendy turned a page and then looked up at Lyn, quizzically. 'You look tired, Lyn. Are the kids OK?'

'Fine, thanks.'

There was an awkward pause before Lyn spoke again.

'I don't want you to say anything to the others, especially Alvera, because she's a bit superstitious, but . . . I think I'm being followed.'

'What makes you think that? Have you seen anyone?'

'No. Not exactly. I just feel I'm being watched – in the street – sometimes when I'm at home.'

'In the streets there is *always* someone watching via a camera, so perhaps the murder has just made you jumpy,' suggested Wendy.

'I wasn't always this flaky but murder hasn't crossed my path before.'

Wendy laughed. 'Hasn't crossed mine either.'

The wind gave a low moan outside and something clattered around the side of the building. Lyn shivered and pulled her cardigan around her. It was two a.m. – the start of the dead hours between two and four. Hours when the night seemed never-ending, when your body grew cold and worries surfaced.

'Do you fancy a hot drink?' asked Wendy, getting to her feet.

'Yeah. Great.'

When Wendy had gone to the kitchen Lyn sat huddled into her cardigan and when she heard a room bell she was tempted to answer it, but she was on her break and, in moments, it had been answered anyway. If it was something Alvera or Pam couldn't deal with they'd fetch her. She listened for footsteps but none came and for a while the wind dropped and, eventually, she could hear Wendy moving about in the kitchen, the click of the toaster switching off and the sound of clinking mugs. She relaxed back into the chair. You're worrying over nothing, she told herself. Carla Robins was in custody. There was no mystery involved. She was just another woman he'd been involved with and he'd paid the price. Even so, Carla had always struck her as ambitious and determined, not the sort to lose control, but there was always that one explosive moment, she supposed.

Wendy had just returned with tea and toast when they heard

the light thud of clogs on carpet and Pam appeared, flushed and breathless. 'Lyn, you'd better come . . .' She paused to catch her breath.

Not Miss Fat-Suck, thought Lyn. She'd been complaining of a headache – please God it wasn't a sub-arachnoid haemorrhage.

'It's Alvera!'

'What's happened?' asked Lyn, whipping off her cardigan.

'She's gone mad,' said Pam. 'She's talking gibberish . . . Says she's seen the Lord.'

Lyn, followed by both Wendy and Pam, rushed downstairs to find Alvera on her knees, holding a single passion flower in her hands and indeed talking gibberish, although, occasionally, a *Praise the Lord* or a *Hallelujah* prised its way through.

'Alvera, what's wrong?' asked Lyn, kneeling down beside her and gently touching her shoulder. There was no response and no halting Alvera's incoherent mumbling.

'What triggered it off?' Lyn asked Pam. She shrugged miserably and Lyn could see beads of sweat glistening on her forehead. 'One minute she was sitting doing her knitting. She was fine – same as ever. Then she said she was going upstairs. She was gone about ten minutes when she came back. She'd taken that passion flower from the vase in the office and she was raving.'

Lyn wasn't quite sure what to do, but when Wendy suggested calling Stan, her response was a brisk, 'No. You go upstairs and have a look round.'

'Me?' queried Wendy. 'There's no way I'm going upstairs on my own.'

'Right. I'll do it,' said Lyn. 'Both of you stay with her.'

Quite what Lyn expected to find on the top floor she wasn't sure, but she flicked on lights and swung open the staffroom door and the room used for lectures. There was nothing unusual. Nothing that might have fired a religious experience, no statues or crosses or shapes. In the staff toilet the windows were closed and torrential rain now joined the weather crescendo. The rain on the roof drummed frantically. Was the stormy weather the reason Alvera had flipped? A teacher friend had once told her that small children react very badly to strong winds. But a grown woman? Not very likely.

At the on-call room Lyn stopped. There was a young agency doctor sleeping in. There was no point in waking him because he'd only suggest phoning a psychiatrist. She felt half tempted to open the door and check he was still breathing but she knew she was being ridiculous.

As she came downstairs, two bells started up together. Pam, less flushed now, seemed keen to answer both. Alvera meanwhile had begun mumbling *Jesus* over and over again. Lyn phoned the duty psychiatrist from the office. Eventually a voice thick with sleep answered. 'Call an ambulance,' he said. 'Get her admitted.' He didn't wait for a reply but slammed down the receiver. 'Thank you so much,' muttered Lyn.

'No joy?' queried Wendy.

'Ambulance job. Who's her next of kin?'

Wendy shrugged. 'No idea. She lives on her own.'

Lyn dialed nine-nine-nine and searched for Alvera's personal record. All staff records were kept in a filing cabinet but this was the first time she'd ever had to look. Alvera's records were easy enough to find. She had named the church pastor – Wesley Kinver – as her next of kin. She picked up the phone with some reluctance; after all, it was two forty-five in the morning. This time the voice that answered sounded wide awake. She explained the situation. 'I'll come right away,' he said. 'I'll be about five minutes – God willing.'

Wesley Kinver's appearance was prompt – it took him six minutes. Although tall, with huge shoulders and a square head, he had tiny eyes that should have been lost in his broad face. Instead, his eyes, the colour of the skin of an aubergine, dominated the situation. He said nothing, just glanced around and then, kneeling down beside Alvera, gently removed the passion flower from her hand. 'Sister Alvera,' he murmured, softly, 'let us pray.' He began whispering the words of the Lord's prayer in her ear. Alvera seemed to be listening even though she was staring ahead blankly. After a few moments she began mouthing the words along with her pastor.

Just as they finished the prayer, two female paramedics bustled in, wet and windswept and weighed down with heavy equipment and disappointed expressions. Lyn guessed that their disappointment was because their call-out was nothing more than a 'psyche' case. Alvera didn't appreciate strangers appearing and began struggling and shouting to God to help her with the devils who were after her. The young paramedics tried to get some sort of response from her by asking her name and address but this merely made her resume utter gibberish. Pastor Kinver whispered something in her ear, held her hand and stroked it back and forth and gradually her utterings reduced to a whisper.

One of the paramedics, who had a blonde ponytail and the figure of a gangly girl, took Lyn aside and asked, 'What happened?'

'No idea,' said Lyn. 'She was her normal self earlier on. It seems she went up to the top floor and when she came down she was raving.'

'Is that her husband?'

Lyn shook her head. 'That's her local pastor. He calmed her down.'

'Has anything like this ever happened before?'

'No, but . . . since the murder here everyone's been a bit jumpy.'

'Yeah. I heard about that. Have they got anyone for it?'

'A member of staff. They were having an affair.'

'Shit happens,' she said, cheerfully. 'We'll do the usual physical tests on her, if she'll let us, and then we'll get her to the psychiatric assessment unit.'

Two bells rang in unison and Pam left to answer them. Lyn watched as Alvera allowed her blood pressure to be taken and then her heart monitored. Wesley Kinver continued to soothe her by stroking her hand.

Eventually, wrapped in a blanket and accompanied by Wesley and the two paramedics, they left the clinic. Wendy busied herself throwing away the cold tea and toast and making more and Lyn stared out on to the front entrance and the receding ambulance. Small tree branches littered the drive and the wind whipping the rain was so fierce it appeared to give life to inanimate objects. It drummed life into dustbins, manhole covers, the walls, the steps. They all made a different sound. As Lyn stared into the darkness she thought she saw a shape in the bushes on the right-hand side. She blinked. There was no one there.

'Mrs Conway in room six wants a couple of paracetamol – says her wound is sore.'

Lyn turned swiftly to see Pam standing at the office door.

'I thought for a moment,' said Lyn, turning back to the window, 'that I saw someone in the grounds – must be the weather.'

'I reckon it's Saul Ravenscroft haunting the place.'

'I'll take Mrs Conway her paracetamol,' said Lyn, relieved to leave the office.

Mrs Alison Conway was a twenty-eight-year-old woman. Twelve hours previously she'd had a breast reconstruction following a mastectomy the year before. Lyn felt real sympathy for her. It wasn't vain to want two breasts.

'I can't sleep,' Alison said. 'It's too noisy. My head's throbbing like a drum.' She swallowed the tablets and Lyn offered her a hot drink, which she refused.

It was on the way back to the office that Lyn caught a glimpse of Stanley at the end of the corridor. 'Stanley,' she called. He hesitated, then walked towards her. Lyn hadn't seen him close up for some time and she had to admit he looked ill. His face was normally pasty but now it was grey. The bags under his eyes were as wrinkled as fat-sucked skin and gone too was the lusting expression. The only word Lyn could think of to describe his expression was – defeated.

'You all right, Stanley?'

'Of course I am. Why shouldn't I be?'

'You look . . . tired.'

'Who doesn't?' he snapped. 'Working bloody nights is enough to make anyone tired.'

'Have you been in the grounds?'

'It's my job – innit?'

'I mean in the last few minutes.'

'Nah. Last time was about two hours ago. Why?' He didn't wait for her reply. 'I'm not going out in this lot again.'

'I wasn't expecting you to. I just thought I saw someone in the grounds.'

She thought for a second she saw a flicker of fear on Stanley's face, but dismissed the idea when he said crossly, 'On a night like this I doubt it. Nothing on my cameras anyway.'

'But they don't cover all of the grounds, do they?'

'What do you mean by that?' he asked.

'Nothing.' She was surprised by the suspicion in his voice.

'Well if that's all you want me for I'll get back to the cameras – wouldn't want to miss anything, would I?'

Lyn watched him walk away. The back of his trousers hung loosely, his shoulders slumped and his head was lowered. He just wasn't the same old lech any more.

Back in the office Wendy agreed with her. 'I think it's all changed here now. Lots of people want to leave. All the police interference has got people down.'

Pam walked in and slumped in a chair near the door. 'Have you heard people are leaving?' asked Lyn.

She undid a button on her uniform and took from her pocket a battery-operated fan, switched it on and sat back to fan herself.

'Sounds like a vibrator,' said Wendy.

'I wouldn't know,' said Pam wearily, 'but I do know *I* want to leave.'

'Has the murder been getting to you?' asked Lyn.

Pam switched off her fan and sighed. 'That's better – another flush bites the dust.'

'You could try HRT,' suggested Wendy.

A look passed between the two that Lyn could only describe as *venomous*.

'I could try a lot of things but I won't.'

Wendy bit into a piece of toast and picked up a magazine. 'So you want to leave, Pam – what's wrong?'

'I've had enough of bloody clients frightened of growing old – I mean, they might look younger, but the years pass just the same. You just can't hang on to youth, can you?'

'So what will you do?'

'God knows. But I can't stay here – it gives me the creeps. Can't you feel it? It's as if we're being watched.'

Lyn murmured, 'I know what you mean. Maybe it's just that a murder is so out of the ordinary it's just shaken us up.'

'I think you two are talking bollocks,' said Wendy. 'Carla's been arrested, she'll be jailed; Alvera's flipped, but she always was a religious maniac. She'll be given tranquilizers and in six weeks she'll be back. A few months down the line Saul Ravenscroft will be long forgotten.'

'You sound bitter,' said Lyn.

'Bitter? I'm not bitter. I won't be leaving. I need this job. One murder isn't going to unsettle me.'

By morning the wind and rain had stopped, leaving storm debris and a sheen of dampness, but the sun shone and by eight a.m. the sky was blue. Lyn felt far more cheerful as she approached her car. She was just getting into it when Una Fairchild drove up and parked alongside her. It seemed churlish not to stop for a chat, so Lyn stood beside her car and waited for Una. As soon as she saw Una she realized she had made a mistake. Una's eyes were red with crying and her hands shook as she tried to lock her car door.

'What's wrong, Una?' she asked.

In husky tones Una murmured, 'Could I sit in your car for a minute?'

Lyn thought of hot tea and toast, seeing the children off to school, then the hottest bath she could handle and, finally, bed. Once Una got going she found it hard to stop.

'Of course you can.' Lyn sat beside her.

'Hugh's left me,' she managed to choke out.

'Why? What on earth happened?' Lyn was genuinely taken aback. Hugh and Una were regarded as an example of that breed, a happy couple. Una had, by now, begun to cry, silently, in a ladylike fashion. Lyn wasn't sure what to say or do but eventually asked, 'Has he found someone else?'

'Oh yes,' she said, bitterly. 'Some bitch who came to him to give up smoking. No younger than me it seems and the bastard thought that would be some sort of consolation. Couldn't he see that made it even worse?'

Hugh worked as a psychotherapist from an office in town. Lyn had met him twice at the clinic. He was tall and lanky, grey-bearded, a committed vegetarian and had the air of a benign vicar. Via the clinic grapevine, Lyn had heard he was particularly good at treating eating disorders and helping people to give up smoking. He'd never struck her as being a womanizer.

'I'm really sorry, Una. I don't quite know what to say.'

Una burrowed into her jacket pocket for a paper tissue and then dabbed at her eyes. 'He's only known her for a few weeks . . .' She took a deep breath, as though trying to steady herself. 'Everything's gone wrong since Saul died.'

'How do you mean?'

'We were both upset – obviously – but Hugh got really down about it, saying he was past it and he might not have much longer to live.'

'What would make him think that?'

'Just his age, I suppose. He's fifty-six and a few of his friends have started to have health problems. He says he wants to take a chance on happiness.' Una wound the tissue around her fingers and then murmured sadly, 'I thought he *was* happy.'

Lyn sighed. She knew what Una was going through. Or at

least she knew about unhappiness and for a short while she'd also known marital happiness.

She was so tired that she found Una's distress was depressing her – she wanted sleep.

'I'm sorry, I'll have to go,' she said. 'The kids are expecting to see me before they go to school.'

'Of course.'

Una opened the car door, got out and stood looking towards the clinic. 'Did you know Saul introduced us?'

Lyn shook her head. She watched as Una walked away, trying to imagine how she would have looked years before. She failed. They had all been so different years ago – in different lives. Their only connection being Saul.

Eleven

Running in extremes of weather, Rydell decided, was more risky than a plate of egg and chips, but he needed exercise so he'd ordered himself a treadmill. He'd waited a month but now, at last, he'd installed the beast in his bedroom and began a campaign to improve his cardiovascular system. He decided that he could easily fit in thirty minutes of brisk uphill walking twice a day. Not in the same league as running but if the weather was good he could run as well. Somehow thirty minutes on the treadmill seemed equivalent to two hours running, at least in terms of how the time passed. He thought of nothing but the little windows in front of him – speed, kilocalories, distance, time – but most of all he took pleasure in how little his pulse rate altered.

Afterwards he thought of sex as he showered. It entered his head more frequently, as if his libido had been on sabbatical and, with its return, he noticed women as if seeing them for the first time. He had even, much to his disgust, noticed Carla Robins.

She had skinny legs but great tits. And something about the cold glint in her eyes aroused him. She was an arrogant bitch – once, during an interview, she'd observed him so carefully that he'd lost his train of thought and she'd smirked as if to say, *You dirty bastard – I know what you're thinking*! She was right. Thoughts of her naked on the bed had intruded, but instead of him being the recipient of her attentions, he'd been merely watching – a voyeur. That had disturbed him. He saw himself as a man of action, not a passive onlooker. He'd realized then that his dealings with Carla could never be truly objective. And he had, for no good reason, opposed bail. It wasn't just that he disliked her for the feelings she stirred in him. He did think she was guilty. The forensic evidence was there, she'd lied about sleeping with Ravenscroft that night and she had a motive. It was enough in the eyes of the Crown Prosecution Service, so the decision was nothing to do with him anyway and bail was granted. He'd felt a real sense of anticlimax, especially as, resolutely and even arrogantly, she'd insisted she was innocent. *Why couldn't the murderous bitch just confess*? That way it would have been tidy. Resolved. Everything in its place. As it was he felt anxious, unsettled, sometimes even feeling his heart race.

He was equally bothered by the fact that Denni was convinced she was innocent and Ram, ex-accountant-like, was still adding up the pros and cons. Rationally there was no reason for them all to agree, but if the team were undecided, where would that leave a jury? Might she even be acquitted? The seed of doubt planted by a good defence lawyer could easily flourish with good rhetoric and an appeal to the jury's emotions.

Rydell could imagine the scenario –

Strange isn't it, members of the jury, that although the defendant's fingerprints were found in the room, the murder weapon itself was clean. There is no doubt my client had sexual intercourse with the victim on the night he died. But it was her habit not to breakfast with her lovers . . . *pause . . . to allow laughter from the court*. She says she left the clinic about one a.m. The pathologist can only give an approximate time of death – within two hours. Anyone, and I repeat, anyone, could have entered that room after she left. And yet the police have offered no other suspect. Ms Robins is a tough, modern young woman, with a good job, her own home and car, money in the bank and one or two lovers. In all conscience, could you convict someone because of her lifestyle or personality? If so, many of us would stand convicted. You've seen her in court – cool under fire. A woman who *can* control her emotions. Admittedly she did lie to the police, but that was to protect Mr Ravenscroft's wife – the fact that he had been brutally murdered was surely enough for her to bear. And did the police find anything incriminating at the home of the accused? They did not! No bloodstained shoes or clothes and yet the perpetrator could hardly have cut throat and wrists without being at the very least spattered in blood.

These doubts, ladies and gentlemen of the jury, will stay with you. My client protests her innocence and, on her behalf, I do beg you to consider the *real* facts of the case. All the forensic evidence proves is that she was with the victim *before* he died. That is her only link and I think I have raised enough doubts in your mind to acquit my client. Anything else would be a complete miscarriage of justice.

Rydell wiped the last of the shaving cream from his face and wondered why, in his mock courtroom scene, he hadn't been on the side of the prosecution. He spent a few minutes polishing the sink and taps, then dressed and checked each room of his flat. He made his final inventory – plugs, lights, water, gas, all doors closed and car keys – then he slammed the flat door. He gave it only one push to check it was fully closed and then he glanced at his watch. He'd managed everything in forty-five minutes. Usually it took him around fifty to fifty-five minutes. He was on a roll. It was going to be a good day.

After the storm of the night before the sunshine and blue sky seemed to have a good effect on everyone. In the office both Ram and Denni were cheerful, so much so that he asked Denni if she had anything to celebrate. 'I think so. My mother seems to have acquired a fella.'

'How did she manage that? I didn't think she went out,' said Rydell.

'She doesn't. A handyman came calling and she's found him a few jobs to do. A real friendship seems to be developing. They've got things in common.'

'Such as?'

'Age and a love of booze and fags.'

Rydell laughed. 'As long as you're happy.'

'I couldn't be more happy,' she said, 'if I'd met someone myself.'

Ram sat at his computer. 'I don't want to burst any bubbles here but, overnight, we've had three burglaries.'

'Same perp do you think?' asked Rydell.

'Same MO. Looks like a professional – empty places, nice and neat, cash and jewellery only. And nobody heard a thing.'

'Anyone naming names?'

Ram shook his head and was about to speak when a uniformed sergeant put his head around the door. 'That Carla Robins hasn't checked in yet, guv. She always turns up at ten on the dot. Thought I'd better let you know.'

Rydell glanced at his watch. It was eleven fifteen. 'Thanks. We'll give it till twelve, then we'll check her out.'

Rydell tried to concentrate on his paperwork, but couldn't. *She always turns up at ten on the dot.* Suddenly it made sense to him. The reason he disliked her so much. She shared some of his traits. The compulsive need to be tidy, to check and recheck – to be on time – to be in control. Not to need anyone, or at least to give that appearance. If he were in her position would he stay meekly or make a run for it?

Make a run for it, he decided. It was a gamble but, if you were going down for murder anyway, there was only bail money to lose.

He straightened the papers in front of him. 'Denni, get your coat – I think Carla's done a runner.'

Carla's blue sports car was parked outside her cottage. There were no lights on and the curtains were all open. Rydell knocked loudly, using first the brass knocker then his fist.

Lifting the letter box he saw fresh flowers on a circular table and a pair of black high-heeled shoes placed side by side on the floor. When there was no response they walked to the back of the house to peer into the narrow kitchen and try the back door. There was no sign of a hurried exit and no signs of life inside.

'We'll have to go in,' said Rydell. 'I've got a crowbar in the car.'

'I'm impressed,' said Denni.

'So you should be.'

The back door gave easily. The kitchen, long and narrow, was white on white. The gold handles on the cupboard doors and a bunch of pink carnations in a red vase only partially alleviated the starkness. Carla was no cook, Denni decided. The cooker was unblemished, the fridge contained a half bottle of white wine, a bottle of champagne, a bag of lettuce leaves and two yogurts. The living room and back room cum office were clean and tidy – nothing was out of place. Rydell was first upstairs, checking the bathroom. A slight smell of bath oil hung in the air, a towel neatly folded over the towel rail felt slightly damp.

Denni, by now, felt as she usually did in an empty house on a search – a mixture of excitement and apprehension. She followed behind to open one of the fitted cupboards on the narrow landing. Inside were three matching suitcases. She picked them up but had already guessed they were empty.

In the bedroom Rydell saw the body first. 'Oh Christ!' he muttered. Denni swallowed hard. It didn't matter how many corpses she had come across, each one was a shock, each one unique. It was obvious Carla had put up a real fight for her life. The room was in disarray, two lamps and the bedside table were overturned. Books and blood-spattered paper surrounded Carla's prone body. Denni knelt down, hurriedly slipping on a pair of latex gloves. She lifted the bloodsoaked hair from Carla's face. Her eyes were closed, her throat had been cut, but not neatly, there were several slashes to her arms and across her face. There was no sign of a weapon but the cuts looked to Denni like scalpel wounds. She was hardly cold. Instinctively Denni felt for a radial pulse, then a neck pulse. 'Oh my God – she's still alive!' She turned her gently into the recovery position, yanked the duvet over her and asked Rydell to fetch either clean tea towels or an ironed sheet.

It seemed a long time before the paramedics arrived but, in fact, it was twelve minutes. Soon she was intubated, given oxygen, an intravenous infusion was set up, but as they carried her out the word was, 'Don't think she's going to make it.'

Rydell sent for the scenes of crime team and they arrived within half an hour. There was nothing more for them to do but drive to Harrowford General.

For more than an hour they sat in the accident and emergency department waiting for news. A continuous health video droned softly in a high corner of the room. Well children ran around or fidgeted, sick children screamed and grizzled. Old people were wheeled around, pale and wheezy. Others held injured limbs, or pads to their eyes, and the triage nurse quickly dispatched some out of sight to sit behind curtains and wait so that the others didn't panic if blood dripped on the floor. The only factor shared by all were the mixed expressions of shock, painful resignation and anxiety.

Eventually the senior registrar came out to give his verdict. 'I don't hold much hope,' he said gently. 'The blood transfusions will make a difference but she may have brain damage – she's arrested twice. We're still trying to stabilize her. What about her next of kin?'

There was no answer to that and both Denni and Rydell felt uncomfortable. 'We'll deal with that,' said Denni. 'And please let us know when she regains consciousness.'

Once a uniformed WPC arrived to sit with Carla there was no point in their remaining, so they drove back to the station, with Denni struggling to remember the name of a friend Carla had mentioned. She had been asked about next of kin as it was part of the personal identification form, but there was no law which said you had to name an individual and Carla had declined at first, but finally had given a name. It would be on tape, it wouldn't be a problem, but Denni still wished she could remember.

Neither of them said much in the car. Rydell felt he had let himself and Carla down. Denni still felt slightly sick and depressed. Somewhere along the line the case had gone horribly wrong.

The news had already spread and Ram was waiting for them. 'Come on, you two, let's get out of here to the pub – the super's still in a meeting. He wants to hold another one at four. Sod all to be done till we've been briefed.' At first, Rydell's expression was faintly disapproving, but finally he nodded. 'Good idea – I could do with a drink.'

Ram insisted on driving out of town and when they reached the Bell Inn in Oatshall he announced, 'I'm buying. An uncle of mine died in India and he's left me a bit of money.'

'That's great,' said Denni. 'I bet your mum's pleased.'

'Oh yeah,' he said. 'Makes me really hot property in the marriage stakes.'

'How much?'

Ram smiled, showing his even white teeth that still managed to survive despite the bombardment of mint humbugs. 'All of a hundred quid but, when I marry, there'll be considerably more.'

'So you're really on the lookout?'

Ram laughed. 'I've been looking for years.'

Rydell meanwhile stared glumly ahead. 'I'll get the drinks,' he said. 'Will you drive back, Denni?' Denni didn't feel she had much choice. 'Make mine a Coke then, please,' she said.

The pub had that indefinable atmosphere of a good pub. Whether it was due to the soft lighting, the coal fire or the comfortable sofas in the lounge, or merely the friendliness of landlord and customers, Denni didn't know. But she immediately felt more relaxed. The horror of finding Carla hadn't gone but it had receded. That was *outside* the pub. This was *inside*, a place with *bonhomie*, where outside didn't exist for a while.

Not that Rydell let them forget that, in his eyes, it was a working lunch and strategies were to be discussed and planned. Ram and Denni sat together on one black leather sofa. Rydell sat opposite on the twin sofa.

'We have to go back and start from the beginning,' he said, staring at the menu.

'You mean a reconstruction?' queried Ram.

'Too expensive. No, we have to go over the PDFs again and every interview and do it *all* again. Somewhere along the line we've missed something. And we have to go back to Carla's. If she doesn't make it, it's a murder scene.'

'There is the possibility,' said Denni, 'that one of the group who came to the open evening hid somewhere – maybe in the theatre – and waited for their opportunity – saw Carla leave and went in and did the deed.'

'I *had* thought of that,' said Rydell, obviously peeved that Denni had too, 'but we didn't interview the guests personally, did we? We concentrated on the staff and fixed our sights on Carla Robins.'

'If she survives,' said Ram, 'she'll give us a name and our troubles will be over.'

'You're such an optimist, Ram, you make me sick.'

'Sorry I look on the bright side, guv, but she obviously knew her attacker – there was no sign of a forced entry, was there?'

'No, it certainly looks as if she let him or her in.'

'Maybe forensic will turn up something?' suggested Denni.

'We thought forensic had solved it before,' said Rydell, staring glumly into his pint of beer.

When the food arrived they decamped to a table. They ate in silence for a while until Ram said, 'I reckon if we concentrate on Ravenscroft's wife we could save ourselves a lot of grief.'

Rydell put down his knife and fork and, ignoring Ram's comment, asked, 'How do you think Ravenscroft's death differed from the attack on Carla?'

Denni thought back to the moment they had found

Ravenscroft. 'Surgical precision.' She hesitated. 'But then Saul was taken unawares, whereas Carla managed to put up a fight.'

Rydell nodded, picked up his knife and fork and continued eating.

Once the meal was over Rydell felt himself relax. He was even more relaxed once the plates were removed and the table wiped. 'We mustn't conclude that Carla didn't commit murder. This could be a copycat attack, maybe for revenge. Ram was quite right in thinking that Amanda Ravenscroft could be responsible. Carla opened the door to her – she would have expected a row – she would have been primed.'

'If Carla dies, who inherits the clinic?' asked Ram.

'No idea,' said Denni.

'It could be a Ms C. Croft,' said Rydell, 'her next of kin. We don't know anything about her at the moment, but we're working on it.'

'Perhaps she's the pair of capable hands he wanted for his beloved clinic,' said Denni. 'He obviously didn't trust his wife enough.'

All three were heading back towards Carla's cottage when Rydell's cellphone rang. 'He'll have to wait. We'll catch him later.'

'That,' said Rydell, clicking off his phone, 'was the nick. Our man Stan has something important to say.'

Twelve

G raham had taken up jogging. He'd been out to buy himself a black jogging suit and black trainers, not a well-known brand, but he didn't care about that. He'd also bought himself a black cap. The day he'd bought the gear he'd stood looking at himself in his wardrobe mirror. He was impressed. His nose, although still slightly swollen, was now normal looking. Everything about him had improved. He'd gained weight, not fat but muscle. He'd got his own exercise regime going – press-ups early morning and evening and a bit of weight training in the middle of the day. He used large tins of baked beans to encourage his biceps to develop. He wasn't going to pay good money to go to a gym when he could do it in the comfort of his own home.

Every morning now he was up at seven and straight into his running gear. Not that he ran the full distance. He went by bike. A mountain bike he'd nicked at a local park. It belonged to a teenage boy who was chatting up a girl by the swings. Well, you careless little sod, he thought. I need that bike so you've seen the last of it. He'd had to repaint it, of course, customize it a bit, scrape off the serial number as best he could, but, when eventually it was finished, he knew if the lad did see him riding it he wouldn't recognize it.

The weather had been a problem lately, so Graham had toured the charity shops for some waterproofs. A twittery little woman had said she'd put some by for him if any came in. A few days later he was greeted by her like an old friend. 'Hello there, dear – look what I've got for you.' She held up a pair of black waterproofs. She wanted to charge seven pounds fifty for them but when he said he wasn't working she said, 'All right then, dear, five pounds.' It wasn't often people called him dear, but that was before he'd had his nose altered.

Graham had never had a trade. At school he was bullied and called Beaky or Hawkshit, so he stayed away as much as possible and, although he learnt to read, writing he found difficult. He could only write in capitals and he was ashamed of that and, although he could sign his name, he became flustered when he had to. And, of course, he had picked up a few words of Italian. He felt sure that would impress Lyn.

He'd seen a lot of her lately. He knew where she worked. He knew where she shopped and, best of all, he knew where she lived. So close by he didn't even need to use his bike. He just jogged. The man in black who knew where to stand to be unobtrusive.

And his luck wasn't running out. He'd been buying his daily *Sun* newspaper at a newsagent near the clinic and there was a sign saying: *Wanted: Evening Paper Boy*. The money was a bit extra on top of his social but, best of all, he delivered the evening paper to the clinic. Not that the timing coincided with Lyn's arrival, but it made him feel good just to step over *her* threshold.

Something else buoyed his spirits. He hadn't seen her with a man. Not once. He'd seen her with a girlfriend and her kids, but he was pretty sure there was no man in her life.

Money, of course, was a problem. You couldn't impress a woman like Lyn without money. But he could sort that. The main thing was to get that little bit closer every day and to do this he'd use the telephone. She'd have an answerphone. He could listen to her voice – imagine what she was wearing, how she stood, how her boobs strained against her bra, how her soft hair clung to her shoulders. How she smelt – warm and humid – soap and sweat. Just thinking about her made him tingle all over. '*Bella, Bella,*' he murmured to himself.

Stanley Goodman sat drinking a mug of cocoa in the kitchen, staring at a blank piece of wall. Freda knew him well enough to know something was wrong and he was aware of her casting surreptitious little glances at him. He stayed silent so she stopped asking him what was wrong and encouraged him instead to eat more. That didn't work. Instead, he ate less and drank more. She could smell the whisky on his breath and she knew he was keeping a stock under the bed, where he thought she couldn't find it, but she'd seen him put it there. He must think she was stupid.

The mug of cocoa was only half finished and cold by now, but he still sat staring at the wall. His behaviour was beginning to frighten her. 'Should you see the doctor, pet?' she asked, tentatively.

'What the hell for? What can he do?'

Freda knew there was no point in saying any more. Stan's mouth was set in a thin line of miserable defiance. What was she going to do? What could she do? Stan didn't like doctors anyway. He thought they were all stuck up and arrogant. He delighted in cases where doctors were in some kind of trouble. *Stan doesn't like doctors.* That thought kept going over and over in her head. She pretended to read the paper, but that didn't stop the thought recurring. Stan wasn't violent. He'd had a bit of a temper when he was younger but, since she'd been disabled, he'd been as quiet as a lamb.

Stan was in bed when the doorbell rang, but it was difficult for her to answer the door and she peered out of the window to see who it was. She pushed open the bedroom door. 'Stan, it's the police.'

'I'm coming, I'm coming,' he said, snatching up his dressing gown and barging past her wheelchair.

The inspector and the woman sergeant smiled at her and followed Stanley through to the living room. Just as her wheelchair approached the door it was closed on her. Tears of frustration welled in her eyes. Had they come to arrest him? What would happen to her?

Half an hour later they left. Stan saw them out then patted her cheek. 'Guess what?' he said. 'She's confessed?' Freda asked, hopefully.

'Nah. Not that. Someone tried to murder Carla Robins. She's still alive, but only just.'

Freda smiled weakly. She was glad Stan was more cheerful, but she couldn't fail to notice that he seemed a bit triumphant, as if he hoped Carla wouldn't make it.

'Well I fancy another cup of cocoa, love,' he said, 'and a chocolate biscuit – how about you?'

Freda made the cocoa and Stan switched on the television. For some reason he seemed proud of himself. She decided that in some way he must have outwitted the police.

The home of Charmaine Reid was set in acres of land with only one visible neighbour. Denni had met Charmaine once, only briefly, before, and this was the first time she'd been to the house. Judging from the outside it had several bedrooms with a couple more in a cottage annex.

Inside, it groaned with antiques and the sound of grandfather clocks. Denni was convinced that Charmaine was in the wrong house. Her husband Charles, known as Chaz, was in the right house. When they knocked at the front door he appeared from the side of the house. He was obviously the hunting, shooting, fishing type, judging by his surroundings, his Barbour and green wellies. 'Wonderful day,' he said, by way of introduction. It wasn't raining, but the sun was feeble and not the sort of day Denni would call wonderful. Chaz was tall and slim with dark hair, greying at the sides, and warm brown eyes. His skin, the colour of toffee, was evidence of long summer holidays in the Mediterranean. She had to admit he was good looking and his smile was as warm as his eyes. 'You'll have tea or coffee, of course,' he said, in the accent-free tone that public schools seem to produce in those under fifty. Denni guessed he was at least ten years younger than Charmaine. Rydell declined, he wasn't thirsty and he didn't like balancing a cup and saucer when he was concerned with an interview.

In the morning room they all sat in padded high-back chairs around a circular table. Denni felt distinctly uncomfortable.

Posh houses made her feel just as uneasy as the scruffy, dirty type. Pen poised over her notebook, she began taking notes.

'Have you lived here long, Mr Reid?' asked Rydell.

'Do call me Chaz,' he said. 'I was born here – unbelievable good luck. Rich parents who snuffed it rather early and left me the loot.' He flashed a smile at his wife. 'We're spending it quite nicely, aren't we, darling?'

Charmaine smiled in response but nothing creased around her eyes. Although she wore full make-up, her blue silk blouse and cream trousers didn't look particularly clean, as if she'd dressed in yesterday's clothes. It was only eleven a.m. but Denni was sure the tumbler she held didn't contain water.

'We're retracing our steps, Mrs Reid,' explained Rydell. 'I'm sure you remember the Friday night in question.'

'I was trussed up like a turkey. I'd hardly be likely to forget.'

'You told us in your previous interview that you didn't leave your room.'

She laughed. 'Do you think I'm going to change my mind now? Why would I leave my room? I'd had my operation that morning. Veteran of cosmetic surgery that I am, even I wouldn't have the stamina to actually *murder* someone post anaesthetic.'

'Really, Inspector,' Chaz intervened, 'you do seem to be wasting your valuable time. I visited Charmaine that evening and she was out for the count. You hardly knew I was there, did you, darling?'

Charmaine sipped her drink and muttered under her breath.

'Saul Ravenscroft had operated on you before,' began Denni. 'How many times?'

'I've lost count – it's all in my diary. Offhand, I'd say about four times.'

'So you had complete trust in him?'

'Of course. He was a very good surgeon.'

'Did you ever see him socially?'

Denni asked the question casually, but Charmaine was

a striking woman and Saul was known for appreciating good-looking women – did it extend to patients?

'Once or twice – I'm sure I told you this before. He wasn't shagging me, if that's what you're implying.'

'Darling, calm down,' said Chaz. 'The sergeant is only doing her job.'

'Well I'm getting a bit pig sick of it. I met him at a drinks party once or twice, when I was three sheets to the wind, and he rambled on about the cost of his wife's horse. You'd think he was down to his last bale of hay the way he moaned.'

'Did he give you the impression the clinic was in trouble financially?'

'No. But then I couldn't give a toss anyway. As long as he was operating, why should I worry?'

'Is the surgery something you started before or after marriage?' asked Rydell. The idea of anyone willingly undergoing surgery appalled him and he couldn't help wondering if Chaz encouraged her.

Charmaine looked him straight in the eye. 'I couldn't afford it before I married and Chaz totally approves.'

Chaz smiled in agreement. 'I'm happy if you're happy, darling.'

It was a situation Rydell found hard to understand – was she chasing eternal youth or merely trying to steer Chaz clear of other younger women? Maybe, of course, she just enjoyed the actual surgery and the cosseting afterwards. A way of seeking attention.

'One final question,' he said. 'You say you didn't see anything, but did you hear anything that night?'

'I thought at one point I heard Carla's voice.'

'You knew her?'

'Well don't look so surprised, Inspector. For a short time we even worked together.'

'Doing what?'

'We worked for the same travel company about seven years ago. An upmarket travel company, I might add. We weren't doing the eighteen to thirty thing. All lager louts and shagging everything that breathes. It was a villa holiday travel company. I thought I'd give it a whirl. I was escaping from a broken marriage I used to be Mrs Croft. Carla was . . . I don't know what she was escaping from. Anyway, I thought sunshine and booze was what I needed. Instead, I got a little too fond of the booze and found the human race on holiday are just a pain in the ass.'

Rydell was surprised, somehow, that Charmaine had ever worked at anything, but he jotted down a few notes and signalled to Denni to take over. 'Would you say you know Carla well?' Denni asked.

Charmaine gave a short, dry laugh. 'As well as anyone, I suppose. She could be friendly but she gave nothing away. She was promiscuous but only with rich, married men. The hoi polloi to her were just drunken tossers.'

'Did she ever mention her family?'

'Didn't have one. At least she never mentioned anyone.'

'Would it surprise you to know she named you as her next of kin?'

'You're kidding?' Charmaine's blandly attractive face showed the news came as a complete surprise and, strangely, she seemed pleased.

Chaz intervened now. 'Why would she do that, darling? You hardly knew her.'

'How the fuck would I know?' she snapped. 'She's nuts – she killed Saul, didn't she?'

'That's not necessarily true,' said Denni. 'Today we found Carla in her own home with her throat cut. Her condition is very serious.'

Charmaine's shoulders sagged and she took a huge gulp of her drink. 'There is something else,' began Denni. 'Saul Ravenscroft left his estate to Carla. We have yet to find Carla's will but you may well be her beneficiary.'

Thirteen

Alvera Lewis had been in hospital a week before Rydell found out. He'd decided to investigate the on-call arrangements in more rigorous detail. So he sat in Una Fairchild's office, checking dates, times and sources. Una seemed nervous. She sat behind her desk trying to sort various piles of paper. The phone rang constantly and she would slip her glasses on to check details and then take them off and lose them under one pile or another.

Rydell had a chair, the use of a small table and access to a filing cabinet. She'd told him she'd visited Carla and her condition remained critical. Then she'd added, 'At least Alvera is improving.'

'What's wrong with her?' he asked

She glanced at him, quizzically, as if he should have known. 'She had a breakdown here one night. Religious mania, so the psychiatrist said – a provisional diagnosis. She might be schizophrenic.'

'Where is she?'

'The acute psychiatric ward at the General.'

'What triggered it off?'

Una shrugged her thin shoulders. 'Who knows? She went up to the top floor, seemingly normal, and came down again in a disturbed state.'

Rydell hid his irritation that no one had told him and concentrated instead on the task in hand, which was to plough through the mysteries of the on-call system. It seemed there was a bank of three doctors who would sleep in. Two were regulars from the agency, one had been known

127

to Saul Ravenscroft. 'Do they sign in when they arrive?' he asked.

'They should do – and the visitor's book – in case of fire,' muttered Una, looking embarrassed.

'You mean they don't.'

'Doctors set themselves apart,' she said. 'I think they regard it like clocking on and feel they're too professional to do that.'

'How often are their services called upon?'

'That's difficult to say.' Her voice sounded slightly huskier now and, for the first time, he noticed the redness around her eyes and her pallor. 'Are you feeling OK?'

She nodded and looked away as if on the verge of tears. Rydell wished Denni was with him but she'd gone to visit Carla. 'I'd love a cup of coffee,' he said.

'Yes, of course,' she answered, obviously grateful for a chance to leave the room.

When she'd gone he rang Denni on his mobile. 'Why didn't you tell me about Alvera Lewis?'

'What about her?'

'She's on the acute psychiatric ward.'

'I didn't know.'

'Pay her a visit, will you? Try to find out why she flipped.'

'Easier said than done, guv, but I'll do my best.'

'How's Carla doing?'

'She's still critical but stable. The staff think she's more responsive.'

'Good. See you later.'

Una appeared at that moment with a tray of coffee and biscuits. The biscuits lay in a neat circle and, although he would have liked one, they were unwrapped and anyway he didn't want to spoil the arrangement. Illogically, he was glad that Una didn't take one.

'You were telling me,' said Rydell with a smile, 'how often your on-call doctors were actually used.'

'It varies—' She broke off. 'To be quite honest the doctors here do their own thing.'

'What does that mean?'

'If the nursing staff do call them during the night it's written in the bed statement, but we haven't been saving that information separately.'

'I'm surprised everything isn't computerized.'

'Martin and Saul have their own computers. They didn't think it necessary to have any more.'

'In that case you'll need to supply me with bed statements for the past year,' said Rydell.

Una frowned. 'Surely you don't think one of the on-call doctors murdered Saul?'

'At the moment, Mrs Fairchild, I'm wondering how often this clinic *did* have a doctor present overnight.'

'Are you suggesting that the clinic hasn't been properly covered?'

Rydell stared at her for several seconds. 'I think it's a strong possibility. After all, your chief surgeon lay dead for two days before being found. Doesn't that strike you as odd?'

Una looked distinctly uncomfortable but said nothing.

'I'd prefer it,' he said, 'if you didn't involve the nursing staff in this at the moment.'

He was leaving and had his hand on the door handle when he asked softly, 'How long were you friends with Saul?'

'Years and—' She broke off, aware that she'd given herself away.

'Next time, Mrs Fairchild, we'll go into more detail.'

Intensive care was, as always, very busy. Relatives came and went, their faces etched with worry. They sat beside beds and struggled to find somewhere to hold or touch their loved ones through the maze of wires and tubes. They stared in dismay at the back of hands bruised by needles, at the dry cracked lips and closed eyes. They stared at monitors they didn't understand and watched anxiously the steady drip, drip of intravenous infusions. An alarm going off caused them to be startled even if it wasn't their relative.

Denni was Carla's first visitor. She lay under one sheet,

her neck wound sutured but with a tracheotomy in situ. Her skin had the translucent grey tones of a corpse. Her breathing bubbled with secretions and, after ten minutes, a nurse approached and asked Denni to leave while they sucked away the flow of mucus.

On her return Denni asked, 'How's she doing?'

The young nurse, reluctant to say anything, suggested she spoke to the registrar. 'Is he here?' asked Denni.

'No, but I could ring him.'

'No need. You tell me your opinion and I promise I won't say a word.'

The nurse's blue eyes flicked anxiously around before she whispered, 'She's got a chest infection, her oxygen levels are down – it doesn't look good.'

'Thanks for telling me.'

'There's something else, but no one else has the same opinion.'

'What's that?'

'I think she hears every word . . .' She broke off to glance in Carla's direction. 'I don't think that about all of the patients – she doesn't respond to pain but I still get the feeling she knows what is going on.'

'A hunch is something I understand. Thanks again.'

Denni sat down beside Carla and began stroking her hand rhythmically. 'I know you can hear me, Carla. We want to find the person who did this to you. You're doing fine but we need your help.' She said the same words over and over again. There was no response but just as she was about to leave she thought Carla's index finger moved. It could have been a mere twitch, an involuntary movement, but, just as relatives clutch at the tiniest of changes, so did Denni. 'I'll be back, Carla. Hang on in there.'

From ICU Denni made her way down tunnel-like corridors to the psychiatric department. Her warrant card gained her a visitor sticker and access to the acute ward.

The staff nurse on duty wore jeans, a pink sweatshirt and carried the biggest bunch of keys Denni had ever seen. 'We have a motto here,' said Nurse Sally. 'If it opens, lock it! If it's an object, count it. If it's movable – bolt it to the floor. Everything here is a potential hazard – even toilet rolls have to be locked away.' Denni didn't need that explaining. She'd known a patient once choke to death on a toilet roll.

Alvera was in the day room staring out of a barred window on to the car park below. Others sat either watching television or pacing up and down. Many mumbled to themselves. One woman slumped forward dramatically as they approached Alvera. Sally stepped forward and sat her back in the chair. 'Don't do that, Babs. You know it upsets the visitors.' Babs, with grey hair straggling to her shoulders and a gaunt and wild expression, rolled her eyes and opened her mouth like a fish, but no sound came out.

'What's the matter?' asked Sally. Denni waited by Sally's side, not wanting to descend unannounced on Alvera. It was important not to frighten Alvera and it was important to see how she related to a member of staff. Babs eventually decided to answer Sally's question. 'You know I'm dead, don't you?'

'Yes,' said Sally, cheerfully. 'We all know that, Babs.'

'I've been dead a long time.'

'I know that but if you *are*, how come you cause us so much trouble?'

Babs thought about that for a few seconds. 'Death is a mystery,' she said with a crooked grin.

'It is in your case,' said Sally with a smile. 'Nearly lunch time, Babs.'

'Good!' she said

As they left Babs, Sally said, 'Eats like a horse – doesn't gain an ounce.'

'Is Alvera eating well?'

'Yeah. Not bad. She's improved in the last day or so. Could be the medication kicking in but she does seem lucid most of the time.'

Alvera, meanwhile, sat unmoving, still staring ahead. Sally knelt in front of her and touched her hands – they were placed

Christine Green

together as if in prayer. 'This is Denni from the police – you remember her?'

There was no answer but Alvera did glance up. Sally left them alone and Denni pulled up a chair to face Alvera. 'Sally tells me you're getting better, Alvera.'

'She's a nice woman.'

'Do you feel better?'

Alvera nodded. 'I feel okay.'

'Do you hear any voices?'

The answering glance was swift and sharp. 'I've never heard voices. I saw what I saw – I'm not a mad woman.'

'Tell me what you *saw* then.'

'I saw the Lord.'

'How do you know it was the Lord?'

Alvera stared at her. 'When you see the Lord – you just know. Even a heathen would know it was the Lord. I've been praying ever since. It's the second coming – the Lord said He would come again. He's here with us, walking amongst us. Praise God. Praise sweet Jesus.'

Denni nodded and smiled as if believing every word. 'How was he dressed?' she asked, softly.

'In white, of course. A long white robe.'

'Did he have a halo around his head?'

'Of course – my Jesus shone with the light of heaven.'

'Did he speak to you?'

Alvera looked faintly disappointed. 'No. But the Good Lord stretched out his arms to me.'

'What did you do?'

The expression on Alvera's face showed contempt. 'I sank to my knees and prayed, as any Christian woman would do.'

'And then what happened?'

'He gave me the gift of tongues.'

'I see. And then he disappeared?'

'You're a very silly woman,' snapped Alvera.

'Why am I silly?'

'Because He's here with us now.'

'Where?'

'Use your eyes.'

Denni glanced around the dayroom at the amblers, the shamblers and the immobile. No one approaching a Jesus lookalike was obvious to her.

'I can't see him.'

'There,' said Alvera, pointing towards the door. Denni looked towards the door, half expecting to see something or someone. 'Praise the Lord,' murmured Alvera.

As Denni made her farewells and turned to go, Alvera reached out and tugged at her sleeve, saying earnestly, 'The Lord is always with you – don't ever forget that – will you?'

'I'll try not to.'

Back in the office Rydell planned a third run through of the CCTV video recording, with special emphasis on the open evening guests' arrival and departure. By now all of them had been interviewed by the uniformed branch and two were found to have criminal records of the minor sort.

Denni arrived as it was in progress. The blinds were pulled and the room was stuffy with airless central heating and body warmth. The video was of poor quality, as though the camera lens was dirty and, after a while, Denni began to squint at the screen. First, at normal speed, they watched the arrival. Some came on foot, some parking their cars. Then they watched the arrival again in slow motion. By a process of elimination the thirty-one had been separated between either staff or visitors. At the end of the evening they straggled out in little groups. Rydell stilled the video for a few moments and then continued in slow motion. 'Guv,' called out Ram, 'there's a problem.'

'What's up?'

Ram, who was in the front row, stood up and went to the video. 'If you look at this frame, four people are leaving – three men and a woman. If you look closely, one of the men hangs back and, because another man is leaving at the same time, we didn't notice he wasn't there any more. Of course, he might be there on the final count.'

'Right,' said Rydell. 'We need a blow-up and an improved video. Can you do that, Ram – for tomorrow?'

'No problem, guv.'

It was later, as they were about to go home, that Ram caught up with Denni in the corridor. 'Did you notice anything about that group of three leaving the clinic?'

Denni shrugged. 'Not a thing. Should I have done?'

'I could be wrong but I thought I recognized one of the men.'

'Who do you think he is?'

'He's obviously under an assumed name,' said Ram, 'but I've seen him before.'

Denni smiled. 'It's not surprising he looked familiar – that was Ravenscroft.'

'Bugger it,' muttered Ram. 'In that case, as I'm so disappointed, how about a drink?'

Denni felt bad refusing, but she wanted to get home, have something on toast, watch something entertaining but mindless on TV and then go to bed with a good book.

When she did get home there were two messages on her answerphone. One was from her mother – 'Don't bother coming round. I'm going out with Bill.' The other was from her blind friend, Alexis. 'Hi Denni. Missing you like crazy but love it here – the island of perpetual spring – when are you coming out? Friends are describing sights to be seen – doesn't sound impressive, but I just love the warmth and the sound of the sea. Do try!'

Fat chance, thought Denni. Since Alexis had been kidnapped, raped and her dog killed, she'd become agoraphobic – her doctor had suggested Tenerife. She'd rented her flat out and had left Harrowford within a month. Denni had been really upset at the time. Alexis was her best friend. In fact, she was the only local female friend she'd had. But Denni could see that, for a blind person, the warmth of the sun and the sound of the sea year-round was a real bonus. In sunshine, people were happier and Denni guessed from Alexis's cheerful phone calls that she wouldn't be coming back.

Having made tea and cheese on toast, Denni sat with a tray on her lap and watched the news. It was gloomy, with reports of bombings and terrorist threats. She took in the headlines and switched channels to an action movie, which revolved around bombings and terrorist threats. At least it was fiction.

It was nearly eleven p.m. when her eyes gave up, but she could still hear the television droning on and then the sound of footsteps outside. Her eyes flicked open. Immediately she sat upright, poised, waiting for someone to knock at the door. Silence. She slipped on her shoes, stood up and crept across the room to open the curtains a fraction.

At first she couldn't see anyone. Just the trees and the lights of houses opposite. Then she saw a dark shape moving near her porch. She walked into the hall and grabbed her nightstick. I'm ready, she told herself, I'm ready.

Fourteen

Opening the door slightly she raised her nightstick and simultaneously switched on the hall light. The man slumped in her doorway turned his face towards the light.

'You bastard, Ram! What the hell are you doing?'

Ram smiled sheepishly. 'I'm drunk.'

Denni had only ever seen him merry after a few lagers. She was both surprised and worried. 'I can see that,' she said. 'Why?'

'Help me in,' he said, trying to haul himself up. With a hand under his arm she eased him into the hallway and then into the living room. He slumped on to the sofa and smiled apologetically. 'I was going to walk away,' he said. 'When I started out, coming here seemed like a good idea.' His speech was hardly slurred and Denni wondered if he was quite as drunk as she'd at first thought. 'What's wrong?' she asked. 'It's not like you to get into this state.'

'I'm a deprived cop.'

'Deprived of what?'

'The love of a good woman.'

'I can't supply a woman, Ram – good or bad.'

His head slumped forward and, for a moment, she thought he'd fallen asleep, but then he roused himself. 'I'm tired of staring at four walls,' he said. 'I'm tired of takeaway meals, no sex, a cold bed and no one to give a toss if I work sixteen hours a day.'

Denni, never having seen Ram this down before, didn't quite know what tack to take. If she was too sympathetic they might both sink into a morass of self-pity. 'Look on the

136

bright side, Ram – your mother isn't an alcoholic with a new boyfriend who's got missing front teeth and dubious personal hygiene. And you don't have to check and double-check every aspect of your life like Rydell. You can cook, so it's your choice to live on takeaways.' Then she added, 'We're all in the same boat anyway.'

Normally Ram would have answered her with a cheerful quip. This time he didn't react for several seconds, then he struggled to stand up. 'I know I'm whingeing, so I'll be off.'

Denni pushed him gently back. 'You can stay here for the night. It's not a problem.'

'You haven't got a drink, have you?'

'No, it looks as if you've had enough for the two of us. But I'll make you something to eat.'

He didn't argue with that, so she made her way to the kitchen and began beating up three eggs for scrambling. She'd cracked the eggs and had just begun to whisk when she realized Ram really wasn't himself – he was depressed. She was cross with herself for not noticing. He'd been attacked twice in the year, his last attack had left him near to death and he'd been on sick leave for several weeks. He'd stayed with his mother in London, but she was a doctor and was hardly ever there. Denni had telephoned every week and the station had sent him a little hamper of goodies, but she hadn't managed to get to London to see him. He'd put on a good show of being back to normal but he obviously wasn't. And she'd been so embroiled in the case she hadn't noticed he'd changed.

He ate the scrambled eggs hungrily, followed by a stack of toast. 'First thing I've eaten today – thanks.'

'Are you waking up in the early hours of the morning?' she asked.

'Yeah,' he said, surprised. 'I watch telly till I fall asleep and then I'm awake at three a.m.'

'Do you feel depressed, Ram?'

'I'm pissed off with my life at the moment.'

'Enough to finish it?' she asked, quietly.

137

His dark eyes watched her suspiciously. 'Denni, stop it –
I can see men in white coats already.'

'So that's a yes then, is it?'

He didn't answer. She knew there was no likelihood of
Ram admitting to being suicidal. Few men did. Women
would often admit to feelings of hopelessness and a desire
for the ultimate release. Men seemed to get on with the job
of suicide and do it without even arousing prior suspicion. 'I
don't think the men in white coats are needed yet,' she said,
'but I do think you should see your GP.'

'So that he can put me on happy pills.'

'They do work,' she said, 'but you need to be on them for
three to six months at least.'

'I don't want *Depression* down on paper. You know what
the force is like about mental illness.'

'OK. There is one more alternative. You've stayed here
before. You can stay here again. One proviso.'

'What's that?'

'Don't tell anyone. They'll think we've shacked up together
and it could ruin our potential love lives.'

'I'm glad you said potential. Haven't you got any friends,
Denni?'

She smiled. 'I have *you* and one or two old school friends
who live scattered round the country. I stay in touch by phone
and send Christmas cards saying we must meet up in the New
Year – but we never seem to get round to it.'

'What about women in the force?'

'What about them?'

'Don't hedge. There's quite a few women in the nick.'

She thought about that for a moment. 'Most are married
or living together,' she said, 'and they don't want to go
out with me on the prowl. There are one or two lesbians
I quite like and they're friendly, but I wouldn't want to
mislead them.'

'Which ones?' asked Ram, looking quite animated.

Denni described three of them. 'Why didn't you tell me?'
he asked. 'That little dark-haired PC I've tried chatting up.

138

She doesn't look like a lesbian. No wonder she turned me down.'

'They don't all have broad shoulders and a butch haircut.'

'If only life were that simple,' he said. 'Women only see me as a nice friendly bloke. It's just a disguise. Inside me is a rampant stallion – *was* a rampant stallion. I reckon now I'm in the male menopause.'

'Could be.'

Ram's mouth dropped.

'I was only joking,' she reassured him. 'You're still young. I promise to stop talking male menopause if you agree to see your GP.'

Ram muttered, 'OK, OK – you win.'

Later, when Ram had gone to bed in the spare room, Denni sat for a while and fretted about Ram's situation. There was nothing she could do but encourage him to see his GP and keep an eye on him. The one thing he hadn't mentioned was the case. She knew he put in hours and hours of unpaid overtime and he'd spent hours going through the financial records of the Harmony Clinic. As yet he'd found nothing amiss.

She fell asleep on the sofa and woke mid-dream. In her dream Ram was in disguise – he wore a mask. And yet when he took it off it wasn't him at all.

Rydell had stayed in the office watching yet another rerun of the CCTV video. He'd decided there was nothing to go home for and he needed to find out why one potential client had returned to the clinic and, more to the point, left two and a half hours later. What the hell was he doing? And could the time of Ravenscroft's death be wrong? According to the pathologist there was several hours' leeway, taking into account all the variables. And, since Carla had managed to evade the camera, the mystery man was beginning to evolve as a top-rank suspect. Could they have been in it together? Was Carla the lookout and mystery boyo the actual murderer?

In front of him was a neat pile of PDFs – those who had

attended the open evening. The majority, twenty in all, were local. The other eleven came from all over the country. He sorted through them carefully and then began to match them with the fuzzy video stills for identification. The techno boys were trying to improve the definition but, until they came up with an improved version, this one would have to do.

He decided to deal with the PDFs in groups of five. They were all on computer but sometimes the varying handwriting and spelling of the original forms were changed or embellished and mistakes were made. He arranged the forms neatly into six sets of five, the form of client number thirty-one he opened in front of him. Then he began the rerun of the video. It was something he could have delegated. He knew he had a reliable team, but at least doing it himself he could be *sure* nothing had been missed. As the grainy faces came into view he began the matching process.

His mind, though, wandered. The search of Carla's cottage had revealed so little. There was one photograph album but no diary. He presumed the killer had stolen that. Her cupboards had been neat to the point of obsession and that he understood. He'd found her passport and her adoption papers. He'd checked the address and the telephone number. An elderly sounding woman had answered, saying she was Mrs Robins. He'd made an appointment with her for the following day – just routine inquiries. He thought back to their first interview – she'd said her parents were dead – maybe her natural parents were dead. No one had bothered to check. No one had time. And was there any significance anyway? Obviously they didn't get on. Estranged families were getting to be the norm.

He was still working at eleven thirty when the telephone rang to inform him that Carla Robins had died at ten forty-six precisely.

Lyn Kilpatrick found out about Carla's death shortly after midnight at the clinic. A friend from the General, whom she'd met on the school run, phoned from intensive care to tell her the news. Her hand shook as she put down the phone. She felt sick. When she tried to stand up, her knees seemed to buckle and she sat down again.

'Are you OK?' Wendy Swan stood at the office door, looking concerned.

'I've just heard Carla Robins has died.'

'I'm sorry about that – she wasn't a friend, was she?'

'No,' said Lyn slowly. 'She wasn't a friend.'

Wendy stood awkwardly, not knowing quite what to say next. It was obvious that the news had shocked Lyn, the colour had drained from her face and she was rubbing her hands anxiously. 'I'll make you some hot sweet tea.'

A few minutes later when she appeared with the tea, Lyn looked more composed. She sipped at the tea and gradually colour returned to her cheeks. 'I'm just being a wimp,' she said. 'I'm getting paranoid.'

'What about?' asked Wendy as she sat down.

Lyn shrugged, as if a shiver had snaked down her back. 'As I told you before, I've just had this feeling – ever since Saul was murdered – that I'm being followed.'

'Have you told the police?'

'No. Maybe it's the police following me.'

'Why would they do that?'

Lyn paused. 'I've no idea.'

Wendy watched her closely. Lyn didn't lie well. 'You knew Saul before, didn't you?'

Lyn sipped at her tea and then stared into space. 'If it *is* the police, they must have found out.'

'Found out what?'

'That I worked with him before.'

'Doing what?'

'I was a theatre nurse.'

'Sounds more exciting than boring nights at the Harmony.'

'I liked it here before – all this . . .'

Wendy was dying to ask if she'd slept with Saul but it wasn't the right time. 'Why don't you ask that inspector if the police are following you?'

'I'm scared, I suppose. *If* it isn't the police, who the hell is it?'

'So why do you think you're being followed?'

'I've heard someone in the back garden on a few occasions now. Even when I go to the shops I get the feeling I'm being watched. When I collect the kids from school I get the same feeling. And now Carla's been murdered.'

'But why would anyone want to harm you?'

'Why would anyone want to harm Saul or Carla? It makes no sense.'

'I thought she'd murdered Saul,' said Wendy.

'The police did too, but it looks as if everyone got it wrong.'

A room bell sounded and Wendy stood up. For once, she was relieved someone was ringing. A few moments later another sounded. Lyn glanced at the board and her heart sank – room seven housed a woman called Genette Sankis. *I don't want to be a trouble* was her motto. She'd been in for two nights following a buttock tuck, which meant she couldn't lie on her back or her side and she slept only an hour at a time. All Lyn could do was reassure her that the discomfort would ease, unless, of course, it had become infected. Strange, thought Lyn, private patients often thought the NHS had a monopoly on infections, not realizing that private hospitals had perfected the art of secrecy. And she understood that better than most. Saul had taught her well.

Fifteen

U na Fairchild stared at the paperwork on her desk, rubbed her eyes wearily and checked the time. It was eight p.m. and she'd achieved little beyond checking the pharmacy requirements and reordering stocks. She knew she was still in shock but she had to keep going. She had no deputy and in her absence one of the sisters took over. They were trustworthy enough, but it added to their burden and, if corners needed cutting, it was *her* corners they cut.

Since Hugh had gone she had felt physically ill. Sometimes she struggled to catch her breath. It was as though a tight band had been placed around her that held in the tears, but threatened to choke her. She felt neither hunger nor thirst and, if she tried to eat, food was as hard to swallow as wood shavings. The only thing that helped was brandy or gin or vodka. She didn't care what sort of spirits she drank. It all tasted foul, but it steadied her and helped her sleep.

The thought of a drink decided her – it was time to go. She no longer thought of going *home*. It wasn't home anymore; it was merely a house.

Once in her car she could feel tears slipping down her cheeks. She brushed them away irritably. She couldn't cry yet – she didn't want to be seen.

Her expensive town house stood dark and soulless between the bright cheeriness of the rest of the houses in Gentleman's Row. It grieved her that her friends and neighbours had probably known he was seeing another woman. Or at least they would have guessed. After all, he'd been *counselling* her several times a week. Why hadn't she guessed? How could

143

she not realize what was going on? He'd even mentioned her – saying she had a lot of problems. Looking back, Una could see he *had* changed. He'd been happier, smarter, he'd even lost weight due to suddenly wanting to eat more fruit and veg, less cheese and peanuts. Now he'd gone. He'd tried to place the blame on her, of course, saying the only interest she'd had was the clinic and that being with her had denied him children. They had been happy though once, she told herself. Her whole relationship wasn't a lie – or was it?

She opened the door and flicked on the lights. She couldn't see anything different in the hall but she could smell his aftershave. She ran upstairs calling his name. In the master bedroom his wardrobe was wide open. She peered inside – all his clothes were gone. His shoes, his suits, his casual wear – there was nothing left. She sat down on the bed and stared at the empty rails and shelves. He wasn't coming back. She knew that now. She walked slowly into the bathroom and lifted the lid of the laundry basket – his socks and two shirts still waiting to be washed. She picked them up and inhaled his scent. After a few minutes, she took off her coat and slipped one of his shirts over her blouse. Then she walked slowly downstairs and poured herself a very large brandy.

Graham needed money. He wanted new clothes, a whole new image to go with his improved looks. He wouldn't find a job unless he looked the part. What *sort* of job was a problem anyway. He wasn't qualified for anything. He sat scanning the local newspaper and nothing appealed. That wasn't quite true, a thirty thousand pound a year job in computer programming appealed but four pounds an hour in McDonald's didn't. That was the only job he might acquire and *that* wasn't going to impress Lyn. He needed capital. That way he could set up his own business. He quite fancied being a landscape gardener. He could learn on the job and, with money behind him, he could offer his services to Lyn. Her garden was a terrible mess, all overgrown weeds, no patio, and just a garden shed that leaked. He knew because he'd been inside it. Once he had money he could buy a small van and some tools. Even employ someone to drive the van and do the donkey work. He could be the arty one – the one with flair. How to get the money wasn't such a big decision. He had to steal it. His mother didn't have anything left to steal. But he had choices – bank, building society, post office, petrol station. He needed a weapon, of course, and a gun was always the best bet. People didn't argue with a gun. A knife they might decide to grapple with – a gun was worthy of respect. But guns cost money and he had to admit that, even with money, he wouldn't know where to get one. Even buying a toy gun was dodgy – it could always be traced.

He folded the newspaper and stared out of the window. After a while he walked into the bedroom to check on the state of his clothes. He needed to wear something that didn't draw attention to himself, a coat or jacket long enough to disguise the fact he was holding a shotgun. Or something that looked like a shotgun.

There was another drawback of course. Banks and building societies had closed-circuit cameras. He wasn't sure about post offices but he guessed that village post offices didn't. He didn't have a criminal record, but there was always someone willing to shop you for the sake of a few hundred pounds. With a baseball cap on his head, pulled well down, it was a chance worth taking. He'd never been caught before on his burglaries. He'd managed to plan those well enough. He studied the obituary columns, noting when funerals were taking place. Then he checked out the name in the phone book using his mobile phone. Sometimes he would say he was an acquaintance of the deceased from way back. Being distressed, they wouldn't be thinking straight and they would invite him to the crematorium or the cemetery. A short service, they would say, and afterwards at the Hare and Hounds or the Fir and Firkin or just a bit of tea back at the house. Graham hadn't made a fortune this way, but over two years he'd managed the odd luxury and it had financed his operation. Not being greedy was Graham's motto. Just enough. Don't take unnecessary risks. That was why he'd never been caught.

He began checking out a few villages on a local map. The smaller ones wouldn't even have a post office. He circled three of the larger villages. Tomorrow he would take the bus and check them out. He needed to know on which day of the week pensions were collected; he didn't want to be caught by two old ladies and a dog. Late afternoon would be best, growing dark, not many people around.

Today he'd jog round to Lyn's place. She hadn't noticed him hanging around. He was glad about that. He didn't want to frighten her.

'Don't tell him,' said Denni as she drove Ram into Harrowford police station car park.

'Tell who what?'

'Don't tell Rydell you're moving in with me. Just keep your flat on for the time being at least.'

'You mean it might not work out.'

Denni smiled and patted his knee. 'We'll give it our best shot.'

There was no sign of Rydell, but evidence that he'd been working late lay in the neat piles of PDFs. 'What's he up to?' asked Ram.

'Still trying to find out who the mystery bloke is, I should imagine.'

Ram and Denni returned to their office and switched on their PCs but were interrupted with reports every few minutes. Since most were in sealed envelopes addressed to Rydell, the messengers had slightly bemused expressions because the acting chief wasn't at his desk.

He finally turned up at eleven thirty. 'Don't even think about commenting', he said at the doorway. 'Meeting in my office – five minutes.'

'I thought I was meant to be depressed,' said Ram. 'I've seen more cheerful faces in the morgue.'

'Everyone has problems,' said Denni.

'Yeah, yeah, CID more than most. Perhaps we should be thinking of a career move.'

'I haven't got the energy. Come on, don't let's keep the boss waiting.'

As the team crowded into the office Rydell merely announced that there had been a development. 'I'm replaying the CCTV video – yet again. Count bodies not faces.'

They watched carefully, all recognizing the thirty-one people checked in for the open evening, but other visitors may have been coming and going too. The odd man hadn't been identified yet, but Rydell had found out that morning that Mrs Lloyd-Peters and son had had a male visitor. The man had not been seen to leave.

Eventually someone called out, 'I think it's still thirty-one in total, boss.'

Rydell fast-forwarded the film to a group leaving. 'When they arrive, they arrive separately but, when they leave, they're more bunched up. Look at this group at the main entrance.'

Denni felt a surge of excitement. Amongst the group was an extra pair of feet. Carla was standing at the open door, ushering people out, but there were more pairs of feet than heads. Then, as they descended the stone steps, the feet once again corresponded with the headcount. 'There's thirty-two!' she shouted out.

'Correct,' said Rydell. 'One person not accounted for. The mock Doric column occludes the face but, judging from the shoes and size of feet, they belong to a male. Someone who knew how to hide from the camera.'

Rydell soon interrupted murmurs of interest. 'Denni, you interview Mrs Lloyd-Peters and male visitor. The rest of the team, see if any of the group remember seeing a man who didn't leave. Because that man could well be our perpetrator.'

'What about motive, boss?' asked Ram. 'Shouldn't we be concentrating more on disgruntled patients?'

'So far,' said Rydell, 'we have the names of three women

who were dissatisfied with the surgery. Denni, I think they'll talk more openly to you.'

There was a general shuffling of chairs and Rydell raised his voice slightly. 'Before you go, I just want to say this is a very complex case. It will take time. Be thorough, be painstaking and stay alert. No one in that clinic, patient or staff, is beyond suspicion. So ask questions and *listen* to the answers – don't assume anything. And by the way – the PM report is back on Carla Robins. The knife wounds were caused by a scalpel. Nothing much of any significance, other than she'd had a hysterectomy, probably for endometriosis. I don't think we need to pursue that at the moment. We don't want to start collecting unnecessary information. That's all. Go to it!'

When the rest of the team had gone Ram followed Rydell to his office. 'What am I supposed to be doing now, boss? The clinic's been open five years and their finances seem as organized as a nun's knicker drawer.'

'How would you know what's in a nun's knicker drawer?'

'I've got a good imagination.'

'Two things then, Ram – find out what Saul Ravenscroft was doing for most of his life. More importantly, who he's been shagging – not recently, but over the years – and follow up every previous job. A grudge can fester for a long time. And if we're dealing with a nutter, it may be something trivial-sounding to us, but not to the aggrieved. By the way, Ram, do you know what . . . endometriosis is?'

'Yes, guv, it's when the lining of the womb grows in places it shouldn't, like round the ovaries. Causes a lot of pain.'

'It comes in handy having a doctor for a mother.'

'Nothing to do with her. I had a girlfriend once – every month she'd keel over.'

'That's what Carla's adoptive mother said.'

'You've seen her?' asked Ram in surprise.

'That's where I was this morning. I had to tell her the bad

news. She hadn't seen Carla since she was eighteen. She was adopted at the age of seven. She'd been in a succession of foster homes till then. It seems she had a very deprived background.'

'Why the rift?'

'Mrs Margaret Robins is a good Catholic woman. And when Carla showed signs of being sexually interested in both boys and girls, there was an almighty row and Carla left – never to be seen again.'

Denni collected the names and addresses of the disgruntled, but decided to visit Mrs Georgina Lloyd-Peters first. She had, after all, been at the clinic on the night of the murder. Denni checked out the village on the map and guessed it would take her about half an hour. She rang first, having learnt that turning up unannounced only worked in films. Most people were at work in the day, but Mrs Lloyd-Peters worked from home and could spare half an hour.

Traffic was light and Denni enjoyed the open road, especially listening to golden oldies on the radio. The small village of Little Upton in Shropshire had one shop, a pub, a derelict church and, although probably pretty in summer, in the grey November gloom it seemed not to slumber, but to moulder. Most houses and cottages looked empty and even the Lloyd-Peters' cottage at the end of the High Street had no lights on.

Georgina answered the door in a purple caftan – circa 1966. Her long hair hung loose, but Denni glimpsed crescent moons dangling from her ears. She knew immediately that she would be in New Age territory – organic vegetables, feng shui, aromatherapy and perfumed candles. Not that she didn't like perfumed candles, but she dreaded the evangelical approach.

'Do come in,' said Georgina, with a big smile. 'I haven't spoken to another adult in three days.'

Georgina led her into a tiny, dim sitting room. There were two elderly low-slung sofas facing a crackling log fire. The room smelt of damp and there was a faint sickly odour of hyacinths, four bowls of which, with tall sagging stems, were dotted around the room. A round table by the window was covered with school exercise books.

'I'm an ex-teacher,' she explained, in quick nervous tones. 'I couldn't hack teaching after Harry was born, so I asked around various schools to see if there was anything I could do at home. Some bright spark said, "I could do with help marking and lesson plans." I went home and thought about it and I do it on the quiet . . .' She paused, as if remembering Denni was a cop. 'It's not illegal, is it? I do copy the class teacher's style – I mean, the kids don't want to know their own teacher isn't actually marking their work . . .' She paused again, but Denni smiled encouragingly, so she added, 'Although it doesn't pay well it means we don't starve. But it all has to be a bit cloak and dagger.'

'The reason I've come,' said Denni, 'is to ask about your visitor the night of Harry's operation.'

A pensive expression crossed her face. 'I was in a terrible state that night. Harry is my world, you see. My husband, Robert, couldn't stand the competition, I was so besotted. I'd been trying to get pregnant for years and when it happened, at the age of forty-two, you can imagine I was . . . thrilled. That's a word that just doesn't convey the emotion I felt.'

'And your visitor?' prompted Denni.

'Would you like a coffee, Sergeant? I've only got decaff. But you won't notice the difference.'

'Fine,' said Denni, as she settled back into the sagging armchair. Some interviews you couldn't rush. And this was going to be one of them.

Denni had been wrong about Georgina being *totally* New Age – there were chocolate biscuits with the coffee. 'I expect you're wondering,' she said, 'how I could afford a private operation for Harry?'

'I wasn't,' said Denni, 'but do tell me.'

'My husband paid. Unusually for him he had a big win on the horses. He's a gambler, you see. One of the reasons

150

we're separated at the moment. His gambling was something I learned to live with, but he got fed up of playing second fiddle to Harry.' She paused and stared at Denni, as if making sure she was listening properly. 'Harry's at school now,' she added, 'and I'm sure Robert will be back with us soon.'

'So he *did* visit that night?'

'Oh yes, he visited. He stayed about half an hour but I think Harry was just an excuse.'

'An excuse for what?'

'To see Carla Robins, of course.'

'He knew her?'

'Oh yes. She came here to talk about Harry's operation. Robert was here too. He wanted to know about the risks et cetera and if Saul Ravenscroft had a good track record. You have to be so careful with surgeons these days, don't you? Especially cosmetic surgeons. We would have gone NHS only the waiting list was so long and the local surgeon, I was reliably informed, had been good in his day, but he was sixty-five and I couldn't risk Harry being operated on by a surgeon who was past it.'

'So you think Robert wanted to see Carla that night? Were they having an affair?'

Georgina tossed her head back so that the half moons glinted in the firelight. 'He was besotted, but I don't know if they slept together.'

'How do you mean, besotted?'

She thought about that for a moment. 'Like a teenage crush, I suppose. I thought it would just pass and, although he wasn't living here then, we still talked and he admitted to phoning her and taking her out for meals – if he was on a winning streak.'

'Doesn't he work?'

'He was deputy head of a comprehensive school but, when he reached fifty, he simply walked out one day. Sort of a breakdown, I suppose. He did get a lump sum but he frittered that away gambling. He does a bit of freelance journalism now but not enough to keep us.'

'Where's he living?'

'He's got a bedsit in Harrowford – Milford Gardens – number 1a.'

'How long was he besotted with Carla?'

'We met her six months before Harry had his op. As I said, he had a big win, so Harry was able to have the operation straight away. We couldn't wait. The money would have gone to the local bookie.'

'You don't sound bitter.'

'I'm not. Carla Robins is dead now. I read it in the papers. He'll be back.'

'How long exactly have you been separated?'

'It must be four years now.'

Four years! To Denni, whose relationships rarely lasted longer than four months, four years seemed to be stretching hope to an abnormal degree.

'Why are you so sure he'll come back?'

Georgina smiled. 'Some things you just know. I'm a bit of a psychic, you see. I have two babies on the other side – both happy and healthy. Harry has the gift too. He communicates with them in his own way.'

It was only occasionally that Denni was stuck for something to say. Now was one of those moments. The woman was not New Age but stark staring raving bonkers or, in the PC words of her training – delusional. A word which, somehow, didn't convey the same meaning.

'I know it's hard for an unbeliever, but I'd love you to attend one of my meetings – we don't call them seances now – they have such a bad press – there are so many charlatans about.'

Denni finally found her voice. 'Do your psychic powers include being able to contact Saul and Carla?'

Georgina smiled. 'Too soon. The departed have to settle first in the spirit world.'

'Pity,' murmured Denni. 'They could tell us who killed them.'

Again Georgina smiled. 'I'm sure they will – given time.'

Sixteen

Pam had slept for a few fitful hours and, as she got out of bed, she felt quite dizzy. She sank back on to the bed for a few moments until the room stopped spinning, then, gingerly, she walked downstairs to the devastation she knew she would face. The kitchen still smelt of beer and fags, vomit and curry. She'd come home from work to find the boys in drunken stupors, draped over her chairs and sofa. Beer cans and takeaway containers littered the floor. Her pot plants had been used as ashtrays and a vase of flowers had been smashed – the flowers lying broken and trampled on her carpet. 'You little bastards!' she'd screamed and had begun kicking and slapping them into sudden wakefulness. They'd staggered to their feet, mumbling, 'Sorry, Mum – we meant to clear it up – we were bladdered.' That was her eldest. She'd slapped his head and screamed, 'Get out, all of you! I don't want to see you again – ever!' They'd scarpered quickly enough, leaving her crying tears of choking rage.

In a cupboard she found a half bottle of vodka and drank a few swigs. Her stomach twisted as the alcohol hit home. Then she looked for a promising cigarette end. The little sods used a mixture of ordinary tobacco and spliff – they thought she didn't know that. She didn't have to look far. One had been left on the edge of her coffee table – hardly smoked. She lit it from the gas stove using a scrap of paper. Then she inhaled deeply. At first she thought the spliff was of poor quality or too weak a mix but, after a few drags, she got a hit. And it felt so good. Filled her with resolve. She wouldn't be leaving them at night again. They couldn't be trusted. She would claim benefit. See how they liked living in poverty. With any luck they'd leave home.

If not, she'd go. If only she'd had a girl, things would have been different. If only Mick hadn't died. But he had and there was no changing that. What she could change now was her life. She'd only worked at the clinic for a year but now she could leave. There was nothing to stop her. She need only consider herself. What consideration did her sons ever show her?

In the bathroom someone had vomited in the bath. It was the final straw. She stared at the mess for a long time. She wasn't going to clear it up. She washed quickly at the sink then went into the bedroom and dressed. She packed her overnight bag, took a handful of ten and twenty pound notes from under her mattress, stuffed them into the side compartment of her bag and walked downstairs. It took her a while to find a large sheet of paper, but she eventually found a sheet of brown paper and a black marker pen. She wrote three words only in huge block capitals: FEND FOR YOURSELVES. She left the message on the kitchen table amongst the debris, slipped on her coat and left the house.

The sudden impact of cold fresh air matched the euphoric effect of her smoke. She took several deep gulps, then opened her car door, switched on the engine, turned on the radio and eased the car into first gear. She was off and free and she was never coming back.

Rydell expected to find Una Fairchild at the clinic but he was informed she'd called in sick. He deliberated for a few moments then decided he would visit her at home, but not on his own. He rang Denni on her mobile and she agreed to meet him outside the house.

They sat in the car for a while, Denni telling him about her meeting with the weird Georgina. 'It sounds like she could be a suspect for Carla,' agreed Rydell. 'But why kill a surgeon who successfully operated on her son?'

'That's another point, guv. Maybe he didn't.'

'Explain that one to me, Denni.'

'In the NHS you don't get a choice of surgeon. For really major stuff it would be the consultant, but for the run-of-the-mill ops the registrar or even the junior would operate. In the private sector you pay for the privilege of choosing a surgeon.'

'Your point being?'

'Maybe Martin Samuels did the op.'

'This case,' said Rydell, 'is sending my hair grey. Have we got any statements from the theatre staff?'

'Only informal stuff.'

'Well, get the team to get some formal statements.'

'Yes, boss.'

Rydell had just knocked on the door with the ornate brass knocker when his mobile trilled. He listened intently, frowned, switched it off, slipped it into his pocket and then said, 'I've got to go back to the station. There's been a complaint laid against me.'

Denni was shocked. Rydell was obsessional, but he was straight and, if she was totally honest, he was the only senior officer she could trust completely. Politics and ambition drove the others. Rydell had good management skills and, in his quiet way, he motivated the team to work as hard as he did. 'What sort of complaint, boss?'

'No details yet. I'll ring you later. Just carry on.'

He walked off, his head slightly down. And for some reason she was filled with a sense of foreboding.

There was still no reply, so Denni knocked more loudly. She was about to give up when Una answered the door. 'I was in the bath,' she said, pulling her blue towelling dressing gown more firmly around her. Her face was pale, her eyes red from weeping and her hair hung damply to her shoulders. 'You'd better come in,' she said reluctantly.

The house, on three floors, had an odd arrangement of rooms. The kitchen was downstairs, the sitting room up one flight. The room, neat to the point of looking unlived in, was expensively furnished with ornate cream lamps and sumptuous cushions. If Denni had been looking for clues to the personality of the owner, there were none.

'I'm more or less living in my bedroom at the moment. I suppose you know my husband's left me?'

Denni nodded.

'Do sit down. Would you like some tea or coffee?'

Denni sank into the cushions of the sofa. 'No thanks.'

Una sat in an armchair opposite. She looked ill at ease. 'I suppose you've come about Carla's death.'

'Yes. We're trying to establish alibis.'

'I was at the clinic,' replied Una, swiftly.

'We don't have an exact time for the attack on her.'

'I thought she was found in the morning.'

'She was, but someone could have been with her all night.'

'You mean a lesbian lover?'

'I hadn't thought of that,' lied Denni. Rydell had told her. 'Was she bisexual?'

'Might have been. She gave the impression of being man mad but she only used men. Perhaps it was a woman she loved.'

'Have you anyone in mind?'

Una shrugged miserably. 'No. When your world is turned upside down nothing makes sense. I try to see the best in people but, so often, I'm proved wrong.'

'What good did you see in Carla?'

'She was focused, hardworking, reliable, conscientious.'

'And her bad points?'

'Amoral, cold, calculating.'

'Did you see her as a threat to your marriage?'

'No. But maybe I should have.'

'How do you mean?'

'She was seeing my husband – as a client.'

'Why didn't you tell us that before?'

'I didn't know until recently. Hugh rarely discussed any of his clients.'

'So you have no idea why she was seeing him?'

'No. She always seemed remarkably together.'

'What about her relationship with Mrs Croft, aka Reid?'

Una showed no surprise. 'I didn't approve of that friend-ship.'

'Why not?'

'For the obvious reason that I felt Carla was encouraging Charmaine to have more and more surgery. I'm only guessing, but I think Charmaine was in love with Carla and it was her attention she wanted.'

'By unnecessary surgery?'

'Yes. I thought her preoccupation with surgery bordered on mental illness.'

'But Saul Ravenscroft had no such qualms?'

'He was a businessman,' she snapped.

Her tone surprised Denni. 'I thought you two were friends – you helped him set up the clinic, didn't you?'

'Yes. We . . . were friends. I didn't always approve of his actions but you make allowances for friends.'

'Do you mean his extra-marital affairs?'

'Yes, of course. What else would I mean?'

Again the tone, rather than the words themselves, were a giveaway. There was something else.

'Where did you work with Saul?'

'In the north – a private hospital outside Bolton – the Retreat.'

'Was he doing cosmetic surgery there?'

'Some, and some general surgery.'

'And your job?'

'I was a theatre nurse.'

'So, director of nursing here was a real promotion.'

'I was more than capable.'

'I'm sure you were. Why did he offer you the job?'

'Because I was the best candidate.'

'So there were other applicants?'

'Of course.'

For some reason, Una began to look uncomfortable, her arms folded protectively against her chest.

'I know you're on sick leave,' said Denni, 'but we'll be needing Saul's CV. We'll need to know where he was working since he qualified – to eliminate any disgruntled patients.'

'I'll ring my secretary. It'll be ready for you in the morning.'

'Your CV as well, Una.'

'Of course,' she muttered, through gritted teeth.

As Una showed Denni to the door, she said, 'I *am* sick, you know. I'm planning to leave as soon as possible. The clinic will fold anyway. Saul was its backbone and, without him, there is no clinic.'

'You don't think Martin Samuels will be capable of running it?'

Her answering tight smile needed no explanation. No one could be compared to Saul.

Denni had planned to visit the three disgruntled patients in the same day, but she rang all three from her car outside Una's house and only one answered the phone. Luckily she lived in Harrowford itself.

Zena Mann was in her late forties, slim, tanned and wearing lots of gold. Her face had seen too much sun and she chain-smoked nervously. 'Tell me about your operation,' said Denni. Zena puffed away and her voice had a smoke-riddled huskiness. 'I go abroad a great deal. My husband died three years ago and I have the money to go in search of the sun. On the beach I'm slim enough to wear a bikini but my backside was getting a bit slack. I saw the advert for the clinic and Carla Robins – some sort of liaison person – came to see me. She assured me I'd have a tight bum and a mere thin streak of a scar. When in fact I got this . . .' With a quick flick of the wrist Zena had lifted her skirt to show stockings and suspenders, but no knickers. At the join of buttocks to thighs were purple keloid scars. 'Feel them,' she said. 'Feel them!'

Denni ran a finger along the thick ridges.

'Knickers and tights irritate the scars and don't even cover them. I was better off just having a slack arse.' She dropped her skirt and sat down again.

'Did you see Saul Ravenscroft before the operation?'

'Briefly. He said the same thing – he said the scar would

be red at first but would gradually fade to silver. He said sod all about it being thick and purple.'

'Are you planning to sue?'

'Can't sue him now, can I? He's dead.'

'You could see another surgeon.'

She shrugged and half smiled. 'Is there any point?'

'Some people do develop thick scars,' said Denni. 'They're called keloid scars. It's not the surgeon's fault.'

'You some sort of expert?'

'No, I've done some nursing in the past. The type of scar you'll acquire can't really be predicted.'

'So you're saying it's no good me pursuing a claim?'

'I wouldn't start paying lawyers.'

She thought about that for a few moments behind a haze of smoke.

'It could be worse,' she said, with a wry smile. 'At least I can sit down.'

Denni left soon after. Zena had a sense of humour; she was upset, but not murderously so. Denni completed her notes in the car and ticked her off the list.

Then she drove to the station. The atmosphere hit her like a snowball in the face. There was silence in the front office. No one smiled or offered her eye contact. 'Has somebody died?' she asked the desk sergeant. He glanced up at her briefly, and then looked away. 'It's not that bad,' he said. 'But your boss has just been suspended.'

'Why?'

'He'll tell you. He's gone home. The super wants to see you.'

Denni wouldn't have cared at that moment if the chief constable wanted to see her.

'I haven't been in, Sarge – okay?'

He raised an eyebrow, looked reluctant, but nodded. Denni made a quick getaway to the car. In less than ten minutes she was outside Rydell's block of flats.

'What the hell are you doing here, Denni?' he asked. He was slightly breathless and wearing a tracksuit. 'Come on in,' he said. 'I've just been on the "beast". She passed the treadmill in the hall. 'You shouldn't overdo it, boss . . .' She broke off. 'What's the complaint against you?'

'Not going for the subtle approach then?'

'You don't seem very upset.'

'No point. There's nothing in the allegation.'

'What allegation?'

'Let's go in the kitchen and I'll make you a cup of coffee.'

Denni watched him line up two mugs on two coasters, then add the coffee granules.

'Strong, weak or medium?' he asked.

'Like my men – strong!'

He didn't smile. He poured the boiling water on to the coffee, asked her if she wanted milk and then placed the coasters and mugs on the kitchen table. Denni went to sit down. 'Not there,' he said, guiding her to the only other chair. 'I have to sit near the door.'

She didn't ask him why. There was probably no logical explanation anyway. It was just one of his foibles.

'As you know,' he said, 'I've been suspended – pending an identification parade.'

Denni quelled her irritation – why didn't he just tell her?

'The charge is,' he said, 'indecent exposure.'

'Oh! My God.'

'No need to look like that, Denni. It seems some old bat walking her dog is convinced I exposed myself to her in the woods.'

'How did she know who you were?'

'My car was the only one near the woods so she took the registration number. The description was a vague fit, so now they have to go through the motions and find a few blokes who resemble me.'

'It's ridiculous – it's so unfair . . .'

'Don't get on your high horse – the only thing I'm guilty of is the occasional pee in the woods when I'm desperate. But since I'm there at the crack of dawn it's very rare I see anyone.'

'How long will you be off work?'

'No idea. But I'm glad you've come round. I want you to keep me up to date and bring me as much info as you can. I can sift though paperwork here as well as anywhere. And I've cracked who the extra man is on the video – it's Edward Gray. Have a crack at him for me.'

'They'll put someone else in charge, boss.'

'Yeah. A fresh eye on the case might help.'

'I think you're taking it all a bit too calmly,' said Denni, still angry at the injustice.

'You know the way the force works,' he said calmly. 'It's no good railing against their time-honoured procedures.'

After she'd left Rydell, Denni used her mobile phone to inform Ram of the news. He'd been summoned to the superintendent too. They arranged to meet in the station's car park. The day was as grey as an army blanket and slow drizzle began to fall and, with it, Denni felt her spirits plummet. 'Do you think it's a plot to get rid of Rydell?' she asked, as they approached the front office. 'Just put a smile on your face, Denni,' Ram answered, squeezing her arm. 'We've worked hard on this case and the boss has worked his socks off. Don't let the bastards think we're worried.'

'We haven't got very far though, have we?'

'A case like this could take as long as a year,' he said. 'Better to get it right than—' He broke off as a slimmed-down DCI Alec Fenton passed them on the steps.

'I'm back and fighting fit,' he said, with his usual belligerence. 'I hope you two are using your brains. You should have this case cracked by now. Get your fingers out!'

Ram stared at the retreating back. 'He's an absolute arsehole. If the boss isn't reinstated soon, I'm resigning.'

'Me too.'

'Life's a bitch,' said Ram.

'Yeah,' agreed Denni, 'and then you marry one.'

Ram laughed. 'I should be so lucky.'

Seventeen

G raham put his plan to rob a post office on hold. He'd grown tired of seeing Lyn from a distance. He wanted to get closer and he thought he knew the way to combine his burglary skills with some personal pleasure.

Lyn's friend took the kids to school every morning that Lyn worked nights and she was usually back within half an hour, but on Wednesdays she went shopping after the school run. For the last two weeks her Wednesday trips had lasted until twelve midday. That gave him plenty of time.

At ten a.m. the road was quiet. Most people were at work. He jogged along the opposite side of the road, then he jogged back again, this time turning off at the side of Lyn's house. He stared up at the guttering, some of which hung loose. Other sections grew spiky grass – *that* needed some attention. The paintwork on the back door and kitchen window was beginning to peel and soon the wood would warp. She needed a man to look after things – some new UPVC windows would be much less trouble. He looked up towards the frosted glass of the bathroom. The window there was slightly ajar. His hand moved to the kitchen door handle and he wasn't surprised to find it open. Strange, he thought, how often people inside the house left the back door unlocked. The back door key was in the lock. *Tut! Tut! Naughty girl, Lyn.* He left the door slightly open, his means of escape, should it be necessary. Then he stood inside the house of his beloved, taking in the atmosphere, the smell – the sense of her.

The kitchen itself needed a coat of paint and it was untidy – toys and feeding bottles and unwashed cereal bowls

162

everywhere. It was a sure sign there was no man in the house. In the future he would be that man. The house would be freshly painted, neat and tidy. He'd make sure the children put their stuff away, did their own washing up, sat properly for meals and went to bed at a reasonable time – seven at the latest. Children these days were spoilt brats, answering back, swearing and spending all their time playing computer games. He'd be firm but fair. He wouldn't allow them to come between him and Lyn.

Silently, he moved towards the stairs. He looked upwards, imagining her lying in bed, opening her arms towards him, a little smile on her full lips. *Graham, darling – you're here at last.*

The first creak of the stairs worried him but she didn't call out. There was no other sound than that of his own breath.

On the landing he paused, wanting to hear her breathe. He knew she occupied the back bedroom. Her door was open a fraction. He paused just outside, listening to her soft rhythmic breathing. Then he placed his hand on the door and very gently swung the door open. It didn't make a sound. He stood in the doorway and watched her. The curtains were heavy but there was a sliver of space in the middle, which allowed some daylight in, and, best of all, meant he could see her hair loose against the pillow. How long he stood there he didn't know but, as he watched her, he felt himself relax and a rare sense of happiness gripped him. He would be able to see her now whenever he liked.

He made his way downstairs, took the back door key from the lock, closed the door and locked it, then he slipped the key into his pocket and began to jog home.

When Lyn's friend returned she wouldn't notice for a while that the key was missing and then she would assume one of the kids had hidden it. There would be a spare key, of course, and then Lyn would get another one cut. No one would ever know he'd been there.

On the second day of his suspension Rydell guessed he might

lose the plot completely. On the first day he'd cleaned the flat from one skirting board to the other, he'd washed and ironed and tidied, finally going to bed at midnight having only eaten two slices of toast.

So on the second day, when he found he couldn't stop mopping the kitchen floor, he realized he needed help. No doubt the force had a tame psychologist he could have seen, but he wanted anonymity and, somehow, paying the full price might be more motivating. He rang Hugh Fairchild and made an appointment for that day at two p.m. He wasn't the only psychotherapist in town, but he had a good reputation and, as yet, his presence at the clinic's open evening hadn't been properly investigated, as he'd had an alibi for the latter part of the evening. Two birds with one stone, thought Rydell, as he climbed aboard his treadmill. After half an hour he'd had enough of the sheer monotony but he felt better, more clear headed. And he'd decided this appointment was just for him. He was just an ordinary punter looking for a cure.

At two p.m. precisely he arrived at Fairchild's office.

It was a dull room with grey half-closed blinds, an office desk and chair, a filing cabinet and a recliner in soft shades of grey and green for the client. There were no pictures on the walls, no flowers and no plants.

Hugh wore a tweed jacket and brown cords, reminding Rydell of one of his grammar school teachers. They shook hands and Rydell felt desperately uneasy as he was signalled to sit in the recliner chair. Fairchild was in the proverbial driving seat, while Rydell was in the back seat feeling his heart rate increasing and his palms beginning to sweat. If Hugh noticed he didn't comment, but he did get straight to the point. 'I'd like you to tell me what makes you anxious.'

Christ, thought Rydell, where do I begin? When he didn't answer, Hugh tried another tack. 'Tell me your ritual for leaving home each morning. From the time you get up.'

He could manage that. 'I turn back the bedclothes, go to the bathroom, shit, shave and shower, then I clean the sink and the bath, wipe over the shower head, polish the taps, pour bleach down the lavatory bowl. Then I take the towels to the washing machine and switch on. After that I get dressed and make the bed. Then I make a cup of instant coffee and have a bowl of cornflakes. I eat that standing up. I clean my teeth and wipe the sink and taps again. Then I wash the mug and bowl and rinse them under boiling water. I put those away, then I check the gas cooker is off and all the plugs are out. Finally, I check all the windows are closed. Sometimes I see a splash of water on the sink or a mark on one of the units, so I have to deal with that.'

Fairchild nodded and made a few notes. 'Fine. Fine,' he murmured, as if this was normal behaviour. 'Now – any other rituals you follow?'

'Food can be a problem.'

'In what way?'

'I'm fussy. I don't eat meals with sauces or gravy because I don't know what it's covering up. I won't eat the top biscuit of a packet. I peel all fruit. I'd never eat a pie unless I knew who'd made it . . .' He paused. 'Shall I go on?'

'No. There's no need,' said Fairchild. 'I get the picture.'

Fairchild watched him, silently, for a few minutes. 'It might take several sessions to unearth the cause or causes of your problem,' he said, 'but in the meantime, I want you to make a contract with me on the two issues – the obsessive behaviour at home and the eating issue. Is that agreed?'

'I'll do my best.'

'Each morning for the next week I want you to leave your mug and plate unwashed in the sink.'

Rydell felt his stomach twitch at the prospect but he nodded.

'In addition,' Hugh added, sadistically, 'I want you to eat an apple or a pear every day without peeling it.'

The thought alone made Rydell want to heave, but he'd come this far and he knew he was in a no pain, no gain situation. 'I'll do my best.'

'Come back – same time next week – and tell me how

it's worked. Keeping a diary helps . . . as long as it doesn't become obsessive.' Did the man have a sense of humour? Rydell wondered.

Just as he was leaving, Rydell asked the question. 'Was supporting your wife the only reason you attended the open evening?'

Fairchild smiled. 'Can you imagine a better business opportunity than thirty or so dissatisfied people bent on self-improvement? I acquired six new clients that day.'

'And did you see Carla?'

'Yes, of course. I couldn't avoid her – she was the host, after all.'

'Did you visit her in her office?'

'Why should I do that?'

'Maybe you were one of her – admirers.'

Hugh looked at him steadily. 'Sooner or later you'll find out, so I may as well tell you now.' There was a short pause before he added, 'She was a client of mine.'

'Why was she seeing you?'

'That's confidential.'

'She's dead now,' snapped Rydell, 'and it may help to find her killer. So you don't have much choice.'

'I'll look out her notes,' he said, reluctantly, 'but I have to say I was never too sure why she came to me. Sometimes she would be quite flirtatious, sometimes depressed. Mostly she talked about her childhood.'

His doorbell rang at that moment. 'I have another client due,' said Fairchild, looking relieved. 'We'll have to have this chat another time.'

'Tomorrow, ten a.m.'

As Rydell left he glanced at his watch. It was two thirty-two on the dot. Each half-hour session cost thirty pounds. No wonder Fairchild had such a high cure rate.

Back in his flat Rydell longed to run in the woods but he knew he couldn't. The silly old crow probably thought every jogger was a flasher. He'd just have to be patient and wait to be vindicated. Had that been Carla's attitude, he wondered?

At five p.m. he poured himself a whisky and picked up an apple from the bowl. He rinsed it twice under the tap and was about to take a first bite when his doorbell rang. It was Denni and Ram. He caught Denni's eye glancing at his tumbler of whisky.

'No need to look like that. It's my first one of the day.'

'Guv, we came to tell you,' said Ram, 'there's been a development.'

'Yeah, yeah. Don't tell me. I'm being charged with multiple rape.'

'No, the news on that score is good. They've got an identity parade fixed up for tomorrow – midday.'

Rydell had no intention of allowing them to see how relieved he was. 'Fine. What else?'

'Did you know Fenton's back?' said Ram. 'He's breathing out zeal instead of carbon dioxide.'

'Every police force has one,' Rydell said. He thought for a moment. 'This identity parade is bound to clear me, so I've decided the team needs a new approach. I want the CVs of all those either on duty or present on the night in question. And by four thirty I want you two and a couple of others – I don't care who – to do a presentation. Don't confer. Find a bloody motive. And find one prime suspect and two other possibles.'

'We'll do our best, guv, but this is short notice . . .' began Denni.

'I don't want any excuses. Two dead and we've achieved sod all. If I have to work all night I'll come up with at least one decent suspect by tomorrow. Who knows, we might even have a consensus.'

As they left Rydell's flat Ram said, 'Let's go back to the nick and get copies of the PDFs and copies of the CVs.'

'Why not? We'll just make sure we're not caught. And, of course, we're not going to confer, are we?'

'We'll stay up all night if necessary,' said Ram, obviously

relishing the challenge. 'And I've got info on bank accounts which is quite interesting.'

'You didn't tell the boss that, did you?'

'No, it simply makes Carla look even more guilty, but even if she did top Saul, who was miffed enough to retaliate?'

She had no answer to that and they managed to slip into their office unnoticed. They were just about to leave when the phone rang. They both looked at each other. 'It could be Edward Gray,' said Denni. 'I asked him to phone me.'

It was. He asked if she could come to the house. There was something he wanted to say. They left then, again seemingly unnoticed, with Denni carrying away the paperwork in a strong plastic bag. Ram drove to Gray's home about a mile from the clinic. The detached cul-de-sac houses shouted stockbroker belt but the interior didn't live up to the promise. It was shabby and untidy and they were ushered into the kitchen.

'My wife's away,' he said, clearing newspapers from a kitchen chair so that they could sit down. 'You'll find out sooner or later. I was at the clinic the night Saul was murdered. I went in the side door round about ten thirty. Carla had told me the code because I used to see her at the clinic quite often. It added an exciting new dimension to our relationship. I knew Carla would sleep with him that night – not that you get much sleep with Carla. Anyway, I wanted to put a stop to it.'

'And did you?' asked Denni.

'Not in the way you mean, Sergeant.'

'I hid in the lecture room, but for some reason, she slipped into the on-call room so quietly that I didn't hear her. So I rang her on my mobile. Told her I was in the building. That shifted her.'

'And then what?'

'She met me by the side entrance. She was furious. We walked to her car. She'd given Saul a lift. I'd taken a taxi – I'd been drinking.'

'Why didn't you tell us this before?'

'Carla didn't want me to do any more damage to my marriage. She said it would make no difference. She was innocent and in the end, she was convinced, the truth would out.'

His shoulders sagged. 'I've been so weak where Carla was concerned. I know she didn't really care for me. She liked to be spoilt – flowers, perfume, expensive meals. She didn't like to be bored or tied down.'

'Quite the opposite of most women then,' said Denni, unable to contain herself.

'It's a good thing, chum,' said Ram, 'you've a cast-iron alibi for the night Carla was attacked.'

'Will there be any charges?'

'What, for being a wuss?' said Ram. 'You'll have to wait and see.'

Outside, Denni said, 'What do you make of that?'

'At the moment,' said Ram, 'the only thing that's talking to me is my stomach.'

They collected a pizza on the way home and ate that at the kitchen table, then they spread out their notes and began the preparation of their presentation. Ram, in cheerful mood, decided that they should have a random pick of three names and try to build a case if they had the slightest evidence.

'I've never done this sort of thing before,' said Denni. 'I suppose it might help.'

'Come on, flower – be positive. We've got nothing to lose.'

'Except our sanity.'

'As I said, we have nothing to lose.'

Denni began listing the staff present on the opening evening. For some reason she began with Ravenscroft. After all, he wasn't meant to have been there – at least not in the on-call room. Once the list was made they cut out the names and folded them and then spread them over the table. Denni picked first – Kirsty White, the receptionist. It was known she had left the clinic by ten p.m. 'Try again,' said Ram, as he picked up his name. Denni picked up another name – this time she had Una Fairchild. Ram had Saul Ravenscroft.

Denni turned to her notebook and on a sheet of A4 wrote, *Una Fairchild, director of nursing*, at the top of the page. Ram did likewise with Saul.

Silently they filled the page. Once they'd finished, Ram said, 'OK, Denni, convince me of Una Fairchild's guilt.'

'I can't. The camera caught her leaving about nine p.m.'

'Could she have come back?'

'Yes. She could have used the coded side entrance.'

'Would she have been caught on camera?'

'Not necessarily, if she came on foot, or parked her car well away from the clinic – she'd certainly know the blind spots.'

Ram agreed. 'Stan has told us that surveillance of the car parks was top priority. The rest of the grounds aren't covered by the cameras.'

'Apart from that,' said Denni, 'she knew Saul previously. They did work in theatre together at the Primrose Lane private clinic.'

'But what possible motive could she have? Without its best surgeon the clinic could fold and with it would go her job.'

'She's forty-eight, he was fifty-two. They could have had an affair perhaps in the past,' suggested Denni.

'Maybe it was still going on. Just good old-fashioned jealousy. Perhaps he was shagging Carla and Una, or he'd dropped Una in place of Carla.'

Denni thought about that scenario but wasn't convinced. Saul had a pretty young wife, Carla was a very attractive woman, but Una had a strait-laced appearance and very little sex appeal. Still, they were trying to identify a probable suspect and maybe she was jealous enough to commit murder – but which one?

'We know Una's husband has left her recently,' she said. 'So maybe she knew, or sensed way back, he was having an affair. And so she murders Saul as a way of killing her husband by proxy.'

Ram laughed, 'On the basis that any bastard will do.' He

stared down at his sheet of A4 for a few moments. 'No, I think that's psychobabble. She would have been hoping to hang on to her husband.'

'Agreed, but she was a theatre nurse, well trained in avoiding contamination. Cool under pressure and with obvious familiarity with the layout and running of the clinic. Also, Carla would have answered the door to her.'

With some reluctance, Ram agreed she was a second division suspect. He checked his watch. It was nine p.m. It was going to be a long night.

'I've pulled the short straw,' he said. 'I've drawn Saul's name. But in a case like this, doesn't the victim know all the answers?'

'Yeah,' agreed Denni, 'but you're only saying that because you've found something out.'

'I've been looking at his CV. Very cleverly done but there are a few gaps – unaccounted for periods of time – ten months, nine months and six months.'

'Maybe he wasn't working then,' suggested Denni.

'Strange that Carla's CV has similar gaps.'

'She worked abroad, didn't she?'

Ram nodded. 'Is it time for a drink?'

'It'll have to be black coffee. We'll get no sleep tonight.'

'I'm going to ring Mrs Ravenscroft and see if she can shed any light on his previous career.'

'She'll complain you're harassing her.'

'I'll cope.'

Denni went out to the kitchen to make the coffee and when she came back Ram was just putting down the phone, looking very thoughtful.

'That was quick.'

'Yeah. Madam's had a change of heart since finding out about the will. She says Saul worked on cruise ships, and in various places abroad, and alternated that with work at private clinics in Bolton and London.'

'Doing cosmetic surgery?'

'No, doing a hell of a lot of abortions.'

171

Eighteen

The sound of the doorbell made Lyn jump and she dropped the tumbler she was holding and watched it crashing down on to the ceramic tiles of the kitchen floor. She stood staring at the shards of glass and waited for the next ring of the doorbell. Then she rushed into the hall and stared at the front door. I'll get a peephole put in tomorrow, she told herself. It was after ten p.m. It could only have been him. Her ex-husband. It was inevitable he'd catch up with her again. It had been six months this time. He was getting quicker at finding her.

She went back into the kitchen and took out a dustpan and brush to sweep up the glass. The gin and tonic had made the floor sticky and the glass shards seemed to have spread into every crevice of the tiles. By the time she'd finished sweeping up and mopping the floor she'd managed to acquire a sliver of glass in her index finger. She pulled it out and put her finger under running water and watched as it ran pink with her blood.

One day she'd have to face up to the confrontation, but her ex-husband was a dangerous man, out for revenge, and she had the children to think of. He'd only rung the doorbell once. Was that simply a warning? Like the silent phone calls she'd been having? Or had he assumed there was no one at home? The only light on in the house had been in the kitchen and she'd had the door closed. He knew where she lived and he'd be back. If it was his intention to set her nerves on edge – he'd succeeded.

She poured herself another gin and tonic and thought about

the options in her life. She could move again, but this time she had a mortgage and selling her rundown house might not be so easy. Holly was a good friend and good friends were hard to find. If she confided in her, would she too be scared? She had her baby to think about and, if she knew the full story, she might not be so keen to be her friend.

Thinking back over the events of the past few weeks it was the loss of the back door key that worried her most. Sometimes the kids did pick up her car keys but they had no interest in the back door key. If he'd got the key, why didn't he use it? *Maybe he has.* With that thought in mind she knew she had no option but to call the police. As plausible as Nathan was, his criminal record was hardly a character reference. Surely the police would offer her some protection this time?

Her time with Nathan belonged to another life. She'd been nineteen when she'd met him, sharing a flat with other student nurses and only just eking out her student bursary. She'd been on a placement in A&E and Nathan had been a patient. He'd been attacked in the street and had a suspected ruptured spleen. He'd begged her to visit him on the ward and she had done. From then on he pursued her relentlessly. There were flowers once a week, expensive meals out, trips to casinos, holidays abroad. He was kind and attentive and made it clear he wanted to marry her but he didn't want to disrupt her nursing studies. Nathan had private means but worked successfully as a graphic designer. He was tall, good-looking and, more to the point, he adored her.

There had been one drawback; her heart was involved elsewhere with a senior registrar working in A&E. He was some years older than her, but very attractive and he too seemed to adore her. But he had so little time and, although she slept with him when she could, there were rarely any meals out or trips to nightclubs. The decision was made for her when she asked him about the future. 'Do you want children?' he'd asked her. 'Of course,' she'd replied. She wanted at least two. He stared at her sadly for a while, saying he didn't want children and that she wouldn't be happy childless and with a workaholic. 'But I'll always look out for you,' he said. And he'd been true to his word.

She became Mrs Nathan Jackson a week after her final exams. She'd only gradually fallen in love with Nathan but he'd clinched her heart by saying he wanted children.

Marriage changed him. He didn't want her to work and they moved from London to a village in the Midlands. Gradually she lost contact with her friends, her mother died and within weeks of her wedding she wanted a way out. But then she missed a period and Nathan seemed genuinely delighted, especially in the first few months. It was only as she grew bigger that he grew more distant and started going out to the local pub and coming back mean and aggressive.

At first it was no more than verbal aggression, trying to goad her. She didn't argue, but one night, when he was sober and mellow, she'd put his hand on her belly so that he could feel his child move. Instead of delight and wonderment she saw a wave of disgust pass his face – a warning cloud that she chose to ignore.

When Justin was born, after an easy labour, weighing eight pounds and the picture of health, Lyn revelled in the sensual delight of breastfeeding and caring for her son. He was an easy baby but Nathan, once over the novelty of first-time fatherhood, grew sullen and resentful. She recognized that he was jealous, which she understood and tried to make allowances for, but Justin needed her as much as the air she breathed. Nathan was a grown man and, anyway, she didn't neglect him or the house.

A week after Justin's birth they were making love as normal, although she had to admit it was more biological than sexual desire. She wanted to have another child as soon as possible. They could afford it and, if she needed an au pair or a cleaner, Nathan was more than able to pay for one.

Justin had been two months old when a friend rang to say she was in Birmingham for just one day that week and how about meeting up for a meal. 'I don't want you to go,' said

Nathan at first, but the next day he relented. 'Just don't be too late back.'

She'd fed Justin just before she left that evening and she expressed enough milk for another bottle if he woke up before she got back. Nathan had seemed confident enough. He had even told her to have a good time.

She'd enjoyed the meal and the laughter, feeling young and carefree again. Nathan had his faults, but then, no one was perfect. On the drive home she was longing to see them both. She felt she'd been away for ages. Perhaps now she could persuade Nathan to let her find a part-time job.

'Hi, I'm home,' she'd called out. It was midnight. Summer. It hadn't been dark for long. Nathan sat upright on the sofa, pale, staring straight ahead. There was an almost empty bottle of whisky on the floor. There was no sign of a glass. 'Nathan?' He didn't answer. She ran up to the nursery. Her baby lay on his back, colourless, eyes closed. She'd tried to breathe her life into him but it was too late. She'd snatched him up, enfolding him to her body as if, once more, she could give him life. Then she rocked him backwards and forwards, backwards and forwards. Screaming silently. It was when Nathan appeared in the doorway that she'd screamed aloud and run with the body of her precious baby to her neighbours.

Even now, so many years on, she replayed that moment in her mind. The months after were a blur of shock and grieving. The day Nathan was sent to prison for two years for the manslaughter of his own son, she felt a different sort of emotion – an overwhelming hatred. For she knew, instinctively, that Nathan hadn't lost momentary control because Justin wouldn't stop crying. He had planned to murder him. No one believed her. He was so plausible, so remorseful, and so middle class. In court, with tears running down his face, he had the sympathy of the judge. She had been dry eyed and stoical. Numb.

One person had given her the strength to go on – Saul. Now he too was dead. The man who had given her so much. Had

Nathan known about him? She didn't think so. She had been so careful, moved so many times. The possibility of Nathan being the killer had crossed her mind until Carla was attacked. There was no possible reason for him to kill her.

But now she had no choice. She had to tell the police everything. Her children could be in danger. She'd lost one child. Perhaps over the years, not seeing Nathan since his trial, she'd grown complacent. She trusted Holly with her children but she wouldn't be returning to night duty. Tomorrow she would see the police and resign from the clinic.

Rydell looked at the other five men in the line-up. Similar build, height, age group, clean-shaven, blue-eyed. The force had obviously scoured the streets of Harrowford to find them. He'd felt uneasy all morning but the parade itself took less than ten minutes.

Afterwards it was handshakes all round, no apology, but the super did offer him a tot of his best scotch. 'Sorry, Tom, the old biddy now says the flasher had brown eyes and a snub nose. I didn't think it was your style, but maybe running in the woods isn't such a good idea.'

Superintendent Norman made running in the woods sound like a perversion. Rydell was irritated but he was damned if he was going to give him and Fenton the satisfaction of knowing it. 'I've booked my team to do a presentation of the evidence at midday,' he said evenly. 'I trust they'll do a good job.'

'Good idea,' said Fenton, taking a slug of scotch. 'I'll be there.' It sounded to Rydell as if he, too, was peeved, but also disguising the fact. 'Runner' Rydell wasn't the norm amongst CID. Fenton knew his background – boy soldier, army boxer, worked in communications, then joined the police. Ex-army was okay with him but he thought Rydell was a misfit, bleeding heart liberal. He didn't drink much, didn't smoke, didn't womanize, worked hard, and kept fit. In his eyes that wasn't normal behaviour for a cop. Fenton thought he might be religious or gay. He'd keep watching him. One day he'd find out.

Rydell was surprised when he entered his office to hear cheering and shouts of triumph. 'Settle down, team,' he shouted, above the noise. 'Wearing shorts in the summer is the nearest I ever get to flashing, so it was never on the cards I'd go down as a pervert.' He paused. The team looked now as if some nasty bully had burst their balloon. 'I've decided to instigate this type of presentation,' he continued, 'to get you all to look beyond the obvious. With Carla we only looked at the obvious. The evidence seemed to fit. She appeared cold and calculating enough to commit murder and yet she too became a victim. This time we need to be open to all possibilities.' He paused. 'Is there a volunteer to go first?' He looked at the sea of faces. 'Was that a nod, DS Caldecote?'

'Must have been, guv.'

Denni went to the front of the room, looked at the sea of faces and swallowed hard. She'd given talks and presentations before, but then she'd been dealing purely with facts and observations. Her brief now had been to find the facts, make deductions and, in so doing, to find three suspects.

'I want to start with the two victims,' she began. 'Firstly, Saul Ravenscroft, age fifty-two but looked ten years younger. Cosmetic surgeon and major shareholder of the Harmony Clinic. Married to Amanda, aged twenty-eight, for three years – no children. He opened the clinic two years ago. There were few complaints about his work and the complainees have been followed up. Either they had alibis for that night or there was no reason to suspect them. We are still checking Ravenscroft's surgical background and there are periods of time still unaccounted for.

'On the night of the clinic's open evening he spent the night in the on-call room. Forensic evidence shows that he was visited by Carla Robins, who originally lied, but later admitted she'd had sexual intercourse with him. However, she maintained that he was alive and well when she left him about one a.m.

'Later it was revealed she was the chief beneficiary of

Ravenscroft's will. Together with the forensic evidence, which placed her in the on-call room that night, she was charged with his murder but was allowed bail. During this period on bail she was found with throat and stab wounds and died four days later from her injuries.'

Denni looked up from her notes to face her peers. 'Are there any questions so far?' A little foot shuffling was her only answer. Perhaps her review was unnecessary.

'There has been another development. Edward Gray – Carla's lover – was in the building that night and they went home together. He seems a timid guy, totally in Carla's thrall, and he has an alibi for the time of Carla's attack. Not a particularly hot contender for either murder, but who knows . . . More about him later.'

She paused again for questions but there were none. 'I'll go on to those suspects I think had motive, access and means. The first of those are Amanda Ravenscroft and Saul's partner, Martin Samuels. The day before her husband's body was found, Amanda had a dramatic, public and maybe contrived altercation with Carla. She was naturally upset by his affair with Carla but seemed genuinely surprised she had been cut out of his will. However, she may be having an affair with Samuels. There is no direct evidence on that score – but they are good friends.

'That night of the murder she was staying with friends. She could have left the house when they were asleep and met Samuels. They both knew the code for the side door of the clinic. Samuels, although a married man, has been left by his wife on three occasions. At the time of the murder Mrs Samuels was staying with her mother. It's perfectly possible that together they entered the clinic that night, killed Saul and left by the side entrance without being caught on camera.'

'What about the car?' someone on the back row asked.

'I think they came into the clinic at the back, avoiding the cameras, and leaving their cars in a side road near the clinic.'

'Didn't the house-to-house enquiries turn up anything?' asked a woman DC.

Denni shook her head. 'It's a quiet area and the residents are mostly middle-aged to elderly. Behind their curtains and double glazing no one heard or saw anything. Or at least they haven't admitted it.'

There were no more questions or comments. Denni's spirits were sinking fast. She now knew how stand-up comedians felt when the only sound they heard was the shuffling of chairs and the clearing of throats.

Valiantly she continued, 'I think their motive in killing Saul was to gain control of the clinic, but underlying that was Amanda's need for revenge and Samuels' desire to be with the woman he loved. Also, he'd lived in Ravenscroft's shadow and, despite inheriting family money, he'd actually overstretched himself financially. But Ravenscroft had the brilliant surgical reputation and Carla Robins had worked very hard to increase their business. Ravenscroft had everything Samuels wanted.'

Denni glanced steadily at her audience, but before they asked the most obvious question she continued, 'Of course, the most obvious question is why was Carla killed? And a botched killing at that. I think Samuels opted out when Amanda decided that Carla would have to die. Finding out that Carla would inherit would have been painful, but also, finding out there was far less money than she thought would have made her wonder where the large withdrawals had been going. The night Carla was attacked, I think she visited her to find out. We found only fifty pounds in Carla's purse. Her bank account was healthy but there had been no large regular deposits, so it could be assumed a large amount of cash was stolen that night. At the scene we found no fingerprints belonging to anyone other than Edward Gray – which he could have left at any time.'

'Trollop!' someone shouted and everyone laughed.

Denni waited until they stopped. But, unexpectedly, Rydell stepped forward.

'Thank you, DS Caldecote,' he said. 'I think that will be enough for the moment. It's given everyone something to think about.'

Had she gone on too long? Was it all bullshit? She could feel her face flaming. The comments around the room made her feel even worse – *Most men have brains in their cocks. Their real brains are only secondary.* Which was followed by the retort – *Lesbo bitch.* Even worse was the mumbled comment – *What the hell was that all about?*

'OK, that's enough,' said Rydell. 'Don't let's get personal. DS Caldecote has done a great job. Anyone convinced by her theories?'

Not a single hand went up. There were inconsistencies, one or two holes, but she thought her suspect choices were as likely as any others. She did wonder, though, if Rydell was floundering and this exercise was merely to help him out.

Just as Ram was about to present his suspects, a uniformed sergeant came in and whispered something in Rydell's ear.

'Sorry, everyone,' called out Rydell above the increasing level of noise, 'and DS Patel in particular. Someone has come forward with new information. This meeting is now cancelled. Denni and Ram to stay behind, please.'

'What's up, guv?'

'We'll go and find out, shall we?'

Nineteen

Lyn Kilpatrick sat in the interview room, anxiously twist-ing a paper handkerchief. She managed a brief smile before saying, 'There are things I have to tell you, Inspector.' She ignored the presence of Denni and Ram.

Rydell smiled back. 'Take your time. There's no hurry.'

'Since Saul Ravenscroft was murdered,' she said quietly, 'I've had the feeling that I'm being followed. At first I thought it was the press or the police, because they'd published photographs of some of the night staff. When I found out it wasn't either, I thought it might be my ex-husband.'

'What makes you think that?' asked Rydell.

'Because I thought he might have found out where I was living. I have to keep moving.'

'You sound frightened of him.'

'I'm terrified.'

'Has he made any threats?'

'No . . .' She broke off. 'Not exactly.'

'But you have a feeling that he means you harm. Was the divorce acrimonious?'

'No, it was a relief. I divorced him when he went to prison.'

Rydell looked sharply at Ram and Denni as if to say – *Why the hell didn't I know about this*? Denni responded with a faint shrug, as if to say she didn't know either.

'What did he go to prison for?'

Lyn sighed, as if preparing herself. 'He killed his own son fourteen years ago. He was jailed for two years for manslaughter, but I think he planned it. He murdered Justin, my lovely son – he was just eight weeks old. I can't . . .' She broke off again, her eyes filling with tears.

'I'm sorry. It must be very painful to talk about,' said Rydell, understanding only too well. 'So we'll stick to your ex-husband – when did you last see him?'

She glanced now at Denni and Ram, as if realizing she might need them as allies too. 'I haven't seen him since the trial, but I know he's been watching me. I think he rang my doorbell the other night. I didn't answer it. I know he means me harm or at least . . . my kids. They're the ones in danger.'

Rydell smiled wryly. 'Lyn, I appreciate you're scared, but he hasn't made any threats and you haven't even seen him. That doesn't add up to a reign of terror, does it?'

Her eyes, lustrous with tears, stared at him. 'You bastard! Two people have already been murdered on your patch – sounds like a reign of terror to me and, so far, your only suspect was also a victim. Have you any idea how this has affected the people who work at the clinic?' She didn't give him a chance to answer. 'Alvera's had a breakdown, Una's husband has left her and I've just heard that Pam has gone missing.'

'Missing?'

'She's left home, leaving her three boys to fend for themselves. No one knows where she is. The cleaner who found the body has been off sick with her nerves and even Stan is depressed and twitchy. Let's face it, we're not safe and you take the piss!'

Rydell sat back in his chair. He couldn't take his eyes from her face. As sparky as this, she definitely ignited his stove. 'It is a very complex case, Lyn,' he said evenly. 'Most of us are working hours and hours of unpaid overtime.'

She didn't look impressed but she nodded slightly, as if acknowledging Rydell's position.

'A murder takes place because of past events,' he said, 'and Saul Ravenscroft's past hasn't yet been fully unravelled. People can and do cover their tracks, as you did. Saul seems to have brought his past, or at least some of it, to the clinic. And you were part of his past, weren't you?'

She muttered, 'Yes, I did work up north with him.'

The set of her mouth and glint in her eyes showed she was still as mad as hell. 'Are you implying I'm a suspect?'

'You had easy access to the room. You moved between the two floors – the staff wouldn't have missed you for the ten to fifteen minutes it took to acquire the scalpel, gloves, gown, et cetera and do the deed.'

She laughed. 'What motive could I possibly have?'

'Jealousy of Carla.'

'I wasn't jealous. I haven't been involved with a man since my husband.'

'But you have young children – that implies involvement, doesn't it?'

'Do you think,' she said coldly, 'I would in any way jeopardize my children's lives for the sake of a man? Especially as my firstborn was killed by a man who was supposed to love me.'

'I've seen it happen before.'

'Well, maybe you have, but not to me.'

Rydell closed his notebook. 'I can see you're upset,' he said. 'Denni and Ram, would you mind leaving us alone?'

When they'd gone, Rydell debated for a moment on the should he, shouldn't he basis. After all, she seemed less than enamoured with the male of the species, but faint heart and all that. So, trying to be ultra-casual, he said, 'I'm parched. We could carry on the questions here and drink stewed tea, or we could go to a wine bar and talk in comfort.'

She stared at him. 'OK. This place is making me feel claustrophobic anyway.

The Oaks wine bar lay within walking distance of Harrowford police station but it wasn't a favourite of the force. Wine bars were thought of as poncey and the inflated prices were also a deterrent. Rydell ordered bottled beer because the idea of wine from an already opened bottle worried him. It wasn't the taste, although he thought that most wines tasted foul, he just found reassurance in the act of seeing a bottle being opened in front of him.

Lyn wanted coffee and they sat by the window, well isolated from the other three customers, who sat on stools near the bar. The lighting was dim and the place contained more artificial plants than a garden centre, but it did give a sense of privacy and Lyn rated the coffee. Rydell was a leg and eye man and she had great legs and unusually green eyes. Now he was away from home territory he felt awkward. He wanted to chat her up but the voice of reason told him to take it easy, don't frighten her. She was obviously wary of men but, after her husband, there had been the father of her two children, so she wasn't *that* averse.

'Did you marry again?' he asked, aware that the question was put a little bluntly.

She shook her head. 'No – once was enough.'

He swallowed a mouthful of beer, wondering what to say next that would make him sound like a clumsy cop. She smiled, as if recognizing his dilemma. 'After Nathan was sent to prison,' she said, 'I changed my name by deed poll. I wanted a new beginning. I worked abroad, mostly in Greece and as a nurse on the cruise ships.'

'What made you come to Harrowford?'

She stared at him. 'I thought,' she said, 'when you invited me for a drink you might try to chat me up, but I can see now you were only trying to eliminate me from your enquiries.'

'Is it that obvious?'

She smiled. 'Inspector . . .'

'My name's Thomas,' he interrupted. 'Tom, if you like.'

'OK, Tom. I need protection. You don't seem to think I'm in any danger, but I am. I think he's insane. Although I've not seen him, years ago I did have a visit from an ex-con, a fraudster. He went to a great deal of trouble to find me. I hadn't changed my name by then. He told me Nathan was obsessed with getting me back, that he deeply regretted what he'd done and he wanted to give me another child. He also told me I should be on my guard because he thought Nathan would stop at nothing.'

Rydell, partly wanting to reassure and partly wanting to impress her, struggled to find a middle way. He wasn't surprised she was scared, paranoid even, but was it justified? Her ex-husband might well be a dangerous obsessive but where was the evidence?

'We'll try to trace him,' he said, 'and get some mugshots put up at the station, but since he hasn't made any actual threats, the word of an ex-con years ago isn't going to carry much weight.'

She bit her bottom lip in disappointment. And he felt a strong urge to put his arm around her. 'I'll have a word with my superiors and see if they'll sanction some protection but I know the answer already. They'll suggest a safe house.'

'You mean a hostel?'

'Not necessarily.'

'Forget it,' she said sharply. 'I'll just move on again. The house is only rented. I could never buy. I have to be able to move quickly.'

'No, don't do that.'

'Why not?'

'You're part of the investigation. We want everyone at the clinic to stay put.'

'Pam hasn't and if you're not going to help me I don't see any other way.'

'I didn't say I wasn't going to help you. I could always say you were a suspect and needed surveillance.'

She smiled. 'That would be great.'

Rydell realized he didn't care *how* he acquired her trust. That's what he wanted. Anything else would be a bonus.

'I'll get that underway then.' He handed her his card. 'Ring me on my mobile any time – day or night – if you're worried.'

'Thank you, Tom – I'm very grateful.'

He would have invited her out for dinner, but if they were seen together too often there would be questions to answer and it might jeopardize any chance she'd have of getting any sort of protection.

At her car she shook his hand. 'Keep in touch,' he said.

'I will,' she replied, smiling. 'Thanks again.'

Back in his office Rydell took Ram aside and explained the position.

'Don't look at me, guv. Surveillance is a health hazard for me. I eat a ton of humbugs and get arse-ache from sitting so long. Anyway, I've been chasing up Ravenscroft's varied career. And it doesn't look so squeaky clean.'

'What does that mean?'

'He's worked in some iffy places – abortion clinics, on cruise ships – but at the moment I'm checking out connections in Greece, Turkey and Tunisia.'

'Christ,' muttered Rydell. 'We're in week five already and soon they'll be pulling the plug on overtime and the extra staff. And now this additional problem of Lyn Kilpatrick.'

'Not much we can do but plough on,' said Ram, as he offered Rydell a humbug.

Rydell shook his head at the humbug. 'What's Denni up to?'

'She's checked out disgruntled patients and hasn't come up with anything, but it does seem certain staff had been following Ravenscroft around.'

'Who for instance?'

'Wendy Swan worked for a short time at an abortion clinic in London at the same time he was working there. And, as you know, she did have a year on probation. Also, Alvera Lewis said she saw them together in a florist's.'

'Well, a bunch of daffs is no evidence they were having an affair.'

'True, guv, but she could have seen Carla leaving the room and then she goes ballistic.'

'I would have thought she'd have wanted a head-on confrontation . . .'

'As opposed to taking him from the rear?' interrupted Ram, with a huge grin.

Vain Hope

The sudden presence of Alec Fenton in the doorway froze their smiles. 'I'm glad you two can find something to laugh about – no one else can. Where's Caldecote?'

'She's checking out disgruntled patients, sir.'

'Tell her to get a move on. I don't like cases involving doctors. Remember Dr Shipman. There's no suggestion Ravenscroft was bumping off patients, so, in the end, it'll just boil down to him shagging the wrong woman.'

Rydell had taken a particular interest in the Shipman serial murder case of the late nineties, but it was not the numbers of dead that interested him, but how Shipman had covered up his addiction history and sustained his convincing portrayal of the hard-working kind and caring medic. So far, Ravenscroft had the same persona. It was just a question of finding the link in the personal history of the two victims. And, in his experience, someone would talk – and soon. Too many people were keeping secrets but it would only take one to unravel the truth.

When Fenton left, Ram was typing his reports into the computer. Rydell's computer skills were fairly basic but Ram was a bit of a computer buff and could always be relied upon to fix a problem or come up with an idea.

Rydell stood at Ram's shoulder. 'Money being the root of all evil,' he said, 'have we checked the victim's bank accounts yet?'

'I've checked back over five years,' said Ram. 'Carla's doesn't reveal much except she isn't Sainsbury's biggest spender. Her incomings are just her salary and she does seem to have been careful with money. Ravenscroft on the other hand has quite a lot of money coming in and going out that I can't account for. Over the past six months he's taken out three thousand pounds in cash.'

'Some people just manage to spend a lot of money,' said Rydell. 'Expensive wines, dinner parties, meals out, rounds of drinks, presents for girlfriends.'

'Carla didn't seem to benefit, guv.'

'What are you saying?'

'The year previously, at regular intervals he was taking out large amounts of cash.'

'Blackmail?'

'Could be.'

'Well we won't pussyfoot about. Check out all the bank accounts of staff who were on duty that night. Maybe we can nail someone that way.'

Ram continued to scan the screen. He'd already checked several bank accounts. Only one had received regular unexplained cash injections. He just wasn't ready to tell Rydell who it was yet.

Twenty

Denni hadn't managed to visit her mother for two days. When she did turn up she found handyman Bill using the vacuum cleaner and Joan painting her nails.

'You all right, dear?' asked her mother. Bill smiled his gappy smile and made tea. He might be scruffy, thought Denni, but at least her mother was sober and the house boasted a bunch of carnations and a bowl of fruit.

After tea and biscuits, Denni left with a light heart. *Please God, let it last.*

Bill had an old banger of a car but, to her mother, it could have been a Rolls. Whenever Denni had wanted to take Joan anywhere she'd said she couldn't be bothered or she didn't feel well. An unprepossessing man turns up and she's ready for trips around stately homes. Bill, it seemed, along with being a handyman, took a big interest in antiques. Denni smiled. Her mother qualified – worn and ragged round the edges she might be, but she still scrubbed up well.

Rydell had phoned her as she was on her way to the station to ask her to visit Pam's sons. She hadn't known Pam was missing and, although there were no suspicious circumstances, in view of the fact that she was a member of the night staff on duty the night Saul was murdered, she needed to be found.

A tall lad with torn jeans and a filthy-looking tee shirt answered the door. 'You from social services?' he asked.

'Detective Sergeant Caldecote – but you can call me Denni. I'd like a word about your mum.'

'You know where she is?' he asked eagerly.

'And you are . . .'

'Daniel – Dan.'

'I'm sorry, Dan, I don't know where she is.'

His face fell. 'You'd better come in then.'

The living room had socks and clothes on the floor, mugs on every surface and saucers used as makeshift ashtrays. One used plate had been placed precariously on the arm of a chair and the other two boys draped the sofa, their long legs making the room look small and cramped. Two cushions from the sofa had been thrown on the floor. One boy played with a Gameboy, the other one slept. No wonder she'd left, thought Denni.

'How long has your mum been gone?' she asked the only functionary in the house.

'About four days now. She never did have any patience. Silly cow.'

Denni clenched her teeth. 'Did she say why she was leaving?'

'She left us a note telling us to fend for ourselves.'

Looking round the room, Denni said, 'This is fending?'

'We're managing fine. She left us some money.'

'And when that runs out?'

'She'll be back.'

'Why are you at home today – no work? No school?'

His expression suggested a mixture of pity and contempt. 'It's Saturday, innit?'

'How long have you lived here?'

'About a year now. We used to live in London but we had to leave. This place is a shit hole. There's nothing to do and nowhere to go.'

'Why did you leave London?'

'You ask a lot of questions.'

'I'm a cop. That's what we do. So answer!'

'Don't get on your high horse. We left because mum lost her job – the place she was working in closed down.'

'But why here?'

'Dunno. She had the job at the clinic so we came here.'

'What about your dad?'

'What about him?'

'Where is he?'

'He left us years ago – he couldn't stand us either.'

'And you haven't heard from him?'

'Not a dicky.'

'Have you any idea where your mother might have gone? Friends – relatives?'

'Nah. But she left her diary.'

'I'll take that if you don't mind.'

'Do what you want. I miss her you know . . . her cooking and stuff and I can't iron shirts.'

'Tough!'

Outside in the fresh air Denni felt suddenly old. She wouldn't have had the stamina to live with those three for a week. She could have woken up the sleeper and grabbed the Gameboy but she knew she would have had the same sort of response. No wonder Pam had left. If she had any sense she'd keep travelling and not look back. Once in the car she tried to be more charitable. They were only teenagers in male bodies. One day they would grow up and become responsible adults – wouldn't they?

Pam loved her room in Tagton's only pub. She'd found the village purely by chance and, after her four nights' stay, she felt like a new woman. In fact, she was a new woman. She'd made up a history for herself as she went along. She was now Pamela Summers, had painted nails, had recently separated from her husband and didn't want to be found by him. She was in the area looking for work and somewhere to stay.

Her room was large with a double bed, en suite bathroom and shower. There was an electric kettle for making tea and a TV. The curtains were pale green and gold and, when she pulled them back in the mornings, the view of rolling hills and fields filled her with a calm she'd never known before.

Gradually she'd chatted more and more to the landlady, Lizzie Waterman. She too was on her own. She was grey-haired, nearly sixty, widowed and confessed that keeping staff was difficult because the pub was quiet and isolated and the wages were low.

Pam murmured casually that if she ever needed staff she was available.

'Have you done bar work before, pet?' asked Lizzie.

Pam shook her head. 'I did some shop work once and I'm very adaptable.'

It was well after closing time, Pam was the only guest and both women had confessed to not sleeping well. Pam had helped wash glasses and, when they'd finished, Lizzie'd suggested a nightcap. One led to another and they were still talking at two a.m.

Lizzie regaled Pam with her life story and Pam elaborated on her fictional one.

'I'll tell you what,' said Lizzie. 'If you can afford to stay on for a couple of weeks, Noreen, my full-time barmaid, has already been offered a better-paid job in town. She's only staying out of loyalty but, if she thought I had someone else in mind, she might take that job.'

Pam had enough cash to last for a while, since she'd closed her bank account. Cash cards were one way she could be found, another would be to go on Lizzie's books.

'My husband could trace me via my insurance number if I worked here,' she said, taking a large swig of her brandy and lemonade.

'I've been in this business a long time, Pamela – I know how to iron out problems like that. Leave it to me. Your old man need never know where you are. I wouldn't give the drunken bastard the satisfaction.'

They both laughed, mellow with brandy and the pleasure of finding a soulmate.

In bed that night Pam had never felt happier. Tomorrow she'd dump the car. Perhaps over a cliff near the sea. She didn't need it anymore. Lizzie had said she could borrow hers. The car represented her old life and she could be traced by it. She didn't want to leave anything to chance.

Somehow, being a fugitive was exciting, on the edge. Could leaving three hulking teenagers, all over sixteen, be a crime? She thought not, but she couldn't go back to being their skivvy again. She didn't want the responsibility and anyway, what did they have in common? Just an accident of birth. She'd loved them when they were small but as they grew into near manhood she saw nothing in them she liked.

Being a barmaid was hardly different from being a care assistant. You had to be a good listener, smile a lot and be generally pleasant. She could do that. In a country pub people wanted a little respite, a laugh and a chat. It would make a change from blood and vomit and pain. It had taken her a long time to realize she'd always worked in the wrong environments, followed the wrong people, been easily led. Maybe if she'd had daughters her life would have been different. But she'd managed to come to terms with that now. Life dealt you all sorts of blows, but you had to deal with it, take risks, carry on. Finally, she could see the rainbow.

In Harrowford, Rydell, Ram and Denni were compiling a dossier from personal records and CVs. It was Ram who suggested eliminating those with no past connection at all. 'That way, guv, we can now reduce our workload and concentrate on those who might have a motive.'

It was a simple idea and Rydell was convinced that Ram was about to reveal something important.

Waving a sheet of A4, Ram pointed to the list of staff known to be in the clinic that night. There were eleven names. 'Now, if we exclude those with no known past connections to Saul Ravenscroft,' he said, as he crossed out names with a black felt tip pen, 'we're left with three who would have had the opportunity to murder him. If we look at the timing of Carla's attack, the same three names occur. We could add one more name.'

Rydell and Denni were both now aware that Ram had made

a breakthrough and they waited silently in anticipation. 'The names are: Wendy Swan, Lyn Kilpatrick, Pamela Miles – the additional name is Una Fairchild.'

'What about Samuels?' asked Rydell, surprised and worried by the three names. Discounting Lyn, that only left Wendy Swan and Pam Miles. Wendy Swan, with her one conviction for violence, certainly seemed a strong contender.

'There's no evidence he returned that night,' explained Ram. 'His wife said he was home by ten thirty. She hasn't changed her story, even knowing her husband was having an affair with Amanda.'

Ram then handed over a computer printout of Saul's bank accounts. 'You'll see he took out regular amounts. Not large sums, but unusual.'

'You're going to tell me who he was paying off, aren't you, Ram? You're just teasing us by stretching this out,' said Denni.

'Not at all. It's complicated. He's been paying Una and her CV is strange. Did you notice that, Denni?'

'I did. She's never once worked in the NHS since she qualified.'

'Is that unusual?' asked Rydell.

'Very. Most nurses work for a while in the NHS. But I'm in the process of checking out her qualification. It's also odd, at her age, that she's settled for the one qualification.'

'What about the larger amounts he was taking out?' asked Rydell, getting impatient. He could see breakthrough coming and he wanted a result.

'Well, guv, you won't like this one. Whenever Lyn Kilpatrick's account was low there was always a top-up. A large one when she came to work at the clinic six months ago.'

'So what are you saying, Ram?' Rydell tried to control the edginess in his voice.

'I reckon she was blackmailing him, guv.'

'So she's your hot suspect, is she?'

'I've got my opinions. Seems odd she's managed to come

up now with a deranged ex-husband. As if she thought we needed another suspect.'

'She hasn't suggested he was involved.'

'Didn't need to – did she, guv?'

Rydell sat down. He felt heavy-hearted and defeated. He'd thought about nothing but this case for weeks. Even the treadmill had been abandoned. He'd worked, snatched meals and hardly slept. And now this.

'There is something else,' said Ram.

'There would be. Go on.'

'We now know that Ravenscroft worked in Turkey, Tunisia and Greece . . .'

'Yes. We know that. What's the punchline?'

'He concentrated on gynaecology.'

'What are you getting at?'

'Maybe he wasn't a very good gynaecological surgeon. Perhaps he botched a few ops and we've been barking up the wrong surgical tree.'

'Christ,' muttered Rydell. 'What do gynaecologists do anyway?'

'Some of them concentrate on surgery,' said Denni, 'hysterectomies, repairs, abortions. Others take an interest in fertility, although they tend to be better-qualified than Ravenscroft.'

'Is he not qualified in cosmetic surgery?'

'Actually, no – he's a qualified doctor but he's not a fellow of the Royal College of Surgeons.'

'You mean he's a cowboy?'

Denni gave a little shrug. 'It's not illegal, guv.'

'Well it bloody should be.'

Ram, still gazing at his computer screen, muttered, 'This Tunisian connection is what interests me.'

'Don't tell me,' said Rydell. 'Let me guess. Ravenscroft has a villa there and regularly has three-in-a-bed sex romps – no let's make that four in a bed.'

'Lucky sod if that's true,' said Ram, 'but he did work over there for a year – fifteen years ago. In Una's CV, the same year is unaccounted for. It's just been glossed over. And at that time Carla was working as a holiday rep.'

'OK,' said Rydell, with a sigh. 'What's Tunisia well known for?'

'Camels?' offered Denni, trying to lighten the mood, with no effect.

'There's two things I can think of,' said Rydell. 'One is drugs and the other is gender-bending sex ops.'

'If he *was* involved in drugs running,' said Ram, 'it would explain how he managed to afford his share of the clinic.'

Rydell sighed. This was the sort of case that could take years to solve. He needed to be alone to think things through. He also needed to trace Lyn's ex-husband and, if possible, get hold of details of the trial. He wanted to know what sort of man he was dealing with. 'We'll leave that angle for the moment, Ram – it's a good one but we've more immediate things to worry about – bitter ex-husbands for one.'

'OK, guv – what next then?'

'Ram, if you needed details of a trial in a hurry, where would you go?'

'*Daily Telegraph*, guv. If it was a major trial, they do the best reports. Give 'em a ring.'

Rydell turned to Denni. 'I want you to move in with Lyn for a few days. And I don't want anyone to know. Snoop if you have to, but go with her everywhere.'

'Won't she mind?'

'She wanted protection. I'll tell Fenton you're at the clinic but for God's sake keep a low profile.'

Denni cast a glance at Ram, who winked as if to say – *I'll manage without you.*

'Is there something going on between you two?' Rydell asked, sharply.

'No, guv,' they replied in unison.

Twenty-One

G raham began to worry he was being seen too often in the vicinity of Lyn's house. He'd thought about getting friendly with one or two of the neighbours but he'd changed his mind. People ignored joggers anyway. They probably thought they were mad buggers, but it was more likely they took no notice at all. He mustn't draw attention to himself and, after all, he wasn't doing any harm.

His days had fallen into a routine. He jogged round to Lyn's about eight thirty in the morning. It was only rarely he caught a glimpse of her, but he'd see her lights on and he'd *know* she was there. He found that very comforting.

He still did his evening paper round and he'd starting chatting to Kirsty, the receptionist. She'd given in her notice, she told him, because her partner worried about her being out late at night – especially since the murder. Graham decided he'd apply for the job. Now he looked better he had more confidence, he could be polite to people and he could practise his smile. That was something he was working on. He'd stand in front of a mirror, turning this way and that, pretending a camera was snapping at him excitedly. Since the operation he'd turned into quite a good-looking guy.

Only one thing cast a shadow on his life . . . He'd seen a bloke in a car hanging around near Lyn's house. At first he'd spotted him on the opposite side of the road, his head behind a newspaper. Then, two days later, he was there again. When he saw him a third time, late at night, Graham had decided to warn Lyn. He'd knocked on her door but she hadn't answered.

Graham had clocked the man's car number and his face. Why he was so convinced the bloke was watching Lyn's house he didn't know. It was just an instinct. It crossed his mind to tell the police, but why should they believe him? He could try warning Lyn personally – if she didn't answer the door next time he'd slip a note through her door.

Disaster struck on his way home. He was only walking but he slipped on damp leaves and sprained his ankle. He was forced to rest up for two days. Even then, he couldn't jog. He could only hobble, so he came out late, knowing Lyn had a night off. Sometimes, if he was lucky, he could see her moving behind closed curtains. At those times he longed to be with her, his chest felt as if it would explode and that would be followed by feeling sick. He'd never felt this way before and he knew he couldn't go on forever skulking in the shadows.

He looked around. There was no one about. All the curtains were drawn and most houses were in darkness. He knelt down behind a bush on the opposite side of the road, four doors up from Lyn's house. He pretended to be tying up his laces. He waited until Lyn switched off the lights. It was eleven thirty. He'd just started walking home when he heard a car draw up. He knew without looking that it was *him*. He dropped back into a front garden and crouched down. The driver switched off his lights but didn't leave the car.

His legs went into spasm after about ten minutes and, in the end, he sat square on the damp ground. He would wait all night if need be.

Graham began to shiver and he hugged his arms round his body for warmth. His backside was numb and he wondered if he should just ring the police. Unless, of course, it was a cop watching the house. He could make an anonymous call. Try to find out. If he was a cop they wouldn't send a police car and then he'd know for sure. Why would the police watch Lyn anyway? He looked at his watch. It was nearly two a.m and getting colder. He'd be dead from hypothermia by the morning at this rate.

It was then that the driver got out of the car. Graham couldn't get much of a look at his face, but he was of medium height, dark haired, forties maybe. He wore a long dark raincoat – the sort you rarely see nowadays, old-fashioned – there was a name for that style – trenchcoat, that was it.

Graham was up on his haunches now, cold and numbness forgotten. What the hell was he up to, anyway? The figure approached the front door. Graham fumbled in his pocket for his mobile phone. He rarely used it and the only call he had ever had on it was a wrong number, but everyone had one these days. He tried his other pocket – it wasn't there. He moved a few inches forward, thinking he'd heard something. What he hadn't heard was any knocking or calling and there were no lights going on in the house.

Then, suddenly, the man was getting into the car, revving the engine, driving off at speed. Graham was on his feet now going towards the house. By the time he got there, he could see flames behind the stained glass. Smoke was beginning to billow out. Christ! He rushed to the front door, but already the heat was intense and drove him back. He yelled, 'Fire!' but his voice was hoarse and his throat tight with panic. He rushed to the back door, remembering he had the key. He slipped it in the lock but it wouldn't turn. He looked round for something to smash the door down – there was nothing.

'Mummy – Mummy!' Lyn was awake instantly. Smoke was pouring in underneath the door. She could hear the crackling of the flames. She leapt from the bed, grabbing her terrified children under her arms. She knew she couldn't open the door. The window was her only chance. The room was filling with smoke. She could see flames licking at the door. She had to release her grip on the children to open the window. The room was dark, the smoke suffocating. She screamed so loudly it seemed to tear her throat. 'Jump! Jump!' shouted a man's voice from below. The window was small, too small for her. She managed to get her son on to the sill. 'Now! Now!' he screamed. And then once more – 'Jump! Jump!'

It seemed in slow motion that she turned back to look at the flames that now roared into the room. She had no choice.

'Catch her!' she screamed. The man stretched out his arms. Roughly she tore Zoe's hands away from her neck and lowered her. Letting go and hearing her terrified sobs, Lyn recognized in a fraction of a second the awful choice she had made. Zoe's fall was broken as the man caught her and staggered backwards on to the grass. Lyn was coughing and choking, but worst of all, Sean made no sound. Clutching Sean to her, the thought flashed into her head that they should jump together. Below, the man shouted, 'Do it now – come on – she's okay – do it!' She had no choice. She dangled Sean from the window – the man below stood, arms outstretched. She let go. Like a rag doll he sped downwards. This time, his weight being less, the man caught him easily. Both children started to scream and sob. They were alive. It was the sweetest sound she'd ever heard.

The smoke swirled and she knew she was suffocating. Her lungs were clogged and her knees began to give way. She wasn't going to make it.

Suddenly there were more voices. A man's voice – the same man – was shouting, 'We can catch you, Lyn. Dive through the window. Come on. You can do it.'

She had to try. Her head and shoulders managed to fit. Below, three men held out a blanket. The sides of the window scraped her sides, her hands were bleeding.

'Push! Push!' someone screamed. Her feet were burning. She gave herself a final push and then she was free of the window and plummeting downwards.

The blanket broke her fall. As they laid her on the grass she managed to gasp before passing out, 'There's someone else in the house – front bedroom.'

Denni had woken up to a smoke-filled room. She rolled on to the floor, remembering you had to keep low in smoke. She had a glass of water by her bed and she ripped off a pillowcase and soaked it in water. She held that to her face and crawled to the window. She struggled to open the unfamiliar lock on the window. She couldn't see properly and she could hardly breathe, the smoke was so thick and acrid. She crawled to the bedside chair and found her nightstick. Struggling to stand up, she managed to break the window. She saw flashing blue lights but heard no sirens. She could hear nothing and she felt dizzy. Where was she? She could feel her body slipping towards the floor. There was nothing she could do.

Rydell, normally a cautious driver, sped towards the fire. Fire was one of his greatest fears. Ram, sitting beside him, clung on and prayed. 'The fire brigade will be there, guv. Don't panic.'

'I'm not fucking panicking! I'm just getting there.'

Ram kept quiet and silently prayed for Denni and the others. There were kids in the house. He'd seen two children brought out dead from a burning house and it had upset him for months. Even now the memory was vivid. The screaming parents, the sense of hopelessness, the burnt teddy in the dead child's arms.

They arrived as the paramedics were putting Lyn and the children into the ambulance. Denni was on a stretcher in the front garden, a male paramedic by her side. She lay still, eyes closed, an oxygen mask on her face. Ram knelt beside her. 'Denni! Denni!' he said, rubbing her hands. There was no response. 'Is she going to make it?' asked Ram.

'Blood pressure's low, mate,' said the paramedic, 'and her pulse is a bit thready. But the oxygen should make a difference.' Rydell and Ram exchanged glances. 'I asked a simple question,' Ram said angrily. 'Will she make it?'

'Don't lose your rag, mate. The hospital will sort her out.'

'You go with her,' said Rydell. 'I'll have a word with Lyn.'

Inside the ambulance, Lyn and the children were also being given oxygen. The kids were wide-eyed and each held their mother's hand. Lyn took her mask off when she saw Rydell. 'Is Denni OK?' Her voice was hoarse and raspy, hardly more than a whisper.

'We hope so,' he said. 'What happened?'

'I was in bed,' she said. 'I didn't hear a thing. It was just so quick. If it hadn't been for the man catching the children and helping to catch me – we'd all be dead.' The effort of talking exhausted her and she held the oxygen mask to her face. 'That's enough talking,' said the paramedic, giving him a warning glance.

'I'll arrange for a woman officer to sit with you, Lyn. I'll see you later.' She waved one hand weakly at him.

The neighbours had now gathered around in dressing gowns or with coats thrown over their nightclothes. One man, dressed in a jogging suit, walked off as the ambulances drove away.

'Hang on,' called Rydell, at his receding back.

He turned. 'Who, me?'

'Yes. Are you a witness?'

Graham nodded. 'I suppose I am.'

'I'm Inspector Rydell.'

'Yeah. We've met before.'

Rydell looked at him closely. Even then he didn't remember him.

'I'm Graham Coombs. I was at the clinic when the surgeon's body was found. I'd had a nose job.'

'Looks good,' said Rydell, vaguely remembering the black eyes and the strip of white plaster across his nose. 'Let's talk in my car.'

In the car Rydell asked, 'Did you catch the kids?' He noticed Graham's hands and face were blue with cold, so he offered him a can of self-heating coffee. 'Yeah, I caught them,' he said, as he read the directions on the tin. He then pressed the top and rolled the can gently between his hands. 'I've never had one of these before. Thanks.'

'Do you live round here?' asked Rydell.

'Not far. I was jogging.'

'In the middle of the night?'

'I don't sleep well. Once I've had a run I sleep great.'

Rydell understood. 'Where do you work?' he asked, not

202

remembering a thing about him. Graham, it seemed, was instantly forgettable.

'I do a bit of this and that. I get by.' Graham warmed his hands on the tin and then opened the can and began drinking. 'No sugar,' he said, 'but it's hot and wet.'

'So tell me what happened. From the beginning.'

'I came out for a jog . . .'

'Why round here?'

'It's respectable. Some places aren't safe. Everyone in this road goes to bed after the news.'

Rydell wondered if he was a peeping tom, but guessed if that was the case, he would have had previous.

'OK, so you were jogging and . . . ?'

'I saw this bloke arrive in a car. He switched his lights off and then he just sat there. I was further up the road so I hid behind a bush. I would have called the police only I didn't have my mobile with me.'

'How long?'

'About two hours.'

'Two hours?' queried Rydell, in astonishment.

'I couldn't move because he might have clocked me, so I stayed put.'

'And then?'

'Then he got out of the car and walked over to Lyn's house.'

'You know Lyn?'

'Only sort of. She's the night sister at the clinic.'

'Go on.'

'He'd got a long dark coat on. I didn't see him carrying anything. I thought he was knocking on the door. Then he just made a run for it and drove away like a bat out of hell. Within seconds the place was like a torch. I rushed around the back.'

'Why the back?'

Graham faltered. 'I thought . . . I thought I might find a ladder around the back. Anyway, the hall was already an inferno.'

'But you didn't find a ladder?'

'No. I couldn't get in the back door. Lyn was at the window and I caught the kids and then neighbours came and we managed to catch Lyn in a blanket.'

'Well done, mate. You're a hero.'

'Not me,' said Graham. 'What else could I do?'

'I know Lyn is very grateful.'

'Is she? Did she say that?'

Up until now Graham had done quite well but, at the mention of her name, his eyes had lit up. Graham was besotted.

'She certainly did,' said Rydell. 'You're definitely her hero.'

Graham smiled with satisfaction.

'One more question,' said Rydell. 'Had you seen this car before?'

'Yeah, several times.'

'Did you get the number?'

'Of course I did. I know it by heart.' Rydell phoned the number through to the station immediately. He had no doubt the bastard would soon be caught.

'Now then, Graham,' he said, 'you'll have to come to the station with me to make a formal statement.'

'OK,' said Graham, cheerfully. Lyn was safe and that was all that mattered.

As daylight broke, a call came through from a substation in the sticks. A car fitting the description had driven at speed into a brick wall. The driver was dead but a can of petrol had been found in the boot. The car belonged to a Nathan Jackson.

Twenty-Two

A few days later Lyn and her children had been tempo-
rarily placed in a housing association house. They had
no possessions left but Rydell organized a whip round for
money and household appliances. He donated a toaster, a
clock radio, a microwave, a water filter, a dinner service, a
nearly full set of cutlery and a kettle. He had acquired two
of most things over the years and kept one set in reserve.
Appliances going wrong meant he had to go shopping. Apart
from a once a month trip to a supermarket he rarely entered
a shop. He ordered clothes from catalogues once a year and
at Christmas he had been known to visit a shopping centre.

Others in the force offered telephones, irons, one ironing
board, a sofa bed – the list went on and on. One or two
female shopaholics came into their own with clothes still in
their original bags. For the children, the toys appeared in large
black sacks.

Lyn was overwhelmed. But it was when she saw a brand
new smoke alarm that she broke down. She'd had a smoke
alarm but the battery hadn't been replaced, so she was filled
with guilt and, although Rydell reassured her that because
petrol had been used the flames were intense from the
word go, she still blamed herself. Rydell knew that arson
attacks were vastly different to a slowly building ordinary
house fire.

Still being in shock, Lyn felt a strange mixture of numbness
and hyper-alertness. Every time she heard a noise she jumped.
She couldn't sleep at night and the *what if* scenario went over
and over in her head. What if Graham hadn't been there? Tom

Rydell had suggested that he was hanging around because he was besotted by her. If that were the case her gratitude to his devotion would last her a lifetime.

Rydell had visited her every day since the fire. He'd come with her to the mortuary to identify her ex-husband and she'd wished she could have felt a vague pang of regret at his death, but there was none. She was both glad and relieved he was dead.

She sensed Tom was hoping a relationship would develop between them. He'd invited her out to dinner and Holly had offered to babysit, but it was too soon. Tom Rydell was a cop and she had information that she now felt obliged to reveal.

On Monday, a week after the fire, her children were back at school and Tom had rung to invite her out to lunch. Instead, she'd suggested she'd make home-made soup and sandwiches.

They were halfway through the soup when she said, 'Tom, there is something I have to tell you, but I don't think it's anything to do with Saul and Carla being murdered. And I want you to promise that you won't make it common knowledge, not just for my sake, but for the sake of the other people involved.'

Rydell put down his soup spoon and his appetite drained away. 'I can't promise anything, Lyn. You'll have to trust me with the information and I'll do the right thing.'

'You can be an uptight, proper bastard,' she said.

'I know. But I do genuinely care about you, Lyn.'

'Nathan used to say he cared. And he did, but only for me. He couldn't bear the thought of anyone else sharing our life. The concept of sharing sent him over the edge. Saul was the opposite. He wanted a share in everyone's life. He could let go, but he didn't want to. He was like the pied piper. He played the tune and we followed. He collected people. Wanted to protect them. Kept in touch. Sounds admirable, doesn't it? He was a man of many virtues and vices. He wasn't exactly Jekyll and Hyde but he was a contradiction. He built up his little band of devotees and I think he thought he led a charmed life.'

'And I think,' said Rydell, 'you'd better start from the beginning.'

'Fair enough,' she said. 'I met Saul when I was in nurse training. I went out with him a few times. He was a surgical registrar. I was flattered. I was twenty, not very experienced, and it began to get serious. But then, one day, Nathan Jackson arrived in A&E. He'd broken his leg badly in a motorbike accident. Weeks later I was transferred to the orthopaedic ward and he was still there. He was very good-looking and, more and more, Saul seemed consumed in his work and Nathan and I got closer. When it came to telling them that they had a rival – Saul caved in and Nathan remained persistent. I think I did love Nathan, but it's hard to remember that now.'

'So you married?'

'Yes, I was twenty-two. I worked in the NHS at St Mary's in London. By that time Saul had moved on. He said he wanted a different sort of life. He sent me postcards from Turkey, Tunisia, Greece. All over the place. And he worked on the cruise ships. He'd phone me at work sometimes during the day. There was nothing romantic about it. He said, "Once a friend, a friend for ever. And no matter what, I'll always be around."

'Even Nathan accepted that we kept in touch. And then along came my beautiful Justin. I had him for such a few short weeks. And all these years later I still think of him. Still feel the loss.'

Rydell watched as her eyes filled with tears. Mention of Lyn's son brought sharply into focus memories of his own son and with that came the guilt he felt at having been unable to accept his son as he was. Not physically perfect. A spastic. Cerebral palsied. Whatever name you gave his condition – the words were ugly. And, God forgive him, he hadn't been able to take the emotional battering that seeing his son had caused him.

'Are you OK?' she asked, watching him.

'Yes. I was thinking about my son. I haven't seen him in a long time.'

'I didn't know.'

'I'll tell you about him one day.'

They'd both abandoned their soup as it began to congeal and, without saying a word, Lyn returned the bowls to the kitchen and came back with two mugs of coffee. She'd obviously been crying.

'I'll be fine now,' she said, trying to smile. 'After Nathan went to prison, I couldn't work for a year. It was Saul who bailed me out when I had no money. It was Saul who rang me every week and wrote often. After a year he persuaded me to work with him in Tunisia.' She sipped at her coffee. 'He and two other surgeons had bought a run-down clinic. It was basic but they had plenty of clients.'

'Private?'

'Oh yes. And it was very expensive.'

'What sort of surgery?'

'Anything that was required. Mostly cosmetic . . .' She broke off. 'To be honest, he wasn't fussy. I was his scrub nurse, so I know.'

'You'll have to spell it out to me, Lyn.'

She sighed. 'He did operations on transexuals, abortions, female circumcisions, removed organs for transplants, changed the faces of criminals. And he cut corners . . .'

'How?'

'He got everything on the cheap – surgical gloves, antibiotics, even anaesthetics.' Then she added quietly, 'He used a new anaesthetic called Rotox. It was very cheap and patients were telling us that they were still awake during their operation. He listened, asked them to write down their experience of surgery. Then he gave them several injections of a Valium-type substance, so that they slept for a couple of days. When they came round in a complete daze he explained, very convincingly, that it had all been a bad dream and that all they could possibly remember were the last few minutes as the anaesthetic lightened. Most patients believed him.'

'Most?'

'There was one that didn't.'

'Carla Robins?'

Lyn shook her head. 'You'll find out sooner or later. It was Una Fairchild. Una Fairchild isn't married to Hugh. And she wasn't born Una. She took her mother's name. Una was born Brian Pattingham. She went out to Tunisia in the late eighties. Brian, as he was then, was a charge nurse. Saul did the sex operation. That went well, and with the help of hormone treatment, Brian became Una. She stayed there for two years perfecting her womanhood. Everything was fine except her nose looked very masculine. Saul operated again but this time using Rotox. She wasn't pacified by sedation and suggestion and she threatened to expose him. He persuaded her to say nothing in exchange for a false passport, glowing references and help from him whenever necessary.'

Rydell tried to visualize Una. She was boyishly slim and had an unusually gravelly voice, but he would never have guessed. Never.

'She came back to England, then?' he asked.

'They came back together. He vouched for her and she worked with him in various private clinics. By now he'd amassed quite a large amount of money.'

'From the ops?'

'Some of it. It was very lucrative. I'm not sure, but I think he was drug running as well.'

Rydell whistled long and low. 'He covered his tracks well.'

'Yes. The CVs were not exactly truthful and, even at the Harmony, he cut corners. There is hardly ever a doctor on the premises at night. That was a major saving. And of course, sleeping in, he could see Carla.'

'Why are you telling me this now?' asked Rydell. He was beginning to feel angry. She could have saved them weeks of work, hours of fruitless overtime, hours of reading and writing reports. 'Why now?' he repeated.

Christine Green

'A brush with death, I suppose, and wanting to protect Una. I thought maybe things could be hushed up . . .'

'Hushed up! You've got to be joking, woman. She's obviously a suspect now—'

'She wouldn't kill Saul,' Lyn interrupted. 'She suffered because of him, but he introduced her to Hugh, found her jobs, invited her to be nursing director. She didn't approve of everything he did, but she was extremely fond of him.'

'Hugh obviously knows she's a transsexual?'

'Oh yes. He's gay but they did love each other. And as far as I know he's been faithful to her – until now. I think the shock of Saul's murder had an effect on both of them. I think she'd have coped better with Hugh's leaving if another man had been involved – but another woman came as a real blow.'

Rydell felt depressed now. He hadn't guessed Hugh was homosexual, although if he was non-practising – did it count? Was it like claiming to be C of E and never entering a church? Could you count yourself as gay or a Christian if it was in name only?

'Well, Lyn, you seem to know all the answers. Tell me about Carla. We know they were having an affair – you're not going to tell me *they* were just good friends?'

'No. He adored her. They first met on a cruise ship. She was working as a travel rep. I met her in Tunisia. I never liked her, partly because of the heartache she caused Saul. He would confide in me that she was his soulmate and that he'd asked her to marry him on several occasions. She would neither marry him nor live with him. She had terribly painful periods due to the endometriosis. It was Saul who encouraged her to have the hysterectomy. Afterwards she told Saul she'd never felt better or happier.'

'I think Saul would have liked children with Carla. He was worried about the op. A friend of his did it in Germany.'

'Where does Amanda fit into all this?'

Lyn shrugged. 'I think Saul finally realized Carla wouldn't change her mind. Freedom was her husband. So he met

210

Amanda when she was temping as a medical secretary and yearning for a large house and a horse. She was young and pretty and didn't irritate him too much and I think he wanted to indulge her. But when it came to his last will and testament he couldn't forsake Carla.'

'You knew about the will?'

'He'd told me that Carla knew, but he wasn't convinced that she believed him and he made her promise to continue to help Una and me out if necessary.'

'And would you have trusted Carla to do that?'

'Oh yes. Carla had her own code of ethics. If she made a promise she would keep it.'

'So Amanda's protestations of his determination to give Carla up were a complete fabrication.'

'Oh yes. Amanda knew about the affair from day one. But she'd convinced herself it was purely sexual and, of course, Saul didn't give her the full background. She didn't realize they'd known each other for years.'

Rydell swore to himself. He tried to remember his first interview with Lyn. Butter wouldn't melt then, now he saw a different side to her. 'What about Amanda and Martin Samuels? When did their affair start?'

'I didn't know they were having an affair,' she said. 'I think Martin is being opportunistic. We had a party here once, his wife was with him, but I did notice he couldn't take his eyes off Amanda. I should imagine she's very needy at the moment and he's taking advantage of that.'

'Do you think he was jealous of Saul's success with women?'

She smiled. 'I couldn't possibly say. I would think it more likely he admired his surgical prowess rather than his sexual prowess. Saul wasn't a sex addict – he actually liked women. He was chivalrous. If he knew a woman was in trouble he'd do anything he could to help – a job, money . . . a . . .' she broke off.

'What?'

'I don't suppose it matters now,' she said, 'but he did offer

211

to warn Nathan off. He said if Nathan bothered me in any way he would *see to it*. I knew what he meant.'

'Okay – so he was a knight in shining armour,' said Rydell, caustically. 'But he rattled somebody's cage.

'Nathan couldn't have . . .' she began.

'No, I did think of that but it seems he was in Ireland at the time.'

Rydell should have felt pleased that he had more information. But he wasn't. He felt a knot of anger in his chest. He was no nearer to finding the killer than he was before and, as investigating officer, he took full responsibility for the rest of the team. He'd once done a short stint with the fraud squad, their cases took years to solve. This one was going the same way. The old adage of *six weeks and a quarter of a million pounds* for murder cases meant that, with no result, there was a gradual winding down. There were other cases to solve and he'd heard the whispers at the nick that the bosses were looking to replace him.

'Is there anyone else with connections to the victims that you haven't told me about?' he asked coldly.

'I am sorry, Tom. Una's a nice person and a good manager. Surely you can see that I didn't mention it before because there was no way she would have harmed Saul.'

'What about Carla?'

'Or *her*. They weren't friendly but they respected each other's abilities.'

'You don't think Una could have been jealous of the sexual nature of their relationship? You tell me Hugh is gay, so I presume Una isn't getting any and could therefore be a very bitter, frustrated woman.'

Lyn's eyes narrowed. 'So a woman, who may or may not be sexually frustrated, is by definition bitter and liable to hack people to death with a scalpel.'

'I didn't say that.'

'You didn't need to.'

'I don't want to fall out with you, Lyn, but you have

hampered this investigation. And I would have thought that you would have wanted Saul's killer to be caught.'

'Oh yes,' she said, quietly. 'I do.'

Rydell sat back in his chair and stared at her. She was either lying to him or withholding something. It was the same slightly uneasy expression his wife's face had shown when she was about to uncover some minor deception.

'Is there anyone else Saul or Carla had a connection with either personally or professionally?'

'It's only gossip, but Wendy Swan was seen with him a couple of times.'

'Would that have made Carla jealous?'

Lyn looked at him, quizzically. 'You mean, Carla kills Saul through jealousy and in retaliation someone kills her?'

'It's a possibility,' said Rydell. 'Have you got any better ideas?'

'I think someone set Carla up and then, when she wasn't charged quickly enough, she too had to die.'

'I had thought of that,' said Rydell, feeling irritated. 'All the speculation in the world doesn't add up to evidence. Come on, Lyn. Who else is there? I know you're keeping something back.'

Twenty-Three

'Well?' said Rydell, sounding irritable.

Lyn thought for a moment, still with that wary, uneasy expression. 'There is only one other person I can think of that worked at the same clinic as Saul a few years back – she told me she worked in the sterilizing department of the Mayflower Clinic in London.'

'What happens there?'

'Cleaning instruments, autoclaving them, making up surgical packs and dressings, that sort of thing. But I don't think she was one of his conquests. Not his type.'

'Who?'

'Pam Miles.'

Rydell frowned, only vaguely remembering her. During her interview she'd fanned herself most of the time, she'd seemed harassed by her three boys and she certainly wasn't the femme fatale type.

'So how come she's working at the Harmony?'

'Pure coincidence, I think.'

Lyn again looked uneasy and there was a long pause before she said, quietly, 'You'll find out sooner or later, Tom.'

'Find out what?'

'I did have rather a strong bond with Saul.'

'I gathered that much.'

'No. More than just friendship. After Justin was murdered you can imagine I wanted nothing to do with men. My trust was gone and, although Saul was one man I did trust, there was also a shady side to his character. As the years went by, I grew more and more desperate for a child, but not desperate for a man . . .' She paused. 'Saul offered me a chance I couldn't refuse. He offered to father my children. He wanted no involvement and that suited me. He did help me out financially and I know I sound like a hypocrite, but it seemed the only answer. A part of me will always grieve for Justin, but having more children has been like sunshine after rain. Saul's death was a blow but I couldn't tell anyone how much of a blow. I really miss just knowing he was there. After all – he gave me life itself.'

Her eyes had filled with tears and Rydell looked away for a moment.

'Does anyone else know about this?'

She shook her head. 'No, we were very careful.'

Rydell wanted to say something about bringing up kids without a father being irresponsible, but then, he too was being hypocritical. Both of Lyn's children seemed happy and healthy and one happy parent was surely better than two at war.

'Is there anything else left to tell me?'

'It's only a suspicion.'

'Go on.'

'Do you know Mrs Lloyd-Peters?'

'Yes, of course,' he said. 'She was in the clinic with her son Harry the night Saul was murdered.'

'Well, I think,' she said, slowly, 'Harry could also have been fathered by Saul. He looks very much like him and I do know that Saul had his ears corrected as a child. He looks nothing like his supposed father. Having seen two of Saul's children, I think I'm a good judge.'

'Christ Almighty. What was he building? His own dynasty?'

'I don't think her husband knows – you will tread carefully, won't you? If he doesn't know, it could wreck their lives. They're separated anyway, but I think she has hopes of a reconciliation. If this gets out, Harry will be left without the man he thinks of as his father.'

Rydell smiled wearily. He'd thought the case difficult

enough without Ravenscroft's offspring appearing all over the place. He'd been shocked many times in his career but somehow these revelations had affected him personally. He'd been attracted to Lyn but now he realized he hadn't known her at all. The complications of her seemingly straightforward life were, to him, like an untidy room and there was nothing he could do to tidy it up. He had no option but to rummage even further and make things worse.

Back at his office someone had moved his in tray and his pens. 'Have you touched my desk?' he asked Denni.

'I only put your post in the in tray.'

'Well, don't in future.'

She glanced thoughtfully at him. He looked pale and strained. 'Are you feeling all right, guv?'

'No. I'm pissed off. We're wasting hours and hours on telephones, delving into bank accounts, checking CVs and, after that, we're none the wiser – except that Lyn, having had a narrow escape, now wants to yield up the secrets of all and bloody sundry. And all that does is make everything a bloody sight more difficult.'

Denni hadn't seen him quite so angry and despondent. 'I'll fetch you a coffee,' she said, 'and some sandwiches from the canteen. Then I'll find Ram.'

'Typical of you,' he said. 'I suppose you think I've got a low blood sugar.'

She was already on her way out of the door. She knew Ram was in the canteen and she found him tucked away at a corner table, reading a newspaper and eating a cream cake.

'Our boss,' she said, 'is not a happy bunny.'

'What's happened?'

'I don't know. He came back from seeing Lyn muttering about secrets and wasted hours. The case is getting to him.'

Ram licked cream from his fingers. 'I've seen senior detectives on long murder cases tipped over the edge.'

'You're cheerful. Are you saying a couple of cheese and

tomato sandwiches and a cup of coffee isn't going to do the trick?'

'Nothing short of a result is going to help Rydell. Do you wonder I'm addicted to cakes and humbugs? It keeps me sane.'

'You told me living at my place kept you sane.'

'Men are such liars,' he said, laughing.

Rydell looked no more cheerful on their return. 'Right,' he said, 'we have three people to concentrate on. And I want them here for questioning. It's background, background, background. Were they shagging Ravenscroft? Had he double-crossed them in the past? Do they harbour any resentment? Ram, you bring in Wendy Swan. I'll bring in Lloyd-Peters and you, Denni – you find Pam and bring her in. Now, if it's not one of those three – we start all over again.'

Both Ram and Denni were slow to move. 'Go on, go on, go on,' said Rydell with a grin. 'And when you find me a hot suspect, we'll search their place and I'm sure we'll find what we're looking for.'

Less than an hour later Ram sat with Wendy Swan and a WPC in an interview room. 'I've been interviewed twice,' she said. 'I'm getting a bit fed up.'

'Yes, love, well *I'd* rather be doing other things.'

'Can I smoke?' she asked.

'It's OK with me. What about you, Jackie?

Jackie in the corner nodded. 'Fine by me.'

Wendy Swan puffed nervously on a cigarette. 'I'm only a suspect because I hacked a bed to death. I've never been violent to a person. Anyway, what reason could I have to kill Saul? I liked him. He wasn't a snob. He was a great bloke.'

'When did you first meet him?'

'I worked in a clinic in London. I worked in the kitchens there. I used to take him a tray when he was working late or sleeping in. We used to chat for ages. He said I should work as a care assistant for a while and then do my nurse training. He said I was bright enough.'

'So you were just good friends?'

Wendy watched a smoke ring sail upwards. 'Look, I know that mad old biddy saw me in the florists with him but that meant nothing. When he opened the Harmony he wrote to me in London – said the clinic was great, the money good and he would offer me a job if I wanted one.'

'So he had your address?'

'He was like that. He kept in touch with people. He was a people person.'

'As long as the people were female?'

'It's not a crime to like women.'

'That's true,' agreed Ram, 'but he upset someone for sure and, knowing his background, it was probably a woman. Tell me about Alvera. He wasn't shagging her, was he?'

Wendy laughed. 'Don't be ridiculous. That fat old cow?'

'Not your best friend then?'

'She's a barmy bitch but I didn't mean her any harm—' She broke off, blushing at her gaff.

'You'll have to explain that,' said Ram. 'Won't she, Jackie?' Jackie nodded dutifully.

Wendy stubbed out her cigarette angrily. 'It was only a joke. I didn't realise she was *that* barmy. I rigged up a figure in a white sheet. It was only made of a mop and a mask with a halo above it. From a distance I suppose it was a bit scary but I didn't think it looked like Jesus Christ.'

'But she did.'

'Yeah. I reckon she thought it was the second coming. Her Church believes in that. Anyway, she turned into a gibbering idiot. I didn't expect that. I mean, I only wanted to get back at her for grassing me up about seeing me with Saul.'

'I'll ask you again,' said Ram, putting his hand over her packet of cigarettes just as she made a move to take another one.

Wendy sighed. 'What's the sodding difference? Yes – I slept with him. Several times, if you must know. But he didn't lead me on saying he loved me or anything. He made it clear he had other women and it was just sex. That suited me. Sex is recreational, isn't it, these days? Just like having a few drinks or going to the gym.'

Ram didn't share that view. He was British born but Asian in his attitudes to sex and marriage. He couldn't help it but he was shocked by the sexual mores of some young British women. He thought sex should be a damn sight more special than a couple of pints of lager. He also thought fatherless homes were one of the main causes of crime. He kept his opinions to himself, but he thought few woman were strong enough emotionally and financially to keep older children under control.

'So you weren't jealous of Carla?'

'I was a bit.'

'Because he was in love with her?'

'No. You've got me wrong there. I was jealous of her because she was really together – know what I mean? Great figure and looks, good job, house of her own, men at her beck and call and no socks to wash. She had it all.'

'And you wanted to take it away?'

'No! You're twisting what I'm saying. I admired her. I wanted to be like her. I didn't kill her. I didn't!'

'Calm down, Wendy. No one said you did.'

Her mouth set in a straight line and she reached for the cigarettes.

'You found the time and the ingenuity, though,' said Ram, pushing the pack of cigarettes towards her, 'to frighten Alvera half to death. Ravenscroft's murder also needed time and ingenuity. Let's face it, you did have a violent outburst when you found your man in bed with another woman. You see Carla leaving his room and the same red mist comes up . . .'

'You're just making it up,' she snapped. 'You fat git!'

'Insulting my size will only antagonize me,' he said, calmly. 'Luckily, I'm known for my good nature.'

'Well even if you're a bloody saint you're not pinning this on me. You all thought Carla had done it and look what happened to her.'

'Which is why we have to keep you here until we're satisfied you're innocent.'

She snatched at the cigarette pack and tried to remove a cigarette but she fumbled and couldn't manage it at first. When she came to lighting it her hand trembled. She took a deep drag. 'You can't keep me here for long.'

'It depends if you think thirty-six hours is a long time.'

'You black bastard!'

'Did you hear that, Jackie?' he asked.

'I've made a note of it, Sarge.'

Ram was used to racist comments. And he had to admit it didn't worry him one bit, unless the person yelling abuse was coming at him with a machete – then he *was* worried.

'It's no use name-calling, Wendy. All you have to do is convince me you're innocent.'

Wendy fell silent while she smoked her cigarette. When she'd finished she said, 'The cameras . . .'

'What about them?'

'Stanley has them fixed. Anyone can get out of the building at the side and get through the fence. And if anyone can get out without being seen, they can also get in.'

'Have you got anyone in mind?'

'I dunno – a jealous man. Carla wasn't just sleeping with Saul – she was a real tart.'

'A few moments ago you were telling me how much you admired her.'

Wendy smiled. 'I do. But she was a tart and tarts make enemies, don't they?'

Ram, knowing there was no evidence against her, tried another tack.

'It might be helpful,' he said casually, 'if we searched your place.'

She smiled, unconcerned. 'Go ahead. I've got nothing to hide.'

Ram was disappointed. Her reaction was so spontaneous he knew a search would be a waste of time. He decided she could sweat it out a little longer.

'Jackie – keep an eye on our guest. I need to see if we need the big guns on this one.'

He was pleased to see she looked worried as he left.

In the canteen he drank coffee and allowed himself a few moments to reflect on the fact that being called a black bastard didn't worry him, but 'fat git' did. He unwrapped a humbug, then changed his mind. He wasn't fat yet but he could get that way.

Wendy Swan, he decided, would have to stay a little longer. She was not his most favourite person, but the thought that rankled was that he suspected she was innocent. In a fair world she would have been guilty. In a fair world, sweet-eaters wouldn't get fat.

Twenty-Four

D enni roused the boys after loud knocking. Again it was Daniel, the eldest, who answered the door.

'Yeah. What is it?' He had a slight growth of downy hair on his chin and an outcrop of spots on his forehead. He wore jeans but nothing on his top half. Strangely, the hair on his chest was much more rugged than the hair on his chin.

'I'd like to come in.'

'What for?'

'Not for health reasons,' she said. 'We need to find your mum.'

The house was a further step forward to total chaos. Takeaway containers had been left on the living-room floor, there were grease marks on the sofa, a waste bin full of empty lager cans and it stank like a brewery.

'We'll clear it up,' he said.

'Have you got any black bags?'

He shrugged his bony shoulders. 'I dunno.'

'Go in the kitchen and look. If this place isn't cleared up by the end of today, I'm getting environmental health in.'

'It's Mum's fault . . .' he began.

'Do you live here?'

'Yeah – you know I do.' He looked mystified.

'Then it's your responsibility. Of course, you could always be taken into care.'

A horrified look crossed his face. He didn't realize he was too old to be taken into care.

'Black bags,' repeated Denni.

When he went to the kitchen Denni began looking around.

She wasn't sure what she was looking for, but a photo or an old diary would be more than enough. She found tapes and CDs and computer games thrown into a plastic box. From the kitchen she still heard the sound of cupboard doors opening and closing, so she crept upstairs and peered into the bedrooms. In the front there were two divans with the occupants huddled under their duvets, and on the floor socks, underpants, girlie mags and cigarette ends in saucers. The room smelt foetid with overtones of testosterone and it was a relief to find Pam's room – neat, tidy and sweet-smelling. In the bottom drawer of the dressing table Denni found a photograph album. She took that downstairs, wondering if Daniel would make a fuss. He didn't, he was busy throwing rubbish into a black bag. 'Have you been nosing around?' he asked.

'Yep. I want a recent photo of your mum. You'll have to help me choose one.'

'I don't think she's had one taken for a few years. We lost our camera.'

'Come and sit down and we'll find the best likeness we can.'

'What about all this rubbish?'

Not wanting him to lose momentum, she said, 'Deal with that first. You do know where the dustbin is?'

'You think you're so funny, don't you,' he said, trying to perfect a sneer, but failing. 'I've cleared rubbish before.'

'Don't forget the kitchen, will you?'

'You're worse than my mum.'

'I think your mother is a saint to put up with this.'

'Well she hasn't, has she! She never wanted boys anyway.'

Denni could see her point. Teenage boys at close quarters were the best contraceptive she could think of. Her contact with young boys had been mainly dealing with vandalism, taking and driving away, drug abuse and violence. Pam's boys weren't criminals, unless making a mother's life a misery could be called criminal. You are getting seriously warped, she told herself.

Daniel eventually sat beside her on the sofa and squirmed at various baby photographs. 'That's me dad,' he said, pointing to a tall, handsome man in swimming trunks, with a very attractive young woman in a bikini by his side. 'Is that his second wife?' she asked.

'That's me mum.'

Denni hid her surprise. 'She was very pretty.'

'Yeah, well she's old now.'

The last photo of Pam and the boys was dated seven years ago. Denni would not have recognized her. 'There's nothing more recent?'

'Nah. That's it.'

'When did your father leave?' she asked.

'Ten years ago – I was eight.'

'Do you see him at all?'

'No. Last I heard of him he'd gone abroad.'

For the first time Denni saw the pain in his eyes and the child he still was. She smiled. 'We'll soon find your mum, I'm sure.'

'I hope so. We miss her,' he said, adding defiantly, 'but we can manage.'

'I'll be in touch,' she said. 'I'll take just one photo of her. An artist can produce a more recent likeness for us. I'll also need her car registration number.'

As she was leaving, the other two boys, Sam and Tim, were staggering downstairs in their underpants. They looked at her questioningly, but actual speech seemed beyond them.

Rydell's interview with Mrs Lloyd-Peters was not going well.

'Do you really think I would leave my son, who was still recovering from surgery, to go off and kill the man who had operated on him? Do I look like a psychopath?'

Rydell kept a dignified silence for a few moments. He'd interviewed many suspects and seen other officers conducting interviews. Television and films did not reflect reality. Experience helped, of course, but there were moments of embarrassment, moments when the next question failed you. Sometimes there came a point in an interview when an answer's clarity was the defining moment – when the answer hit home. This was one of them. He knew he was wasting his time. For the sake of his own pride and the fact that there was a WPC in the room, he had to carry on with an interview that would go nowhere and be painful for her.

The best he could do was make it brief and be tactful. 'Could you tell me why you failed to tell us of the true nature of your relationship with Saul Ravenscroft?'

She looked up sharply. 'There was no relationship. I don't know what you're talking about.' When he didn't answer she stared at him, realization slowly dawning. 'For God's sake – what has that sergeant told you? – that I'm some sort of crackpot? And suddenly I've become a suspect. I'm not a murderer. I would never risk going to prison. I love my son far too much to endanger his welfare. I waited many years to be a mother. It was all I ever wanted.'

'I don't want to distress you, but there is a suggestion that Saul could be the father of your child.'

Her mouth dropped and her surprise was more than obvious. 'I don't know who has been talking,' she said. 'I did have fertility treatment and artificial insemination, but I can assure you the donor was my husband. I'm more than willing to have DNA testing.'

Rydell apologized for upsetting her. There was no evidence against her for either murder. None of the staff saw her wandering about the night Saul died and she had an alibi for the night Carla was attacked. The fact that her son looked like Ravenscroft was down to coincidence and Lyn's paranoia.

After she'd gone he went back to his office and began rearranging his paperwork. He couldn't settle and the phone ringing came as a welcome diversion.

'There's a Stanley Goodman in the front office, sir. He'd like a word.' Rydell replaced the phone thoughtfully. Maybe this was the breakthrough they'd been waiting for, he thought, but that was stretching optimism a bit far.

Stanley wore a baggy, hand-knitted brown jumper, brown trousers and black shoes. His sparse hair looked fluffy, as if he'd just washed it, and his eyes ranged around the room anxiously. 'I had to come,' he said miserably. 'I can't sleep. It's getting me down. I was brought up to tell the truth and old habits die hard, don't they?'

'That's true,' said Rydell. 'You'd better sit down and confess all, then.'

A horrified look passed across Stan's face and he slumped heavily into the chair.

'Inspector – I've got my wife to think of – bless her, she's had a lot to put up with over the years.'

'You too,' said Rydell.

'Till death do us part. I'm old-fashioned. I believe in that. She hasn't been well for years. She's like a very old car – first one bit goes, then another. She's beyond patching up now.' He sighed heavily and Rydell noticed he was shaking slightly. 'I've had some bad news, see – the doc doesn't think she'll last more than six months – he says her kidneys are packing up.'

'I'm sorry.'

'It's been a struggle at times, I can tell you. But it's time to come clean now, because losing my job doesn't matter any more. I gave in my notice this morning. I can't leave her night after night now. She's got so little time left.'

'What do you want to tell me, Stan?'

'They pay me for a twelve-hour shift – I'm not meant to leave the premises. I start at eight and finish at eight. My Freda can't be all night without me. She doesn't want to go to bed at eight o'clock so, since I worked at the clinic, I've been nipping home round about midnight to settle her down for the night. Carla knew that. I don't reckon anyone else did. Mr Ravenscroft often slept in if he was worried about a patient or if he wanted to see one of his women friends. He was a good bloke. Even if he had known, he wouldn't have sacked me, but now he's dead – Samuels and Frau Director wouldn't hesitate to get rid of me. But it doesn't matter anymore now, does it?'

'What time did you see Carla leave that night?'

'She used to get out through a gap in the fence and leave her car outside my bungalow – the other residents are all elderly, curtains drawn, tellies up loud – they never noticed. I'm surprised your blokes never noticed that bit of loose fencing. Anyway, that night my Freda took longer than usual. I got in just after midnight and her car was there then. When I came out at one thirty it was gone but I didn't hear her drive away. With double glazing you don't hear much.'

'It's a pity you didn't tell us this before,' said Rydell, tersely.

'It wouldn't have changed anything – would it?'

'We thought Carla was lying about the time she left,' said Rydell. 'It might have made us less keen to think she was the only suspect.'

'Sorry,' murmured Stan. 'Will I be charged with anything?'

'I could charge you for withholding information but that wouldn't do your wife much good. So think yourself lucky.'

Stan gave a wry smile. 'Depends on the way you look at things. What will my life be like without her?'

There was no answer to that, but Rydell shook his hand and wished him the best of luck and, at the unexpected kindness, Stan's eyes filled with tears and Rydell's spirits sank even further.

Denni was disappointed to find out that the police artist would take at least two days to come up with an age-enhanced likeness. Demand varied, but he was working on two missing children for the Birmingham police, and computer generated pictures took time to get just right.

In the meantime, Pam's car registration number was being forwarded to all traffic cops across the country. Maybe that would bring a result, unless, of course, she had the car garaged or had decided to abandon it. It really depended on how much she wanted to disappear.

When Rydell saw Pam's photograph he too was surprised. Seven years had made a huge difference in her appearance. She would have been forty-four then and she looked young and vibrant. The longer Denni looked at the photo the more she realized that the expression in her eyes was something unusual. The boys growing into difficult teenagers were not the only reason for the dimming of that look in her eyes – she was in love seven years ago. Living in London, working in the same clinic as Ravenscroft, and they were both single. It made sense.

'Guv,' she said excitedly. 'She's the one!'

'Just because she looked pretty good a few years back doesn't mean she killed Ravenscroft and Carla.'

'Maybe she couldn't take rejection – perhaps jealousy made her kill them both. That night she could have seen Carla leaving and it was too much for her, especially as she was so physically changed. It was no coincidence she moved to Harrowford. If Saul was running true to form he would have kept in touch with her.'

'But she has an alibi for the night Carla was killed.'

'She was off duty that night. Those boys wouldn't have known if she was in the house or not. They would have taken it for granted she was in. They sleep like the dead and they're half stoned most of the time.'

Rydell thought about it for a few moments. 'Wherever she's gone she must have told someone, even if it was only a vague direction, an old holiday haunt . . . maybe abroad. Has her passport gone?'

'I don't know, guv – I didn't do a proper search.'

'OK, I'll get a warrant now. We'll do it together.'

Pam had still done nothing about the car. It was parked at the back of the pub and she knew, as long as it stayed there, she'd be tempted to use it. She loved her car. It was freedom and the open road, but if they were looking for her it was best she got rid. She'd got stuff in the boot, but she supposed she could set fire to it and, once that was done, no one need ever find her. She had enough money to buy another cheap second-hand car and then she could move on if she wanted to. The sense of freedom was like being tipsy. All her worries were behind her. Already she looked better. She'd dyed her hair a soft auburn colour, she'd lost weight, grown her nails. Even her hot flushes had diminished. She felt like a new woman. Life may not begin at fifty, she told herself, but it certainly seemed like it. One of the customers had asked her out and tonight was her night off and he was taking her out for a meal. He was a good-looking guy and it had been years since she'd been on a date. She felt like a teenager again.

She'd see to the car later, there was plenty of time.

Twenty-Five

Pam's date, George Harper, called for her at seven thirty. She'd dressed with care and her low-cut blue sweater, black skirt and high heels were rewarded by a low whistle of appreciation.

'I've booked us a table at the Grange Hotel,' he said. 'You'll love the food.'

She did indeed love the food and the faded grandeur of the place. There was a huge fire, oak beams, damask tablecloths and a smell of age about the place. Pam happily relaxed, drank wine and chatted animatedly about her life. Except that it wasn't her life she talked about.

George in turn talked about his garden, his motorbike and his camper van. He'd been a widower for four years and Pam was his first date. They were holding hands when the coffee arrived.

'What did you do before you took early retirement?' she asked.

'Don't let it put you off,' he said smiling. 'I was a cop.'

It took a supreme effort for her not to drop his hand. 'I bet that was interesting,' she managed to say.

'It was better when I first started,' he said. 'We had a few laughs then. Now everything is politically correct and police black humour isn't PC. But I get a good pension and I'm still young enough to enjoy it.'

Now she couldn't wait to get back to the pub.

'You've gone quiet on me,' he said.

'I've talked too much,' she said, managing to give his hand a friendly squeeze. 'It's tired me out.'

Vain Hope

It was past closing time by the time they returned to the pub. At the back door George obviously wanted to linger. 'You have beautiful hair,' he said, as he moved towards her to kiss her. Pam kissed him back enthusiastically. The sooner it was done the sooner she could make her escape. 'When can I see you again?' he asked.

'My next night off,' she said. 'But you'll see me in the pub.'

Since he came in every evening she could hardly avoid him. 'It's not the same though – is it?' he said. 'I have to share you.'

Eventually, as she waved, he drove away. Maybe he'll be breathalyzed, she thought, but it was a forlorn hope. She crept upstairs wondering if she should give Lizzie the girly gossip, but she decided against it.

In the early hours she planned to leave. She didn't want to, but now she knew George was an ex-cop, how long would it be before he began asking awkward questions?

It didn't take long for her to pack her two suitcases. She thought about leaving a note for Lizzie, but decided against it. Better that she left no trace.

She crept down the stairs and out towards the garage. It was two a.m. on a clear cold night and she couldn't help but feel exhilarated to be on the run again. She didn't plan to go back to the boys ever.

She drove fast along the empty country roads, deciding that Wales and the coast would be her next haven. She was driving at fifty miles an hour through a deserted village when she saw the blue lights flashing. She had no choice but to pull over. A young policeman approached the car. She wound down the window. 'Do you know the speed limit, madam, for a built-up area?'

'Yes, officer. Was I doing more than thirty?'

'Nearer fifty, I would say.'

'Does that mean a speeding fine?'

He stared at her a moment. 'Speed limits apply, madam, day or night. Step out of the car, please.'

231

By now his companion had arrived and produced a breathalyzer. Pam could feel a hot flush coming on. She felt sick but she breathed into the bag, knowing it would be positive. She'd drunk several glasses of wine and finished off the evening with two large brandies. *You fool*, she told herself. *You stupid bitch*!

The officer who'd approached the car first was now using his mobile. They were checking out her car registration number. It was over. Her little bit of freedom lost for the sake of a few wines with an ex-cop.

'Lock up your car, madam,' he said grimly. 'You'll have to come with us.'

The search of Pam's house found nothing. The boys were anxious and surly, fretting that their mother was dead. 'We've no reason to worry about her safety,' explained Denni. 'We just need to talk to her so that we can eliminate her from our inquiries.'

'What would she know about murder and stuff like that?' asked Daniel, sneering and trying to look macho.

'We just have to be sure,' said Denni. 'Just sit down and we'll be out of here in no time.'

It was when they asked about her passport that the boys looked from one to another.

'She wouldn't go abroad,' said Daniel. 'She's never been abroad. She hasn't got a passport.'

'You're sure?'

They nodded, solemnly.

'Are you going to put out something on the telly?' asked Daniel. 'I could say, Come home, Mum, we've done the washing up. I mean, that's why she left, know what I mean? Because we're lazy scumbags.'

There was no answer to that. At the moment she was only a suspect because she may have had an affair with Ravenscroft. There was nothing to prove even that. There were no letters or photos – nothing. They found diaries in her drawer for the last three years but mostly she'd used them for shopping lists and the odd comment on the weather.

Eventually they left, dispirited, and it was Rydell who suggested a pub lunch.

'This case is getting me down,' he said, as they waited in the Crown pub for their baguettes and coffee. As a pub it had seen better days. The upholstery on the seats showed the foam beneath through various rips, the carpets were stained and threadbare in places and, more tellingly, they were the only two customers. Denni saw Rydell's uneasy expression. 'You could have a drink, guv,' she said. 'I'll drive.'

'Once I start I might not want to stop.'

'What are the chances of Pam being a two-time killer?' she asked.

'If I was a bookie,' he said, 'I'd be delighted to take any bet because we don't have a shred of evidence against her and we don't have a motive.

'My bet would be on Wendy Swan,' he went on. 'I've read the details of the damage she did to that bed. It was pretty impressive. Luckily her bloke and the girlfriend did a runner – I think if they were there, they'd have been the ones under the axe. Let's face it. That morning the staff were shattered, they hadn't slept all night, they couldn't remember who was around and who wasn't – it was a shambles and that was our crucial time.

'What does Ram think?' he asked.

'He thinks she's clean, but what about Una? She knew the building, knew how to get togged up to avoid getting contaminated. I know she's convincing but, what if . . .'

'I've had enough of *what ifs*, Denni. All the women involved are consummate liars . . .'

'Even Lyn?'

'Yeah. Even her. I thought we might get something going together but not after her revelations.'

'Times have changed, Tom.'

He half smiled. 'I'm still in my thirties, not my dotage. And

I'm not looking for a virgin, but I have to admit I wouldn't want to bring up another man's children.'

'Lots of men do.'

'Those who fail with their own shouldn't even try.'

Denni was relieved when their meal arrived and they ate in silence. When he'd finished eating, Rydell said, 'Where the hell did we go wrong?'

'We didn't – we had evidence, and a motive and a prime suspect. It was all going too well. Perhaps we just didn't take account of the planning involved . . .'

'That's it!' he said, excitedly. 'Somewhere along the line we assumed Saul was killed because someone found out he was shagging Carla that night. But the point is, the open evening had been planned months in advance. His death was an execution carefully orchestrated. But something went wrong. Could the killer have planned to kill them both at the same time? But Carla left early, and the murderer had expected to find her beside him.'

'But with a scalpel?' she asked in surprise. 'Surely they would have put up a fight.'

'Not if they were sound asleep, taken unawares by someone who knew what they were doing. In the event, Saul was taken unawares, Carla wasn't and put up a fight.'

'It's all guesswork,' said Denni wearily. 'We don't seem to have spoken to anyone who has a bad word to say about Ravenscroft. Even Carla, although she wasn't liked, she wasn't hated either.'

'So we're looking for someone,' said Rydell, 'who keeps their emotions under control until the right moment.'

'Rules out Wendy Swan then?'

'I think so. She would have wanted to see his face – a proper confrontation. There's still Una. As far as I can gather, Carla and Saul were the only two people, other than Hugh, her so-called husband, who knew she'd been born a man. Maybe Carla, for some reason, threatened to expose her. Or she guessed that Hugh was playing away and that unhinged her. Maybe she—'

Rydell's mobile phone rang and he listened intently for a few moments. Then he grinned. 'The traffic boys have found Pam. They're sending a pick-up truck for her car now. If we exclude her – we're only left with Una. This could be our lucky day.'

He sounded jubilant and Denni hoped, for all their sakes, that this was going to be a breakthrough. They'd all worked hard. Rydell had worked sixteen hours most days, he'd had no time to run, she'd had no time to herself, no time to read, and Ram was probably going square-eyed in front of his computer.

Pam looked miserable but composed. 'Have I committed a crime?' she asked. 'My three boys are all over sixteen.'

Denni sat beside Rydell and he asked the questions. 'It's not about the boys. It's about Saul Ravenscroft and Carla Robins. How long were you having an affair with Saul?'

Pam didn't even blink. 'I wasn't having an affair with him. He was always friendly and he took me out for dinner a couple of times. But only when I worked in London. Probably felt sorry for me.'

'Why didn't you tell us this before?'

'No one asked me if I was having an affair with him – it's a ridiculous idea.'

'Why?'

'I'm not his type,' she said, with wry smile.

'A few years back you looked just his type.'

'Did I? If you're looking for a scapegoat, a fat, menopausal woman isn't the type to commit murder either.'

Denni watched her steely expression. Pam's hair had lost its grey and she'd lost weight. She was confident, prettier, calm – maybe totally innocent.

'Why did you come to Harrowford?' he asked. 'It meant uprooting your boys. Didn't they object?'

'We didn't have a lot of choice. I was renting and rents in London started going up. When our landlord put up the rent by a hundred pounds a month I just couldn't afford to stay. I knew Saul was opening his own clinic so I wrote to him and he offered me a job on nights as a care assistant.'

'And did you see him socially?'

'No. Carla was around and he was besotted with her. We had a chat sometimes, that's all.'

'And what did he tell you during these chats?'

'He said he'd married Amanda because she'd fallen in love with him and she was more interested in horses than having children.'

'Didn't he want children?'

'He'd wanted Carla's children. But she'd had a hysterectomy. She suffered from endometriosis. Not that she wanted children anyway.'

'So you knew her well?'

'I didn't say that. He talked about her quite a bit. Sad really.'

'Yes, indeed. And were you jealous of this adoration?'

Pam glanced at Denni. 'Any woman would have been a bit jealous. But I wasn't jealous enough to kill them both, if that's what you're getting at.'

A knock at the door of the interview room stopped Rydell in his tracks. Denni left the room to find Ram outside. 'The car and the luggage seem to be clean,' he said, despondently. 'Clothes, a few books, a CD player and a few CDs, make-up, underwear. No bloodstains. Nothing incriminating, so far.'

Denni shrugged. 'For someone who gets hot flushes, she's sitting in there as cool as a plate of frozen prawns. I think our boss is wasting his time.'

'Tell you what. I'll cook us something special tonight. We could invite him.'

'No,' she said firmly. 'That smacks of celebration. We've got nothing to celebrate. If we don't get a result soon we'll be back in uniform.'

'That's what I like, Denni. A good, positive attitude.'

Ten minutes later Pam was allowed to go. 'We'd prefer it,' said Rydell, 'if you went back to the boys for the time being.'

'Life's a bitch,' said Pam cheerfully as she left, swinging her handbag over her shoulder.

By nine o'clock that evening the delights of cooking curry from scratch had failed Ram and he'd decided to ring up for a takeaway. 'It'll take forty minutes,' he said.

'Good,' said Denni. 'I've got wine in and brandy to follow. I'm going to get bladdered.'

'You won't enjoy the food,' warned Ram.

She'd drunk two glasses of wine when the telephone rang. It was the hospital. Her mother had had a fall. She was comfortable but she was being kept in overnight. Could Denni visit and bring a nightie and dressing gown?

'I'll drive you,' said Ram, as he helped her on with her coat. 'I'll tell the Curry Palace we'll pick it up later.' He rang and explained the position and was told they closed at midnight. Even Ram, who had a robust stomach, didn't feel he could face a curry at or near midnight.

At Harrowford General Jean lay on a hospital trolley. A cut and swelling above her right eyebrow had closed her eye and she had a large bruise over the left eyebrow. Her thin arms were also bruised, her eyes were closed and she looked ten years older. Ram had insisted on being by Denni's side and, when Jean opened her one good eye, she peered at him and said, 'You another Paki doctor?'

Denni felt herself blushing. 'For God's sake, there's no need for that.'

'I didn't mean anything by it, I'm sure. Where would the NHS be without Paki doctors?'

'This is Ram Patel. He's not from Pakistan and he's not a doctor. He's with me in the CID.'

'He looks more like a doctor than a cop.'

Now that Denni stood a little nearer to her mother she could smell the whisky on her breath. It was pungent enough to stop a camel in its tracks.

'Where's Bill and what happened?'

'Poor bugger was too drunk to come with me.'

'So what happened?'

'I fell down the stairs.'

'You don't have any stairs – you live in a bungalow.'

'I know that much. I wasn't at home. I was at Bill's and I forgot he had stairs.'

'So have you been X-rayed?'

'Oh yes, and I haven't broken a thing but they want to keep me in overnight. Have you brought me a nightie?'

Denni nodded. She could tell her mother was still drunk and, although she felt sorry for her, she also felt ashamed. 'Is there anything else you want?' she asked.

'No, I'm all right. Bill's going to take me home tomorrow.'

They stayed a little longer but Jean obviously wanted to sleep. 'I'll go now,' said Denni, 'and have a word with the doctor.' Her mother opened her good eye. 'He'll only tell you I should stop drinking. Before you go – can you find my handbag, my life's in there.'

My life's in there. The words echoed in Denni's head. *My life's in there*.

The young registrar gave Denni a thorough rundown of her mother's condition. She must stop smoking and drinking, her liver was a little enlarged and her lungs were congested. She nodded and agreed but, sadly, knew no amount of warnings would make any difference.

It was nearly eleven by the time they got to the curry house. Denni had been hungry but now she was anxious about her mother and excited by her last words.

Once they were home and with the takeaway in its bag on the kitchen table they both decided on a bowl of cornflakes. 'I'll freeze it,' said Denni. 'We'll have it another night.'

Although she felt exhausted she couldn't sleep. Ram happily snored in the spare room, but for Denni, sleep evaded her and she watched the hours tick by. It wasn't that they hadn't tried to find the missing pieces in the puzzle. The pieces hadn't been there to find – until now. Denni was sure this new day would bring the answer.

Twenty-Six

For two mornings in a row Rydell had left his breakfast bowl and mug unwashed in the sink. The first day he'd felt very uneasy as he left his flat. The second day his resolve slipped a little and he washed the spoon and put that away. He didn't expect a thunderbolt from hell as retribution. He knew his actions were totally without logic and knew he was screwed up, but he could feel an improvement in his anxiety levels. He hadn't quite managed the unpeeled apple, but, as yet, he wasn't in the Howard Hughes league of total paranoid obsession. In fact, he was convinced that if he took things slowly he could get as near to normal as damn it. After all, physical danger didn't worry him at all. A drug-crazed man mountain of a guy swinging a baseball bat hadn't bothered him unduly. And he'd looked down the barrel of a gun on two occasions. So why the hell should mere disorder set his heart racing?

He'd been in the office for an hour when Ram and Denni turned up. 'How come you two always turn up together these days?' he asked. 'Have you been clubbing? Denni, you look shattered.'

'I didn't sleep well. And I haven't been *out* out since this case started. But I have had a thought, guv.'

'Should I get excited?'

'*I* am.'

'Is Ram excited?'

She looked at Ram and smiled. 'We haven't discussed it.'

Now the moment had come to tell him, it no longer seemed quite such a breakthrough. In fact, she now thought disappointment loomed.

'Well,' said Rydell. 'Any ideas are welcome. God knows we need a crumb of inspiration.'

'It was something my mother said about her handbag. She said, "My life's in that handbag."'

Rydell looked nonplussed.

'We didn't search Pam's handbag, did we?' said Denni. 'Her luggage was searched and the car, but if *she* carried her life in her shoulder bag we might find something there.'

'It's worth a try – what do you think, Ram?'

Ram, switching on his computer, looked up. 'Don't forget to include me in the grand opening.'

'There's no reason to wait. We'll go and do it now.'

Pam looked shocked at the sight of the three of them on her doorstep. She was still in her dressing gown, her hair not brushed. 'I'll have to get dressed,' she said. 'I thought you were finished with me. There's nothing else I can tell you.'

'We're happy to wait,' said Rydell. 'Take your time. Are the boys still in bed?'

'One's at school, the other two are shirking as usual.'

The lounge was back to normal. On the floor were two pairs of socks, a couple of empty cans and two girlie mags.

When she came downstairs dressed, she looked with ill-concealed disgust around the room. 'I'm not picking up after them. The place can rot for all I care. My room's fine and, as soon as I can, I'll be leaving again.'

'We have come for a specific reason, Pam,' said Rydell. 'We want to look at the contents of your handbag.'

Pam paled visibly. She sat down immediately, as though fearing her knees might give way. 'Can you do that? Is it legal?'

'It is. Where is your handbag?'

'In my room.'

'Ram, go and fetch it.'

Ram gave a *why me* expression.

'I'll come with you,' said Pam swiftly.

Pam led the way to her bedroom and pointed to the bed. 'It's there.'

Ram looked to the side of the bed and saw the black shoulder bag half tucked under the bed. As he bent to pick it up he heard a slight movement behind him. The instinct for self-preservation kicked in and, for once, he was prepared. He grabbed the bag and swung it round Pam's legs. The lamp she'd been holding fell to the ground with a crash and they landed up on the bed grappling. He was winning until she grabbed him between the legs. He cried out with the pain and, as he struggled to loosen her grip, they both fell from the bed.

Rydell and Denni rushed up the stairs to find them grappling on the floor. Ram's skin had a greenish tinge but he managed to say two words. 'Cuff her!'

'The pervert attacked me,' she screamed. 'He should be locked up.' Ram had hold of her leg but she continued to flail and struggle. Rydell put a foot on her body, which momentarily quietened her, and then deftly slipped on handcuffs. As he and Denni hauled her to her feet he began cautioning her. The cuffs and the caution quickly had a sobering effect. She looked both defeated and confused.

Ram was by now hauling himself upright to his feet. 'I'm improving,' he said. 'She didn't get a crack at my skull.' He didn't add that she'd nearly twisted his balls off.

With Pam in a cell they used an interview room to examine the contents of the shoulder bag. It was as neat as her room. There were bundles of cash, a set of car keys, a make-up bag, a diary and her purse. The diary contained names and home addresses of various people, including those of Carla and Ravenscroft and, strangely, Lyn Kilpatrick. It was in the wallet-type purse, tucked away with various credit and store cards, that Denni found the photo – a polaroid – of a premature baby lying in a kidney dish. On the back it said: Zoe.

Although it seemed cruel ammunition, Denni guessed the photo was Pam's Achilles heel.

Subdued and tearful, Pam sat in the interview room and Rydell explained the interview would be taped and did she understand. She nodded. Her shoulder bag was placed in front of her. 'You can check the contents if you like,' he said. She swiftly placed both hands on the bag but didn't look inside.

'Now, Pam, let's go back to when you worked in London at the Mayflower Clinic. Did you enjoy the job?'

'Yes.'

'And that was when you first met Saul?'

'Yes.'

'You had an affair with him?'

'Yes.'

Rydell was only a little surprised at the swiftness of her reply for, in his experience of interviewing suspected murderers, amongst the lies and subterfuge the truth nearly always leaked out. In her case she'd taken out the stopper.

'Tell me about the affair,' he said. 'How did it start?'

Pam stared down at her hands and played with a plain silver ring on her right hand.

'He asked me out to dinner,' she said eventually. 'We'd both been working late and I was just leaving and he said, very casually, he was starving and would I like a bite to eat.'

'And you got on well?'

'Yes. Very well. He was talkative but he also listened.'

'What did you talk about?'

'Does it matter? Do I need a solicitor?'

'That's your choice, Pam. It's not too traumatic for you, is it – telling the truth this time?'

'I *am* telling the truth.'

'Fine, then we don't have a problem. You had this meal together – what happened next?'

'He asked me out a couple of nights later. And we made love.'

Rydell noticed the phrase – *made love*. It wasn't a description much used anymore. He'd noticed too the way her eyes softened when she spoke about him.

'You fell in love with him?'

She smiled wryly and fidgeted with the strap of her bag. 'Yes. I was forty-four then – I was like a teenager. He was a great lover. I'd never been so happy. He didn't lead me on or anything. He said he wasn't the marrying kind. He also told me about Carla – how much he loved her and how she'd refused to marry him. The bitch didn't know how lucky she was. I suppose they were two of a kind.'

'So jealousy drove you to kill them?'

Pam looked up sharply. 'You can't trick me like that. You have no evidence against me. Just because I was in love with him doesn't mean I would kill him or her.'

Rydell glanced at Denni, a signal for her to take over. Denni slapped the photo on to the table. 'Who is Zoe?'

Pam's lower lip trembled. 'She was my daughter,' she murmured. 'She was born at twenty-six weeks. She weighed just under a pound.'

'She was Saul's child?'

'Yes.'

'Did he know?'

'Yes. It wasn't his fault I got pregnant. I told him I was on the pill. I was so happy to be having his baby.'

'What was his reaction?'

'He said he would help me financially, but he would never want to see the child.'

'Did you accept that?'

'Yes. Because I knew my baby would be a girl . . .' she broke off. 'I always wanted girls. I never loved the boys – not properly. After Daniel was born, I got pregnant again within three months. I was convinced I'd have a girl and yet, as time went on, I knew it was a boy. Then along came Samuel. I could hardly cope. I suffered from post-natal depression but I convinced Mick, my husband, that another baby was likely to be a girl and that I'd be cured. Only the next baby was another boy, Timothy. I tried bringing him up as a girl but it didn't work – the male genes won through and Mick left because he thought I was nuts. And then after all those years I had another chance to have the girl I'd always wanted. I was so happy, I was convinced this time . . .' She broke off.

'What happened?'

She sighed, her eyes bright with tears, and began twisting the ring on her finger.

'I sailed through those first months. I did have a bit of bleeding occasionally but I thought it had something to do with carrying a girl. I didn't tell anyone. Then it got heavier and I knew something was wrong. I took myself to hospital – of course, I was losing the baby. I gave them Saul's name and he came in to see me after the baby was born. I wasn't in my right mind. He told me I'd had a boy. He was trying to be kind. I knew I'd had a girl. You see, because I was so hysterical, they took the baby away before I'd seen her. One of the staff gave me that photo, but she's so small I couldn't even tell what sex she was. I had to know – you can understand that, can't you?'

Denni nodded. 'Go on,' she encouraged.

Pam gulped down her tears and continued in a voice sometimes so quiet that Denni had to lean forward to hear.

'So when I was alone for a few minutes,' she said, 'I managed to get out of bed and stagger into the sluice. And there was my baby lying in a cold metal dish. My baby girl – smaller than my hand and perfect. She'd been left there like a piece of rubbish waiting to be thrown out, or . . . put in the incinerator.'

By now Pam's voice had cracked and tears were streaming down her face.

'Would you like a break and a cup of tea?'

She shook her head. 'No . . . I want to go on. I want to tell you everything.'

'Take your time, Pam.'

She took a few deep breaths and wiped her eyes with the tissue Denni offered her.

'A year after Zoe, I was still a wreck. I couldn't stop thinking about her, how she might have been . . . anyway, I had to carry on. The boys were younger then and not quite so obnoxious. Saul wrote to me and sent me money occasionally but, when the landlord put the rent up, that was it – we had to find somewhere cheaper to live. Saul suggested coming to Harrowford. So I came. We hadn't seen each other in years and I know he was shocked at the change in me, but he was kind as ever and told me I looked well.'

Pam's face began to get pinker and beads of sweat broke out on her forehead. She fanned her face with her hand.

'A cold drink?' suggested Denni.

'Yes, please.'

By the time the plastic cup of squash arrived, Pam's face was its normal colour. She drank the squash in silence. 'Everything was going okay until Lyn Kilpatrick arrived,' she began, without being prompted. 'But I can't blame her – can I?'

'For what?'

'For what happened. One night, I'd gone for my break upstairs and I saw Saul and Carla going into the on-call room. They hadn't closed the door properly and I stood outside and listened.'

Pam stared into space for several seconds. 'If I hadn't done that . . . It doesn't matter now, does it?' she said bleakly.

'What did you hear, Pam?'

'Carla did most of the talking. I could hear them clearly. They were just standing by the door. She said, "I've just seen that fat old cow you used to shag." He said, "Don't be unkind, Carla – you know she's had a rough time." They sounded as if they were kissing then and I heard her say, "Lyn's working here now, I see. She still looks good. How's your Zoe, by the way?"

'I nearly fainted. His Zoe? What was she talking about? I was so confused. When he'd seen me after she was born I told him that Zoe was my choice of name. He'd thought it a lovely name. And suddenly another woman had a child called Zoe. And, of course, the penny dropped. It was his child. Then he said, "I've only seen them both from a distance. She's a little peach and Sean is nearly as handsome as his father." They

both laughed, and then she said, "Come on, Daddy, take me
to bed now."

'They moved away from the door then and I couldn't hear
any more. Of course, I found out later it was Lyn's children
who were called Zoe and Sean.'

'That must have been very upsetting.'

'Of course it was!' she snapped. 'I was devastated. But I
made up my mind, there and then, to kill them all. All three
of them. I didn't even expect to get caught. I planned it so
carefully. I stole a sterile theatre cap, gown, mask, gloves,
plastic overshoes and a scalpel. Most places only do a stock
check once a year. I knew he would be guest of honour at the
open evening and they'd probably spend the night together.
I also knew Stan was never around between twelve and one.
The night before, I hid the stuff in an old storage cupboard
on the top floor, behind a load of boxes. It was about twelve
thirty and I was outside the door. I waited. I couldn't hear a
thing. I opened the door so quietly and was shocked that the
bed was empty – then I realized Saul was in the bathroom and
she must have gone. He had his back towards me – he was
peeing – half kneeling. I crept up behind him. He didn't hear
a thing. I cut his throat and, as he sagged to the floor, I cut his
wrists. Then I got out of the gear and had a shower.'

Pam sighed as if exhausted. Denni felt the same way. 'Tell
me,' said Denni. 'Killing by cutting someone's throat isn't
easy – how did you manage it?'

Pam smiled for the first time. 'My dad was a soldier. I
had two older brothers. We played war games. Dad taught
us with plastic knives and plastic guns. "Be bold," he used
to say, as he showed us how to take someone from behind.
"Go in hard. Go in deep. Make sure they're dead." We loved
it. We played jungle games, cowboys and indians, we went
camping and learned how to track and make fires. Both my
brothers joined the army. One's dead now, I don't hear from
the other one.'

'You didn't want to join the army?'

'No, I didn't. What I wanted most in all the world were

two daughters to wear pretty frocks and to leave all that macho stuff behind. I couldn't compete with my brothers but, somehow, my dad tried to make me as tough as them. Strange, isn't it – he'd be proud of me now – that's the sort of man he was. You kill your enemies.'

'So, having killed Saul and knowing Carla was on bail, why did you have to kill her? She would probably have been found guilty.'

'I did think of letting the cow live, but death is tidier, isn't it? As the years went by and she was in prison I'd have thought about her. Dead, I didn't need to think about her.'

As she stopped talking, Denni wondered if this full confession was a prelude to a plea of insanity. If she'd committed murder within a year of Zoe's birth she might have been lucky, but, years down the line, it was unlikely. There was no doubt she was fully aware of her actions – *with malice aforethought*.

Denni glanced at Rydell. He looked pale and worried and in other circumstances she'd have asked him what was wrong.

Pam had paused for only a few seconds. Now she cleared her throat and started again.

'I was geared up to kill her that night but, if she'd apologized, I might not have done it, but she was a cool bitch. I put on the theatre garb in front of her. She didn't bat an eyelid. I reckon she thought – fat old cow isn't fit enough to take me on. Even when she saw the scalpel she thought she'd win. I have to say she put up a good fight. I just forgot one thing really.

'What was that?'

'I went in bold, I went in hard, but I didn't check she was dead.'

'What did you do then?'

'I took the gear off, except for the gloves, then I went home, put them in a black bag and put that out for the dustman.'

Denni sat back, relieved it was all over.

'Tell me,' said Rydell. 'Was it the fact that Lyn had Saul's children, or that one of them was named Zoe, or was there something I missed?'

Pam looked him straight in the eye. 'I hadn't stopped loving Saul. I suppose I'm mad, but I thought when I came back we might get something going again. I mean, you hear of women having fertility treatment in their fifties. I thought there was still a chance until I overheard them – then I knew it was just a vain hope. I was a stupid, fat menopausal woman. But worse was to come when I realized his daughter, Zoe, was eight years old. Eight! Born before my daughter. He'd agreed that Zoe was a lovely name and yet he already had a child of that name – was that a sick joke, or what? The baby girl I'd always wanted was given the same name as his child by another woman. That hurt the most. I knew then that all hope was gone and that I had nothing to lose. Like my dad used to say – be bold. And I was, and I don't regret it.'

Rydell and Denni sat without speaking for a while. Then Rydell said, 'I can't understand why you didn't kill Lyn.'

She shrugged. 'I wanted to. Believe me, I wanted to at the time. I didn't want to risk another killing at the clinic. I might have been caught and anyway you lot were all over the place. I knew Lyn would be difficult. That friend of hers, Holly, was always around. One night I was going to do it. I went round to her place and knocked on the door. I knew she was in and that Holly was next door. She didn't answer the door and I thought better of it. Lyn's Zoe was the child of a man I loved. It would have left two children alone. That didn't seem right.'

Later, when Pam had been formally charged and the paper-work was underway, Rydell, Ram and Denni went to the canteen for lunch.

'What bothers me,' said Rydell, 'is that she very nearly got away with it. It was pure chance that traffic cop stopped her.'

'Sod's law, guv,' said Ram. 'That's the way they caught Sutcliffe, the Yorkshire Ripper. We work our balls off and someone else gets the satisfaction.'

'Yeah, but let's face it, she wasn't even a suspect,' said Rydell, as he inspected the interior of his sandwich.

'They do say,' said Denni, 'that middle-aged women feel invisible. We went wrong because she was invisible to us. She was always around but we didn't notice her. She was too ordinary.'

'Come on, you two,' said Ram. 'We got her in the end – how we did it doesn't matter.'

'It matters to me,' murmured Rydell. 'I always thought I would recognize someone raised in an army family. I should have seen the signs.'

'What signs?' asked Denni.

'The planning, the checking, leaving nothing to chance. The fear of the disorder her sons caused. It scrabbles your brain.'

'Do you think she's insane?' asked Ram.

'Yes. But I doubt whether a psychiatrist would agree. She knew exactly what she was doing.'

'You sound sympathetic towards her,' said Denni.

Rydell smiled sadly. 'I wouldn't call it sympathy. But prison won't be such a hardship for her. Prison is routine and order and rules and regulations. She'll fit in, no problem.'

A few days later the team decided to celebrate, if that was the word, with drinks at Denni's place. The end of the case seemed like an anticlimax and a party signified closure as much as any self-congratulation.

News from the clinic suggested it would fold within days. Now that the case was over, the medical and nursing bodies were looking at the discrepancies. The fraud squad were taking an interest in Martin Samuels and Una had already resigned. Lyn was planning to return to work at the General and Alvera had been discharged from hospital and was working for her Church.

Graham Coombs had, in the meantime, been caught mid-burglary, but Rydell had suggested he might put in a good word for him, so he was ready to admit to several more.

Pam's sons were still at home and Daniel was doing his best to keep the other two in line. Pam, meanwhile, was on remand in prison and appeared to be taking life in prison in her stride.

Denni took two days off and spent the time reading and eating. Ram visited his mother and Tom Rydell took to the Welsh hills for a long solitary run.

The latest gossip at Harrowford nick was that Denni and Ram were an item. Neither of them minded and Tom wasn't in the least bit surprised.

Denni didn't enjoy the rest and recreation as much as she'd thought she would. It was no fun at all without Ram.